TOO SOON OLD,
TOO LATE SMART

TOO SOON OLD, TOO LATE SMART

A NOVEL

REX COLE

This is a work of fiction. Names, characters, organizations, places, events, and incidents are either products of the author's imagination or are used fictitiously.

Copyright © 2025 by Rex Cole

All rights reserved.

No part of this book may be reproduced, or stored in a retrieval system, or transmitted in any form or by any means, electronic, mechanical, photocopying, recording, or otherwise, without express written permission of the publisher.

Published by GFB™, Seattle
www.girlfridayproductions.com

Produced by Girl Friday Productions

Design: Paul Barrett
Production editorial: Kylee Hayes
Project management: Sara Addicott

Image credits: cover © Shutterstock/guruXOX, Shutterstock/Somsak Thapthimthong, Shutterstock/Rustic, Shutterstock/Andreas Novandi Irawan, Shutterstock/aljosa2015

ISBN (hardcover): 978-1-959411-93-2
ISBN (paperback): 978-1-959411-94-9
ISBN (ebook): 978-1-959411-95-6

Library of Congress Control Number: 2024918819

First edition

*To my wives
To Stephanie, whom I lost
To Suzanne, whom I found*

I stepped from plank to plank
So slow and cautiously;
The stars about my head I felt,
About my feet the sea.

I knew not but the next
Would be my final inch,—
This gave me that precarious gait
Some call experience.
　　　　　　　　—Emily Dickinson

Life can only be understood backwards;
but it must be lived forwards.
　　　　　　　　—Soren Kierkegaard

And, yes, I know the prologue customarily goes in the front.

Chapter 1

The One Hundredth

Backward

I opened my eyes, rubbed them, and looked at the alarm clock on my bedside table. Six o'clock. Just like always. The alarm never went off. I never set it. I simply always woke up at six—or at least I had for the past twenty-five years. *How strange is the human mind,* I thought. There must be a clock with a very dependable built-in alarm up in my brain. God probably put it there just for the hell of it.

I sat up and put my feet on the floor. Today was special. It was the first time in my life I had ever been a hundred years old. I hoped they wouldn't make too big a deal out of it. Since I had been living at Sunset Acres Assisted Living Facility no one had ever had a one hundredth birthday, so I had no idea what to expect. I would much rather be living at Sun*rise* Acres Assisted Living Facility, but I wasn't in charge of naming the place. They had already warned me that a reporter from the local newspaper was going to interview me in the afternoon. They said he would arrive around two. I already knew that from when the paper called me. I guessed they'd thought I had forgotten. The paper had called me up and asked if they could send a reporter over and I said yes. I'll bet he's going to ask me what my secret to a long life is. I think I'll tell him prune juice. If he doesn't laugh, I'll pretend I'm deaf and make him yell at me.

As I did every morning, I reached over and lightly caressed my favorite photo of Joanne. It was on my bedside table next to the clock. She was holding our dog, Pepper—well, actually Pepper was her dog. Joanne had passed away twenty-five years ago. I'd moved to the assisted-living facility six years ago because I wanted some company and because I can't cook. They let you have a dog, or else I wouldn't have come. Lady was lying in her bed next to mine. Her rheumy eyes were open, her head was up, and she was watching me. She didn't move. She was old too. Bless her heart for that.

I got up, took my meds, showered, shaved, and went down to breakfast. It was a big deal that I could still do the little things in life to remain independent. It made you feel like you were still worth something. Maybe not much, but something. But eventually you had to be willing to ask for help if you needed it. I didn't mind getting older. I just didn't like being old.

Here, you'd sit down, and they'd come and wait on you. The waiter's name was Willie. We always said the same thing to each other in the morning. Willie would say, "Morning, Bob. How are you today?"

Then I'd say, "Morning, Willie. I'm better than I deserve."

He'd chuckle and touch my shoulder. Yes, I know it was predictable and mundane. But the touch always made the moment special. Human contact. It was a good thing. Definitely not overrated.

I always had the same thing for breakfast. A cup of yogurt, a hard-boiled egg, a cup of coffee, and a little glass of orange juice. I hated prune juice.

Everyone there was nice. I made sure I sat at a table with people who wanted to talk about something other than their health—or lack thereof. I couldn't stand the tables where you listen to nothing but "organ recitals." How long did you have to be on this planet before you learned that people don't like people who complain all the time? Why in the world would someone think I found their gallbladder fascinating? I didn't find my own gallbladder the least bit fascinating.

I was the only one at my table at that hour. Everyone left me alone, so that was a relief. I was not a morning person. I wasn't in the mood to sparkle.

After breakfast, I took Lady for her walk. She was a terrier mutt. I was partial to the breed. She used to be feisty. Now she was not. She loved me. Of that I was sure. What more could you ask of a companion? She tottered a bit, so we took our time. We both had plenty of that.

Then I went back to my apartment and watched the news, read the newspaper, and started a new book.

At lunch, everyone at my table wished me a happy birthday. They didn't sing "Happy Birthday," thank God. Joanne and I had made an agreement. There were only two grounds for divorce in our marriage. One was that neither of us could ever arrange to have "Happy Birthday" sung to the other spouse in a restaurant. The other was that neither spouse could ever buy a cuckoo clock. They did, however, say they were going to sing it to me that evening. I hoped they didn't hear my little groan. Maybe they'd forget. We talked about gardening and birds. Nice folks. When people get old, some get meaner, most get nicer. They knew that life kicked you in the ass from time to time, and they empathized. They knew things didn't always go according to plan.

I went up to my room to wait for the reporter. I didn't know why I'd agreed to do this. I sure wasn't looking forward to it.

At two thirty, there was a knock on my door. I opened it,

and a nice-looking young woman of about twenty-five was standing there. She was dressed very neatly. She looked competent but a little unsure of herself. She smiled and stuck out her hand. "Dr. Carson, I'm Mindy Wilson with the *Record*. May I come in?"

"Sure. Come on in. I didn't realize you were going to have so many X chromosomes. Not that I'm disappointed. I've often felt that I have been cursed to have to lug around this Y chromosome. It weighs a ton. I'm ready for the inquisition. I've got chairs and chains and everything you could possibly need."

She laughed and said, "No chains. Just a chair will do. Lance couldn't come. He's sick. I'm a substitute. I'm glad I'm not a disappointment." She looked around a bit. "This is nice. And you've got a great view of the hills." Then she saw Lady and said, "What's your dog's name?"

"That's Lady. In dog years, she's even more ancient than I am."

"Does she bite?"

"No. But she can gum you pretty good."

Mindy knelt down and scratched her behind the ears. "She looks so sweet. My dog is old too, but probably not as old as she is. It's hard when they get old, isn't it?"

"In some ways. If they're healthy, it's a lot easier. Same with people."

"You look healthy."

"I am healthy . . . and I think it's in large measure because I believe in short TUF units."

"You believe in short tough units? What's a tough unit?"

"Not a tough unit, a TUF unit."

"I'm sorry. I don't understand."

"That's because your brain was spelling TUF as t-o-u-g-h, not the proper way, which is t-u-f. It stands for Time Until Funny."

"I'm sorry. I still don't get it. Time until what's funny?"

"Well, almost anything aggravating. As long as it's not funny at the time it happens. Let's say you're outside the church before your wedding, and the photographer is there waiting to take your picture. From out of nowhere, a bird flies over and craps on your head. Now, at some time in your life, that will be funny to almost everyone. 'Hey, Mindy. Remember the time that bird took a dump on your head right before you got married?' And then everybody laughs. Well, some people are going to laugh about that sooner than others. Some will have a short TUF unit and laugh about it fairly quickly. It may take a long time for some people to see the humor in it. They will have demonstrated a long TUF unit. Some may never laugh about it. It will ruin first their wedding, then their honeymoon, then their marriage, then their life. That's sad. It's good to have short TUF units."

Mindy smiled. "Well, it's disturbing to learn I don't know how to spell 'tough.' I'll remember that if a bird poops on my head just before my wedding. I wouldn't want it to ruin my life. But I see what you mean. I'll work on getting my TUF units nice and low."

Mindy looked around and stopped at Joanne's picture on my bedside table.

"What a pretty lady. Was she your wife?"

"Yes, she was. We were married fifty years. A wonderful woman. I still kiss her good night every evening. I still miss her every morning. I kiss her and miss her. When you lose someone you love, you heal, but you never forget. Even if they're no longer here physically, they're in your mind." I waved both arms around. "They're in the room with you. They swirl in your air. It's a special feeling."

"I hope to be able to say that someday. Right now it's not looking too good. Some men can be such jerks. But this guy I'm dating now is really good-looking, has gorgeous blue eyes, and is easy to talk to. And I feel safe with him."

"If you want to feel safe, why don't you just buy a gun? Or better yet, get a pit bull."

She laughed. "You're teasing me, aren't you?"

"Yes. And I would like to say I'm sorry, but I can't because I'm not."

"You're funny. He's not. He's so serious about everything. But I think I love him."

"No, you don't."

"Do you mean I don't think I love him?"

"No. I mean you don't love him."

"How can you say that?"

"Because you know you love someone when you don't have to ask yourself if you love them. You just do and you have no idea why. It's one of life's greatest mysteries. 'The heart has its reasons, which reason does not know. We feel it in a thousand things.' A Frenchman named Pascal said that. Frenchmen can be right sometimes. I ought to know. I'm half French, if Cajun counts as French."

"That's beautiful. Maybe you're right."

"Of course I'm right. I'm a hundred years old, aren't I? And the Frenchman would be even older if he were still alive."

She laughed. "We're having some problems right now. We agreed not to see other people, but I saw him texting his ex. When I confronted him about it, he lied and told me I was crazy. My girlfriends say different things. Then he got mad and slapped me. It wasn't hard. He doesn't want me to see my friends anymore. He says they hate him and want to break us up, and it's not fair to him because they barely know him. I don't know. It's all so confusing. What do you think?"

"Well, first, since you ask, the lying is huge. Liars always get found out, and then trust goes, and then you have no meaningful relationship. But mainly it depends on the answer to one question."

"What question?"

"How much control over your life do you want to give to the jerks of this world?"

"My dad used to do that."

"Do what?"

"Answer a question with a question."

"It's your question to answer. And it's important that you do. Who you decide to marry, if you see yourself getting married, is easily one of the biggest decisions, if not *the* biggest, you will ever make."

"I'm sorry. I'm afraid I forgot why I'm here. I'm supposed to be interviewing you."

"That's okay. You can just make stuff up."

"You mean you want me to lie?"

I laughed. "No. I was just kidding."

"Well then, will your family be here for your birthday?"

"No. They're all gone now. I had a younger brother, but he died two years ago. I'm the last of the Mohicans."

Mindy got out her pen and notepad and said, "What is your favorite memory?"

"I don't have a favorite memory. I have thousands of wonderful memories. I try not to live in the past, but sometimes I just sit in my chair and think about my life. I love people. I love being outside. I love problems. I always think things are going to turn out well in the end. And they usually do. I'm just lucky, I guess."

"You love problems?"

"Yes. Well, I love solving them. It gives your mind something to do that's useful."

"Any favorite food?"

"I'm particularly fond of Jack Daniel's and butter. Just not together."

"Would you say that you've had a happy life?"

"Oh my, yes. I laugh a lot. There are a lot of things in life that are funny if you just think about them and don't take yourself too seriously. It cures a lot of maladies too. Life's not worth living without laughter. But, as important as laughter is, life's most important lessons are seldom learned while laughing."

"Did your life turn out the way you thought it would?"

"No. Not at all. Not even close. When you're young, especially if you're ambitious, you make a plan. I know I did. Now it almost seems cute. You can make a plan if you want, but then you'll look back on it when you're old and chuckle. I'm not saying you shouldn't make plans to better yourself, but the details are unknowable. Your philosophy of life changes in many ways throughout your life. For some reason, it's rather disturbing to me to realize that. Life is like a huge buffet. There are so many choices. You step to the head of the line thinking you'll have the salmon, but when you get to the entrée section the salmon is all gone. So . . . try the goulash. Maybe you'll find out you like goulash better than salmon anyway."

"Do you have any regrets?"

"No. None that matter. There's nothing I wanted to do that I haven't done—or at least tried my best to do. But I do have a lot of questions. I was thinking the other day how some of the little decisions I have made have had such a profound impact on my life. And I wondered what might have been different had I been a little wiser. What if I could live my life again, only backward this time? You know, from death to birth . . ."

I sat there quietly for a moment. I guessed it made her a little ill at ease.

She spent the next thirty minutes doing her reporter thing. She was very good at it. Then she said, "Just one more question: To what do you attribute your long life?"

"Prune juice," I said.

She laughed so hard she dropped her pen. Then she dropped her notebook when she tried to pick up her pen. When she had all her stuff back in order, she headed for the door. As she reached it, she turned and said, "Do you mind if I come again sometime? Just for a visit."

"I would really like just a visit."

"I'll do a good job on the article, Dr. Carson. Trust me."

"I do trust you. I really do. I trust most people. I'd rather go through life trusting people and being disappointed on occasion than go through life with a cynical attitude and occasionally being pleasantly surprised."

She stuck her hand out again. "Thank you so much. It was so much fun, but I have to go now. I need to go buy me some prune juice."

At dinner that night, they sang "Happy Birthday" to me. You might've noticed I didn't say "*for* me." They wanted me to put on one of those conical hats with the rubber band, but I wouldn't. A man's got to have a little pride. The cake was good. I got a corner piece since it had the most icing. For candles, they had a one and two zeros. I guessed they didn't want me to catch fire trying to blow out a hundred of those little things. Thank God for small favors. I got all three of them in one breath.

I went upstairs to my room and got ready for bed. I scratched Lady, told her what a good girl she was, and bid her good night. I stopped by the bedside table, lightly caressed Joanne's picture, told her I loved her, and turned off the light. I sat in my chair and looked out the window. There was a full moon and I could see the hills. Mindy was right. It was a beautiful view and one that I never grew tired of.

I had lived to be a hundred. It makes a person a bit pensive. I thanked God for my life. I told Him I was glad I had been born. I hoped other people could say the same about me. I hoped that I had been a good person. At any rate, I tried. I really tried. "Oh God. I have been so lucky," I whispered.

I thought again about Joanne. "See you soon, sweetheart." I felt tired. So tired. I closed my eyes.

I contemplated what I had said to Mindy about little decisions. I knew one thing. The best decision I ever made was to marry Joanne. But I felt I hadn't explained very well to Mindy what I had meant about living your life backward. I didn't mean that if you did, you would know all the incidents in your life. I only meant, what if you could enter each day with the knowledge, and hopefully wisdom, that a long lifetime of experiences and perspective gives you? How might that impact the decisions you make—even the little ones? Of course, that's not possible, but what if? I mean, really, what if . . . ?

Chapter 2

The Rainbow

Forward

I climbed the stepladder, reached up, and pulled on the cord. The attic stairs appeared from the ceiling and unfolded, hitting the floor with a soft clack. Momma (that's how we spelled it—you can spell it "Mama" in your brain if it makes you feel superior) had asked me to get a box of her old clothes, which was stored in the attic. My little brother, Frankie, decided to tag along. I didn't really mind having him follow me around. He thought I walked on water, and I wasn't about to set him straight. In the meantime, I decided to put him to good use.

"Why don't you go up first and turn on the light," I said. I was afraid of spiders and thought I would let him walk through any webs that might be lurking in the attic. Besides, he kind of liked spiders.

"My *Golden Book of Spiders* says they eat bad insects," he'd said a while back.

"Not if I can get to them first with a shoe," I'd replied.

I was following him up the attic stairs when he suddenly

slipped and fell. His butt hit me on the top of my head, and I dropped about two feet and hit my right elbow on a rung of the ladder. The pain was so bad I couldn't say anything for a few seconds.

"Oh, sorry, Bubba. My foot slipped," he said. "Are you okay?"

My arm, little finger, and ring finger felt numb but also hurt, if that made any sense. I flexed my fingers to see if they still worked, and they did. "Yeah. I think so," I said.

I waited a minute until I got some feeling back and then climbed into the attic behind Frankie. It was summer in Corpus Christi, and the attic was hot. We found the box Momma had wanted. It weighed a ton. As I wrestled it over to the stairs, something caught my eye.

Sunlight poured through the vent in the attic, and I noticed there were small rainbow-colored lights refracting here and there. Some were on the floor, some on other boxes, and some on the undersides of the roof. It was so pretty. I put the box down by the attic opening and walked over to see what was causing this. It proved to be a cylindrical piece of glass with a lot of small facets on its surface. It was about as big as my thumb and had a hole in the center of its long axis.

I reached over, picked it up with my right hand, and enclosed it in my fist. Electrical bolts went through my hand, especially some of my fingers. It was so hot it almost burned.

"Wow!" is all I said. Then I opened my fist and closed it again, and again I felt the electricity. "Wow," I said again. This time softly.

"What is it, Bubba?" said Frankie.

"I don't know. There is some kind of power or electricity or something in this thing. I think I'll keep it." I put it in my pocket and went over to the ladder. I went down a few steps, pulled the box over, and went down the steps holding the box over my head. It was easy! It was light! It was a lot easier to get it down the steps than it was carrying the box around before I touched the crystal in my pocket.

Frankie came down, and we closed the attic door. I canceled my other plans for the day. "Frankie," I said, "I need to take this to Momma's bedroom. Then let's go to the tree house. I need to tell you something."

I picked up the box to take it downstairs to Momma's bedroom. The box had gotten lighter still. I was getting stronger. It was amazing. Then we went out in the backyard and climbed up to the second floor of our tree house. I pulled the towel that we used as a door closed, and we both sat down.

I said to Frankie, "Do me a favor. Hold this crystal for a second." I handed it to him. "Do you feel, like, an electrical power coming out of it?"

He waited a couple of seconds and said, "Do you?"

"I did."

"I think maybe I do too," he said.

I took it from him and held it in my left hand. It was warm, and I felt power in my left hand too. I put it in the pocket of my jeans. "I think my crystal has special powers," I said. "I suddenly got stronger after I touched it. We need to keep this a secret. Maybe it was given to me for a special reason."

"What reason?" Frankie said.

"I don't know. Maybe to help people."

"How?"

"I don't know. But if it's real, I bet I'll find out. Let's go down. I know my arms are stronger. I want to see if I can run faster."

We climbed down from the tree house and went to the alley behind our house. This was where we had our races. For our hundred-yard dash, we would run from a crack in the pavement to a telephone pole. We had no idea how long it really was. I handed my watch to Frankie. He knew to yell, "Ready. Set. Go!" when I told him I was ready. Not three months ago, I had run this in nine seconds.

I went to the crack, took the crystal out of my pocket, and rubbed it on my left leg and then my right leg. I put it back in my pocket and signaled to Frankie, who was standing by the telephone pole, that I was ready. Then Frankie yelled, "Ready. Set. *Go!*" and off I went. I felt powerful and smooth. My strides were eating up the pavement. I had never run this fast before. I crossed the finish line and was not even breathing hard.

"What was my time, Frankie?"

"Seven seconds! You looked superhuman!"

"I feel superhuman. Frankie, do you suppose I really do have special powers with my crystal?"

"I guess so. Maybe you ought to have a name."

"Yeah. That's a great idea. What do you think?"

"How about Rainbow Boy?"

"Nah. Too girlie. I felt electricity when I first picked it up. How about Electro Boy?"

"Yeah. That's great! Say, you could make a special T-shirt, and you could wear it with that western shirt you have with the snaps instead of buttons on top of it, and then you could just yank on your shirttails and it would pop open and there would be . . . Electro Boy!"

"Great idea!" And it was. Frankie was little. He wasn't stupid. "Let's go make one now," I said.

We ran into the house and got my last yellow T-shirt. I found a black and a red marker and used the black one to draw a big capital *E* just to the left of center and a capital *B* just to the right of center, but I left off the vertical line in the *B*. Then with the red marker, I drew in the vertical line of the *B* but made it look like a lightning bolt. Then I drew a jagged red circle around the letters.

"What do you think, Frankie?"

"Cool! Super cool!"

I took off my regular T-shirt and put on my Electro Boy T-shirt, then my western shirt on top of that. I closed the snaps, leaving the shirt untucked.

"Let's go, Frankie," I said. "We need to go find some people who need Electro Boy's help."

We walked down our street, Elizabeth Street, to Morgan Parkway and then turned left and went to the elevated pedestrian walkway that crossed the street. We could have turned right instead, but that was where a lot of Mexicans lived, and I was afraid to go there. Mexicans carried knives. Everybody knew that. Morgan Parkway was the busiest street in town. It had six lanes separated by a narrow, grassy median. Momma and Daddy wouldn't let us cross this street except by the walkway at the light, and we needed to cross Morgan to get to the part of town where I was sure we would find all kinds of people needing Electro Boy's help.

As we walked along, Frankie started to sing the "Notre Dame Victory March." He had no idea what the proper words were, so he had made up his own.

> Come on, you baby, come on you dah
> Come on, you everlasting rah rah
> Round the fields of drowned clover
> We're out on the fields to win.

I should have made him shut up, but I was feeling so magnanimous that I didn't. I suddenly realized that I had a sidekick. Every superhero needed a sidekick. I'd have to tell him about that idea when we got back home. We could have another secret meeting in our tree house. He'd need a name, of course. Maybe I'd let him come up with one himself. Just so long as it wasn't Rainbow Boy or something uncreative like that. It had to be cool, but not as cool as Electro Boy, as if that were possible.

We walked down street after street with no sightings of anyone in distress. It was late in the afternoon when I looked down a long driveway and saw an old lady unloading her groceries, or at least trying to. She must have been at least fifty. Her car trunk was open, and she was struggling with a bulging paper bag. I could see a small tear developing and that meant disaster was just around the corner.

I said to Frankie, "You wait here. This looks like a job for Electro Boy!"

I took off running at a blistering pace, reaching down and grabbing my shirttails to jerk them apart. My western shirt flew open and revealed my Electro Boy T-shirt.

As I neared the old lady, I saw the bag split slowly open and a few cans of beans fell on the driveway and started rolling down a slight incline toward the house. As I passed her, I yelled, "Electro Boy is here! Stand aside, ma'am."

I think I startled her, as she gave a little squeak, straightened up suddenly, and banged her head on the underside of the open trunk.

"Oooh. What th—?" she said.

I was forced to repeat, "Electro Boy is here!" Then I ran off to chase down the errant beans. She sat on the edge of the trunk and held her head.

When I came back with the cans, I saw that she didn't look too good. "Are you all right?"

"Yes. I think so. You startled me. Thank you for trying to help."

"Glad to," I said. "Let me help you get this stuff inside."

"Okay. I do feel a little woozy."

I led her into the house, and she sat down at her kitchen table.

"Can I get you some water?" I said.

"Yes. As a matter of fact, that sounds good. The glasses are in that cabinet over there."

I got the water and handed it to her.

"Do you want some yourself?" she asked.

"No, ma'am. I need to get the rest of your groceries in."

I went back out to the car and brought the rest of the groceries in. I put them all on the kitchen table.

"Thank you for your help. What's your name?"

"Electro Boy." I pointed to my T-shirt. "See, here's the *E* and the *B* with the lightning bolt on it. I think I may be a superhero. I was trying to find out today if I really am one."

"Well, you sure do act like one."

"Thank you, ma'am. Well, I'd better be off. My mother and father are probably wondering where I am."

I was halfway out the door and in the act of closing it when I heard her scream. It was a loud, high-pitched, terror-stricken scream. I recognized it. My mother shrieked like that on occasion. It was her spider scream. I whirled around, and the old lady was standing there with one hand over her mouth and her other hand pointing at the floor. I was right. It was a spider. Unless I missed my bet, it was a brown recluse. I recognized it from Frankie's *The Golden Book of Spiders*.

I'm sure I hated spiders as much as she and Momma did, but I had been forced to kill them whenever Daddy wasn't around. I said, "Don't worry, ma'am, I'm good at this. I'll get him for you."

With that, I began to stalk him by sneaking up on him from behind. I had learned to take baby steps for this part. When I was a couple of feet away, I suddenly slapped my right foot down for the kill. For those of you not familiar with the breed, let me tell you a brown recluse is extremely fast and has superb reflexes. He shot out ahead of me about five feet and stopped. The lady let out another spider scream and pulled her feet up into the seat of her chair.

I sneaked up on him again and slapped again, and he shot out again and she screamed again. It was unnerving, especially for me. The spider looked unconcerned. I was starting to get flustered. This wasn't supposed to be happening.

I charged the dang thing, slapping with my right foot, then my left, then my right, then my left. I was basically walking around her kitchen like a wild man with a severe problem with his gait. Her screams became less and less loud, and eventually I noticed that the screams had turned into laughter. I looked over, and she had her face in her hands and her shoulders were shaking.

Well, shake away, sister, I thought. Then I smashed him and gave a howl of triumph.

"Take that!" I said.

I got a paper towel and cleaned up the spider guts.

"No kidding, Electro Boy, you are my hero. I don't know when I've had so much fun being scared to death." She came over and tousled my hair and gave me a hug. "Thank you from the bottom of my heart. I'm sure you'll be a wonderful superhero."

I walked back up the driveway to where I had left Frankie, snapping my shirt closed. As we headed back home, I told Frankie all about my exploit. He was impressed. And, to tell the truth, the way I told the story, I was impressed too.

We got back to Morgan Parkway a little after five. The traffic was awful. We crossed over the walkway, then walked down to the corner of Elizabeth and Morgan. I was tired. I was glad we were only two blocks from home.

Frankie turned right for home, but I glanced to my left and saw something that made me come to a sudden halt. There was a puppy all alone on the median. He was trembling, and his tail was tucked between his legs. Each time a car would whiz by, he would flinch. Occasionally, he would take a small step like he wanted to run. He was so cute. He had big, soft eyes, floppy ears, and a black patch on his white chest.

I turned and yelled, "Frankie. Look over there."

Frankie turned back and came over. "Aww. Poor guy. What'll we do? Maybe the police can help."

"I doubt it. And he needs to be rescued now. Not in thirty minutes. Look. He looks like he wants to run. He'll get run over. I have to go get him."

"No, Bubba. *You'll* get run over. Let me go get Daddy. He'll know what to do."

"He's probably not home yet. I have to go get him now. Don't worry. I feel really strong."

I took the crystal out of my pocket and quickly rubbed it on both arms and both legs and then put it back in my right pocket. Then I jerked on my shirttails again and became Electro Boy. A surge of extreme energy coursed through my body. I looked to my left to size up the situation. The cars were whizzing by one after the other. I judged that there was not going to be a break long enough for me to cross all three lanes at once. I was going to have to cross this street one lane at a time. I waited for an opening big enough to get across one lane and went for it. A car honked but kept going. I stopped right on the line separating the right lane from the middle lane and waited. I had almost flown across that first lane I was so fast.

The cars were veering a little away from me so that my space on the line was a little bigger than when I had first arrived. This made the space on the line between the middle lane and the left lane smaller than before. I saw I was going to have to cross the last two lanes in one dash. I reminded myself how fast I had run my hundred-yard race earlier that day. I thought I saw my opening. I tore off the millisecond the first car's bumper was past me and just kept going. The second car honked and the driver slammed on his brakes. I dived for the median and came to rest within a foot of the puppy. I would like to say that he was glad to see me, but I think he was too scared to be grateful.

I scooped him up, and he quit trembling. "You're gonna be okay, fella. Electro Boy is here. You're gonna be okay. You'll see."

Now all that remained was to get back across. I thought I would just do again what had gotten me across the street the first time, but that was so close that I had almost gotten hit, and now I was carrying a puppy. I decided to do it one lane at a time. The first lane was easy. This time, I didn't wait long on the first line. I charged again and made it to the second. Just one more lane to go. I saw an opening and went for it. Just as I started, the puppy tried to squirm free. I hesitated to regain control over him, and I realized the car I had been sure I was going to miss was going to hit me. The driver slammed on his brakes, and just before impact, I turned my back to the car so the puppy wouldn't get hurt. I kind of danced to the side a bit, and the right-front headlight hit the back of my left thigh. I spun around and wound up on my back on the sidewalk. I watched as my right pant leg turned red in the area of my thigh. My left leg was all wrong. It was not pointing where a leg was supposed to point.

Daddy and Momma and Frankie were sprinting down Elizabeth Street, and the next thing I knew, Momma had my head in her lap. Daddy looked worried. Frankie was crying, "I told him not to go. I told him. He wouldn't listen."

Daddy went to call an ambulance. The driver of the car came running up. She looked worried. She kept saying how sorry she was. She was crying.

My leg hurt so bad. I thought I might throw up. Momma stayed right with me. She was crying too. "Why in the name of God would you run right in front of a car like that? You could have been killed. Are you okay? Bob! Talk to me, son."

I forgot about myself for a moment and looked at my mother. "I was rescuing a dog. I thought I could make it because . . ." I reached in my right pant pocket and pulled out my crystal to show her. It was broken in two.

"What's that?" Momma said.

"It's my crystal," I said.

"Why, that looks like a weight for my old ceiling fan pull," she said. "Where did you get it?"

"I found it in the attic when Frankie and I were up there looking for your box of clothes. It was hot, and it made my hand tingle. I thought it gave me superpowers. I thought it had magic in it. I thought it made me special."

"You already are special," she said. "And there is magic out there. You just need to let it find you. You're my baby. I know these things."

The puppy came over and sat down next to me. He put his head on my chest and looked up at me with his big eyes. I stroked his head, and he closed his eyes. He wagged his tail. He looked happy.

"Momma, can we keep him? I think he likes me."

"Sure, baby. I'll tell Daddy we're getting a new dog."

"Thanks. I'll take good care of him."

"I know you will. What do you think we should name him?"

"I think Frankie should name him. Just not Rainbow Boy. Okay, Frankie?"

"Okay, Bubba. How about Lucky?"

Chapter 3

The Seventy-Fifth

Backward

Joanne poked me with her foot. "Bob! The alarm. Turn it off."

I rolled over and turned the dang thing off. We needed to buy a kinder, gentler alarm.

"You were awful last night," she said.

Nothing like waking up in the morning and discovering that you had been a jerk while you were asleep. I snored—or at least I used to snore. I had my dentist make me one of those custom-fitted mouthpiece things you jam in your mouth before retiring for the night. It holds your jaw forward and keeps your tongue from falling back in your throat, thus keeping you from snoring. At least that was what I was told. Surprisingly, it worked. That was the good part. Unfortunately, now, instead of snoring, I made a noise that Joanne called "gakking."

"You gakked last night! Again!"

"Shorry. Shorry all aground," I said. It's hard to sound intelligible with a hunk of plastic in your mouth. I took it out and headed for the bathroom, drool trailing behind me from my anti-snoring, pro-gakking oral appliance.

Joanne threw her knee pillow at me. She missed. She was just teasing—I thought. As I walked away, she said, "I have to pee. Don't make me laugh."

I lifted the toilet lid and leaned against the wall as I relieved myself. Ah! Nothing like an empty bladder to brighten your day. When I was through, I did an absolutely amazing thing that was entirely out of character for me: I lowered the lid. It was, after all, Joanne's seventy-fifth birthday. *I should get an A plus for that one,* I thought. The lid was loose and wobbled a little when I'd lowered it. I needed to fix that someday. It tended to snap from side to side unpredictably when you sat down. I went to my sink to begin my ablutions.

As I was brushing my teeth, Joanne came into the bathroom, laid her head on my shoulder, kissed me on the neck, and popped me on the butt as she walked away. She went into the toilet room and closed the door. I heard the little thwack of the toilet seat suddenly skittering off to one side. "Crap!"

"What's the matter?" As if I didn't know.

"I almost fell in."

"Then that must be the shriek I almost heard."

"Don't be a wise ass, Wise Ass."

She exited the toilet room, strode purposefully to the shower, ran the water, and stepped in. She always unfailingly hummed in the shower. I have a theory why so many people sing in the shower. After all, we did spend the warmest, wettest, safest nine months of our lives in basically a bath. At any rate, she hummed and she was loud. It was always oldies. Today her selection was "Itsy Bitsy Teenie Weenie Yellow Polka Dot Bikini." I hated that song, but it was just Joanne being Joanne. And I loved my Joanne. It used to irritate the hell out of me. But now, like so many of her little foibles, I found it endearing.

I hoped she felt the same about my foibles. Lord knew I had a rich supply of them. I could foibleize with the best of them.

She got out, dried herself off, and began her toe-fungus ritual. She'd had a toe fungus for years. She had seen a podiatrist, and he wanted to remove the toenail. Her response was "No way, Jose." Well, she didn't actually say that. You see, she was a Flip-Flop Queen, and no way was she going to go around in public with a buck-naked big toe. She went to her dermatologist to obtain a more acceptable treatment plan, but he had been no help either. Our housekeeper, unburdened by a medical education, was more helpful. She recommended Joanne soak her foot in a bucket of Clorox, so she was trying that. I recommended she try sulfuric acid, since you couldn't have toe fungus if you didn't have toes.

Her only reply was "Sweetheart, sometimes I feel really rooster pecked."

Her next stop was her vanity table and the Land of a Thousand Bottles, as Dave Barry called it. She had everything from Pond's Cold Cream to something called the Hoofmaker over there. I had read the label on this one: "Intensive protein hoof treatment. Regular use of the Hoofmaker will provide strong yet flexible hooves on your horse. Not for internal use. Keep out of the reach of children." She claimed it made your nails stronger. I told her that probably explained her whinnying in her sleep. She was not amused, so I doubled down by asking if it had improved her time for seven furlongs.

She also had Udder Balm. The instructions here were, and I quote, "Apply liberally to teats, udders, and other exposed skin areas." *Other exposed skin areas?* What did that mean? I asked her if she had been running around town with her udders exposed.

As she examined her inventory she said, "I don't think I'll use deodorant today. I'm not planning on sweating."

I have learned that I am expected to comment on all her

utterances, so I carefully considered my reply to this pronouncement and grunted "Uh" to satisfy the requirement.

She took out a Kleenex and began to blow her nose over and over. I gave her a quizzical look.

"I'm dealing with a rogue booger," she explained. "He apparently likes it up there."

"Are you sure it's a he?"

Next she went to the sink and began to brush her teeth. Shortly after beginning, she stopped and rather mushily said, "Shumshings hrong wish dish tooshpace. Hit dushn't tashe hright. Hit mush be ole."

I picked up the tube and glanced at it. I said, "I think the reason why this 'tooshpace,' as you call it, doesn't 'tashe hright' is because this 'tooshpace' is hemorrhoid cream."

She made a loud noise some might call "gakking" and spit it all out in the sink. Then she threw the toothbrush away, got a new one, and brushed her teeth twice. This time with toothpaste. Then she got out her mouthwash and, taking a big swig, held it in her mouth while she counted to a hundred with her fingers. Each time she counted to ten, she stamped her right foot.

Next she put on a white T-shirt but was unhappy with the way it fit or looked. She complained that the front of it was pressing against her throat, so she took it off and started to hang it up again. Then she noticed she had put it on backward and said, "The front of your neck and the back of your neck aren't quite the same." She put it back on.

Next were the slippers. They were a kind of moccasin, and each looked a bit alike, but not a whole lot. She had put an *X* inside the left one so she would know which was which.

Finally she picked up her wedding ring, smiled, kissed it, and slipped it on. It was a plain gold band. That was all she had wanted. I had simply engraved it, "You are my life." I had a similar gold band, which she had engraved, "Put your damn ring back on." Really.

I always kept an eye on this performance in the shaving mirror. It led to frequent nicks. I got a good one today.

"Dammit," I said. It was a gusher.

As she walked out of the bathroom, she showed her sensitive side by saying, "Don't bleed on the carpet."

I followed her out the door, and I passed by the thermostat. I had been freezing since I got out of bed, but that was no surprise, since she had, as usual, set the thermostat to sixty-five. I was not allowed to touch the thing. It was an unspoken rule, which I rarely broke. The last time I did, I heard this: "Who cranked the thermostat all the way up to seventy?" If I was cold, well then, I just had to put on more clothes. I wondered if her doctor had ever checked her thyroid. I was once again tempted to "crank it all the way up to seventy." I was somehow able to resist the temptation. Ah well. It was just another little thing. Most of your life was little things. Might as well enjoy them.

***

Joanne and I always did something that was fun on our birthdays. Unlike most couples, the spouse made all the plans. You never knew what your spouse had in store for you. The big surprise today was that I had managed to get some tickets to the Willie Nelson concert in San Antonio at the Alamodome. By the time I'd learned of the concert, they were sold out, and she loved Willie. I liked Willie. I felt his best song was "Just as I Am." It was an instrumental. You got to hear Willie without actually having to listen to his voice. At any rate, I had called one of those ticket agencies, and of course they had tickets, and they were only $350 each. "Good" seats, but not "great." Take it or leave it. I took it.

We drove downtown to park. If you had "great" tickets, you could park on the grounds of the Alamodome. If you had "good" tickets, you were on your own. Turns out being on your own was a bad place to be. There was a Baptist convention at the nearby convention center, and with the Baptists and the Willieists in town, there were no parking places at all. I am a Christian myself, but now I was thinking, *Damn Christians anyhow.*

The concert was due to start in twenty minutes. All the lots were full. There were absolutely no places on the streets. Even all the "No Parking" parking spots were taken. All the fire hydrants were blocked. The streets were choked with traffic. Whose idea was this anyway? Oh yeah, mine.

I finally found a parking spot in a residential area about two miles from the arena. We parked, and I got out and went around to open her car door like I always did. I took her hand and helped her out. She was in high heels. She looked great, but she didn't look happy. I said, "You don't look happy."

She just looked at me and said, "Number one."

Oh no! Number one. The crusher. We'd been married long enough that we had decided it would be easier to just assign certain situations numbers so that we wouldn't have to waste time and effort repeating the same thing over and over. For example, "number three" meant "We're going to be late." "Number two" meant "No. I don't care where we eat, but I'm going to veto wherever you suggest." "Number one," of course, meant "This is all your fault."

"Maybe we can find a cab," I said. "Let's just start walking."

We came to the first corner, and a kid about twelve years old rolled by on his bicycle, licking a popsicle. I got an idea. I sprinted after him. "Hey, kid," I yelled.

He stopped and I ran up to him. The bicycle was pretty pathetic. For some reason, he had a chain lock around the handlebars. Like anyone would ever want to steal it. I said, "What's your name?"

"Ja'Corian."

"Ja'Corian, I need a bicycle. How much for yours?"

"I dunno. It's mine. I like it."

"How about a hundred?"

"A hundred what?"

"Dollars. A hundred dollars."

His eyes widened. "A hundred dollars? You'd give me a hundred dollars for this?"

"Yeah, and I'll tell you what. If you tell me the combination to that lock, I'll bring it back here later tonight and chain it to that stop sign over there. You can come and get it in the morning."

He asked what seemed like a very intelligent question. "You got the hundred dollars on you?"

"Yes." I gave him five twenties, and he gave me the combination. It was 0-0-0-0.

I got on the bicycle, and Joanne sat crosswise on the bar in front of the seat, whatever that is called, and away we went. I used to think downtown San Antonio was flat. Turns out it was not. There were mountains there. Or at least that was what it felt like when your wife was sitting on the bar in front of you, and you hadn't ridden a bicycle in sixty years.

Joanne was a big help. "Faster, Bob. Faster." Then she would laugh and yell, "Woo-hoo! This is *fun*! You're gonna get a big tip!"

We pulled up right in front of the Alamodome, and Joanne hopped off in a great mood. Me, not so much. I was drenched in sweat, my legs were burning, and I was breathing hard as I chained the bike to a lamppost.

We went in. The opening act was already at it. We walked by the usual assortment of marketing junk. I was in a hurry to get to our seats. Joanne was not. She stopped and looked over the assortment.

"I think I found my birthday present," she said, and held up a pink T-shirt with a hideous picture of Willie on the front. It was a headshot. Willie seemed happy. On the back was a list of where he would be appearing on this season's tour.

"If you want it, we'll get it, but remember, one of these things tried to strangle you this morning."

"Yeah. I remember. Thank God you were there. But, honey, this one has a picture on it. I think I can remember to put Willie in front."

We got the T-shirt and headed for our seats. As we neared them, it became obvious they were going to be great, despite what the guy at the ticket place had told me. Right in the center and just behind the most expensive section. The seats were in the stadium area, so we were sure to be able to see over whoever sat in front of us. And they were aisle seats. My sweat had begun to evaporate, and my legs weren't trembling anymore. This was going to be great!

When we reached our seats, we discovered they were already occupied by another couple.

"Pardon me," I said. "I think you're sitting in our seats." I showed the guy our tickets. He was wearing a wifebeater tank top, apparently to showcase his impressive array of deltoid tattoos. I didn't study the details, but I did notice that skulls and daggers featured prominently. He also had a beautiful roach tattooed on his neck. I guessed he was in the pest control business. A psychedelic do-rag sat proudly on top of his head. I felt confident they had arrived on one of the Harleys parked outside.

The guy stood. He was huge. "I think not, my friend. We're not going anywhere. Sweetie, why don't you go get security?"

His babe stepped around him and strode past Joanne and me.

So we three just stood there. Joanne and I in the aisle, and he in front of our seats. At least security was coming. Maybe the security guy was bigger than my opponent. He watched the opening act. I glared at him and tried to look tough. Joanne watched the opening act.

A few minutes later, I felt a tap on my shoulder and turned around. There was a guy standing in the aisle in front of Wifebeater's girl. He looked like Barney Fife. He had a vest on with a name tag pinned to it. His first name was in small letters. It identified him as either Perry or Percy. I couldn't tell which. His last name, in large letters, was Periwinkle. I was wondering, *What were his parents thinking?* They must have loved *P*s.

"Excuse me, sir. May I see your tickets?"

"Sure." I handed him our tickets.

He looked at them a minute. "These tickets were stolen. Come with me, please."

"What?" Joanne suddenly got interested. "We have stolen tickets? This is so exciting! We're criminals! Who knew?" And then, to officer Periwinkle, she said, "I'd keep a close eye on him, officer. He's one tough hombre." Nice touch, that. Now he thought I was an "hombre."

We followed Barney, me trudging meekly along. Joanne was holding on to my arm, whispering, "Can you believe this, honey? We've been nabbed by the fuzz."

We walked down a long corridor to a single elevator. We stepped in, he hit the *G* button, and, as the doors closed, Periwinkle uttered a soft moan.

I glanced over at him. "You okay?" I said.

"Yeah. I'm a little claustrophobic. I hate these things."

"We could take the stairs."

"Nah. I'll be fine."

The elevator stopped. The doors didn't open.

An "uh-oh" came out of Periwinkle. "This isn't good."

"Why aren't the doors opening?" Joanne asked.

"I don't know," Periwinkle replied in a shaky voice. He

started pounding on the doors with both fists. "Help! Help! Help! Help!" There was, of course, no response, so he tried reasoning with the elevator. "I'll never ride you again if you'll just open your doors." There was still no response.

Joanne looked at me and mouthed, *Do something.*

I reached over and patted him on the shoulder. "There, there."

Joanne rolled her eyes. "Come over here, and we'll both sit down." Periwinkle let himself be led to the corner, and they both sat down. Joanne said, "Is your name Percy?"

"No. My middle name is Percy. My first name is Perry."

"So your name is Perry Percy Periwinkle?"

"Yes. My parents wanted a girl. I was a big disappointment to them. I still am."

Joanne patted him on the shoulder and said, "There, there."

I rolled my eyes. Two could play that game. Perry began to rock gently side to side. He started to moan.

"Okay," I said. "Perry, we're going to get out of here. I guarantee it. You know that's true. Right?"

"Yeah. I guess so." He kept right on rocking and moaning.

I looked over the control panel. I first saw the big red alarm button. I thought this qualified as an alarm-worthy situation, so I punched it. Nothing happened. Next I tried the "Door Open" button, but no doors opened. Then I saw the "Call" button. It wasn't red, but I liked its message of hope, so I pushed it. No response. Next I tried Perry's initial solution. "Help! Help! Help!"

After the third "help," a voice said, "Can I help you?" *Wow! It works!*

"Yes. My wife and I and Mr. Periwinkle with security are stuck in this elevator."

"I see that now on my controls here, sir. We'll get you out. Don't worry."

"Okay. Thanks. Any idea how long it'll take?"

"It'd only be a guess, sir. Probably an hour or two."

"Okay."

I turned to Joanne and Perry. "Well, here we all are. Any suggestions?"

"What if we run out of oxygen?" Perry said. "What if the cable breaks? What if the lights go out? Maybe we could free it up if we all jumped at the same time." Then he looked up at the ceiling. "Maybe I could crawl out through the escape hatch up there."

"I'm sure we'll be fine if we just sit here and wait for them to get us out," Joanne said.

"Tell you what, Perry, why don't you just do what you were going to do back in the office. We might as well get that out of the way."

"Yeah. You're right. That's a good idea." He seemed to settle down a bit. He puffed himself up and said, "Do you know what the penalty is for stealing tickets of this value?"

"No."

"Well, I'll tell you. You could spend thirty days in jail and be fined up to $10,000."

"Really? That seems a bit harsh."

"Well, check it out."

"Look, I bought the tickets at the Sterling Ticket Agency. You can call them up. I had no idea they were stolen. I purchased them in good faith. Cost me $350 each."

"$350 a pop! Must be nice. Just to see an old singer."

"It's my wife's birthday. She wanted to see Willie. He can't help it if he's old."

"I know. Sorry, I'm not being very professional. I'm just upset. It's been a bad day. I had a wreck on the way to work today. Just a fender bender, but it knocked my left-front headlight out. I had just bought the car. It wasn't new, but it was new to me. A seven-year-old Honda. It only had seventy-five thousand miles on it. I don't have the money to fix it, and I can't drive it unless I do."

"Oh. Sorry."

"Talking seems to make me feel better."

"Good. I'm Bob, by the way. And this is Joanne."

"Nice to meet you."

"So what do we do now?" I said.

"We could have a sing-along, or we could play a game," Joanne suggested.

"I don't sing," Perry said.

"She doesn't either."

"Okay, then," Joanne said. "Let's play a game. It'll be fun. Let's see . . . how about two truths and a lie?"

Surprisingly, Perry perked up. "How do you play that?"

"It's easy. We all think up two things about ourselves that are true and one lie about ourselves. Then we tell all three things, and you have to guess which one is the lie. Since Bob and I know everything about each other, you get to guess about both of us, and Bob and I both get to guess about you."

"Okay. But I'll need a few minutes to come up with something."

Five minutes later, we were all ready.

Joanne said, "It was my idea. I get to go first. The three things about me are these. One—I was voted the most beautiful girl in my senior class when I was in high school. Two—I'm afraid of spiders. Three—I can beat Bob in arm wrestling."

Perry said, "Okay. Well, you are a very attractive woman so I can believe number one. And number two, well, a lot of people, especially women, I believe, are afraid of spiders. Number three, um, sorry, you just don't come across that way to me. So . . . I think number three is the lie."

"Sorry, Perry, you're oh for one. Number two is the lie."

I said, "You were the most beautiful girl in high school? Why did you never tell me that?"

"You never asked. And I resent the incredulous tone in that response."

"I just would've thought you'd have let me in on that little tidbit."

"You'll get over it, sweetheart. Now it's your turn."

"Okay. Here are mine. One—I once strangled a coyote." Perry snorted. "Two—I hate brussels sprouts. Three—if I had been a girl, I would have been named Mable."

"I can sympathize with you on number three," Perry said. "If I had been a girl, and as I said, I was supposed to be, I would have been Melissa Marie. Makes me wish I had been a girl sometimes. I mean, really, Perry *and* Percy. One would have been bad enough. So I think number three is true. And I hate brussels sprouts so I'm going to say that's true. Now number one, well, I'll give you that one took some imagination, but I feel confident number one is the lie."

"Sorry, Perry, you're oh for two. Number two is the lie. I love brussels sprouts."

Joanne said, "You strangled a coyote! Are you kidding me?"

"Nope. I'll tell you the story when we get home tonight. Now it's your turn, Perry."

"Okay. Number one is I live with my mother. Two—I once ran the marathon in two hours and thirty-nine minutes. Three—I won the Congressional Medal of Honor."

I thought he misunderstood and was giving us two lies and a truth. Not the other way around. However, I just plowed ahead as if that were not the case. I said, "Number one seems entirely possible. Number two, my God, that's an exceptional time for a marathon. Still, you look like you could have once been a long-distance runner. So that one's possible too. Three—no offense, but that one seems highly unlikely. So I would have to say number three is the lie. What do you say, Joanne?"

"Yes. I agree with Bob. And, I would just like to say that living with your mom is awfully sweet. I'm sure she is happy to have you around."

Perry said, "Looks like we're oh for three as a group. The lie is number one. I live with my brother."

Joanne and I looked at each other, and I gave her a *Can you believe this guy?* look. Just then, the lights blinked, and the elevator jerked and began to descend. It only had half a floor to go before it stopped and the doors opened.

There were a couple of firemen standing there along with a maintenance-looking guy. We all stepped out into the hallway. We thanked them profusely, and the most beautiful girl in her high school class gave each of them a kiss on the cheek. What a strumpet!

We took a short walk down the corridor to a door marked "Security" and went in. A young lady behind the counter said, "You okay, Perry?"

"Yeah. I'm fine. Meet Joanne and Bob. We actually had fun. Didn't we?"

Joanne said, "Yes, we did."

Perry reached in a drawer. "Here are a couple of tickets. These aren't stolen, by the way. I'm afraid they aren't very good. You better hurry. Willie's probably about through, and he never gives encores."

"Thanks, Perry. Sorry if we caused you any trouble."

We walked down the corridor and took the stairs up to the first floor. Our seats were near the top of the stadium and were at a ninety-degree angle to the stage. Perry was right. They weren't very good seats. As we entered the seating area, we heard tremendous applause and saw Willie shuffling off the stage, waving goodbye. So all we got to see was the south side of a northbound Willie. It was not a pretty sight. Certainly not worth $800 (if you counted our limo chained to a lamppost outside).

Joanne and I both started laughing and had to sit down in our seats for a few minutes. We got up and followed the crowd toward the exit. We had to pass by the merchandise hawkers again, and again Joanne wanted to stop. She wanted a Willie CD to listen to on the way home, since we hadn't gotten to hear him sing in person.

We passed into the night air with all the other concertgoers and held hands as we headed for Ja'Corian's bicycle. It was still there, chained to the lamppost. I unlocked it and pushed the thing along at first to get to an open area with fewer pedestrians. As we got to the parking area behind the Alamodome, I glanced up and saw an old Honda. The left-front headlight was broken and the fender was crushed. I stopped.

"Why did we stop?"

"Look at that. An old Honda with the left-front fender crushed."

"Oh. Perry's car, I bet. Poor guy."

I looked down at the license plate. "Oh my God! Look at that."

"What?"

"The license plate. It's a Congressional Medal of Honor plate. It was the truth. We missed Willie, but we spent the evening with a Congressional Medal of Honor winner." I fingered the ruined fender. "Do you have anything to write with and something to write on?"

Joanne opened her purse and produced a pen and a shopping list. I opened my wallet and took out the one personal check I always had tucked away. I filled it in for $500 and made it out to Perry Percy Periwinkle. I wrote on the back of the shopping list: "If you don't cash this check, I will hunt you down and strangle you like a coyote. I am serious, Perry. We doubted what you told us. Thank you for whatever you did. You must accept this. You are our hero." Then I signed it and handed it to Joanne. She read it and signed it too. I tucked the check and the note under the windshield wiper.

We pedaled back to our car, and I locked the bicycle to the stop sign. We got in and drove home, listening to Willie the whole way.

At home, we sat on the couch, and I poured a couple of glasses of wine. Joanne said, "Now tell me the truth. You strangled a coyote?"

"I did indeed. I was in high school. Dolly and I were driving in my car down a country road. I forget why. It was dark, and I saw something move in my peripheral vision, and then we hit it. We stopped, and I backed up to put my headlights on it. It was a coyote, and I had run over his chest. He was just lying there and seemed to be in a lot of pain. So, to put him out of his misery, I reached down and strangled him."

"Isn't that strange," she said. "I told Perry we both knew everything about each other, and we both had deep, dark secrets that neither of us knew about. Well, maybe not dark or even too deep. But secrets nonetheless. Isn't life funny? So full of surprises."

She put both hands to her temples. "Oh. My head! Oh, Bob." She slumped back on the couch and jerked twice.

❋❋❋

And now there I sat. Alone, in a truly ugly room. It looked sterile. Everything was too clean. It smelled sterile. Alcohol and disinfectant vying for attention. Why did those rooms always smell that way? I'd hated them even when I was still practicing.

They'd put you in a place like this and wouldn't tell you how long you'd be there. Then you'd wait for that plain white door to open, and some stranger would walk in and tell you whether your loved one was dead or not.

I was sitting rigidly in a hard green plastic chair with a chrome frame. It had no armrests. My hands were on my knees. The floor was beige. There was a single exam table with white paper across it and a single white pillow placed perfectly at its head. There was an empty metal bucket on wheels on the floor by the foot of the table. The cabinets were hard and angular. The drawer pulls were stainless steel. There were clean glass containers with metal lids all lined up like little soldiers along the back of the countertop. The only thing on the walls was one of those charts with the cartoon faces on it so you could point to the one that best described your pain level. It was called a pain scale chart. The cartoon on the left was smiling. It was the "no pain" level, level one. The cartoon on the right, level ten, was crying. It was labeled the "unimaginable, unspeakable pain" level. That was me.

I heard a big, booming laugh just outside the door. The door handle turned, and a happy face appeared. This was fantastic. She was okay! What a relief!

The face said, "Oh, sorry. Wrong room." The relief disappeared as the door closed.

Later, a kind doctor appeared and gave me the news. The unimaginable, unspeakable news.

I went and sat in my car. I lowered my head, looked down at my hands, and tried to wish the truth away. Old, cracked fingernails stuck on old, gnarled fingers attached to old, splotchy hands. I was old. And now, for the first time in my life, I felt old. Things began to blur. The world looked scary through a lens of tears. I started the car, then stared straight ahead and wondered what to do and where to go. Home? Where was home now? Then I blinked.

Chapter 4

The Bully

Forward

The best part of school began after the final bell. Free at last. I was walking home with my friends. Mack, Charlie, Bill, and I were doing that on Friday, the best day of the week. Saturday was looming with some kind of adventure sure to be in store for us. Maybe just a movie, but probably something more exciting. We were joking and poking and shoving and laughing and teasing each other as usual when we saw Jerry ahead of us. He was alone—just like always. Plodding along with his head down—just like always. I wondered what he was doing there. He usually didn't walk on our street.

We all hated Jerry. It was another thing that drew us all together. It was fun to hate Jerry. It was also easy. He made it so. For one thing, he tried so hard, too hard, to make friends. It made you uncomfortable to see his pathetic efforts. He didn't have a single friend. But the main thing was his appearance.

He couldn't move one side of his face. The good side was smooth and kind of pulled the bad side off to the left. He couldn't smile right. When he tried, his face got even more lopsided, and it looked more like a grimace. One eye wouldn't close. It just stared at you through a pair of goggles. He wore them all the time. He lisped when he talked, which was seldom. He occasionally spit at you when he talked. He didn't have an ear on one side. There was just a dimple where his ear should have been. The other ear was normal. The worst part, I thought, was that he drooled. He carried a handkerchief with him to wipe it away. There were even rumors that he had six toes on one foot.

This was just perfect. There we were, alone with him. No teachers, or any adults at all for that matter, were anywhere in sight. We were at the corner of Elizabeth Street, where I lived. I decided not to turn off. This was going to be good.

Charlie said, "Hold these," and he handed his books to me. He tiptoed quickly behind Jerry and suddenly grabbed the elastic strap on his goggles, pulled it back, and then let it snap forward to pop Jerry on the back of his head.

"Ow!" Jerry rubbed the back of his head and spun around.

"Hey, Frogman," Bill said, "eat any nice bugs lately?"

That was a perfect nickname for Jerry, so I added, "Yeah, Froggie. How did they taste? Were they nice and juicy?"

"Leave me alone." Jerry straightened his goggles and mopped the drool from the corner of his mouth.

"I see you still have rabies, Frogman," Bill said. He then looked at the rest of us for approval of this witticism.

"I don't have rabies. I can't help this."

"We'd all appreciate it if you'd try," I said. "That's disgusting."

Charlie took an exaggerated step back. "Oooh. Our widdle Fwoggie has wabies. I hope it isn't contagious. Are you contagious, Fwoggie?"

Jerry glared at us. "No. I'm not contagious. I don't have rabies. And I don't have leprosy either."

We knew he didn't have rabies or leprosy, of course, but that didn't stop us from treating him as if he did.

We all walked by. I saw the look on his face, his mouth gaping like a frog. As we passed him, Mack pulled on his books so they fell to the sidewalk. I looked back, and he was crouched over them. He looked like he was getting ready to hop. We laughed as we, the cool guys, strode away. It felt good.

***

We had first seen him on the first day of school, walking down the hallway. It was quite a shock.

"What was that?" Charlie whispered after he had passed by.

We all agreed, all four of us, that we sure hoped he was not in our homeroom. We might get sick just by looking at him. What if what he had was contagious? We were all going to be in Miss Krueger's fifth-grade class. Bill, Mack, Charlie, and I were the Four Musketeers. It would have been a disaster if even one of us had been assigned to another room. Particularly if it had been me.

We found room eight and went in and sat down in the back. I got the desk farthest to the rear. Sure enough, just before the bell sounded, this wonder walked in and sat down in the front row. We all made disgusted faces at one another. Charlie pretended to be vomiting.

At the first recess, Charlie said, "Look. I have a great idea. Actually two great ideas."

"What?" I asked. Charlie did have a lot of ideas and some of them were great.

"I'll tell you later. For now I want us to act like you and Mack don't even know Bill and me."

Kind of mysterious. Typical of Charlie. At recess, Mack and I went to the far side of the playground and joined in a game of keep-away football. We saw Bill and Charlie talking to the freak. Near the end of recess, Charlie gave us our secret sign, and we met up at our special place on the far side of the school building where the trash cans were kept. It kind of stunk, but no one else went there.

"So," Charlie began, "we find him sitting on a swing all by himself, and we tell him our names and he says, 'Hi. Nythe to meesh you. I'm Cherry. This isth my firth day here.'"

"His first name is Cherry?" I was astounded.

Bill and Mack laughed. Charlie said, "No, dummy. His name is Jerry. I was just doing my lisp imitation. He was spitting all over us."

"Next time I talk to him, I'm going to bring me an umbrella," Bill said.

"Good idea. And I'll bring a raincoat," Charlie said. "I told him we had been going to Menger since the first grade, and we thought he might want to learn some of the traditions here." Charlie and Bill glanced at one another conspiratorially, and Charlie continued. "So he says, 'Oh wow! You guys are the gweatisht. Thanks.'"

Bill spoke up. "And I said, the first thing you should probably know is that Audubon's birthday is a big deal here at Menger. You know about Audubon, right? The guy who drew birds. And he said, 'Yeth. I've seen some of his dwawings. They're weally good.'"

Charlie resumed control of the report. "Well, this coming Friday is his birthday. Every year on his birthday, everyone in school dresses up like a bird. You know. In honor of the guy. Every year, the bird is different. This year we're all going to dress up like redheaded woodpeckers."

Bill chimed in. "So I said, 'Yeah. That's right. Last year, it was a yellow-bellied sapsucker. There's a prize for the best costume. Two years ago, it was a loon, and I won and got five dollars. I was a good loon. Real loony.'"

Mack and I groaned, then laughed.

"So anyway. Bill and I welcomed him to Menger, and I said, 'We just wanted to give you a little warning about the bird thing. You know, to give you a chance to come up with something good.'"

"I really think he took the bait," Bill added.

Following Charlie's plan, for the rest of the week, Charlie and Bill didn't have anything to do with Mack or me.

Friday finally arrived, and we were anxious to see Jerry walk in. He was late. The bell rang at eight o'clock sharp, and no Jerry. Miss Krueger called the roll and started the class. At 8:10 a.m., the door opened, and in walked Jerry. Or at least we thought it was Jerry. He was magnificent—if you can use that word to describe a redheaded woodpecker. I half expected him to pull out his number 2 pencil and have a snack.

He had used face paint to make his entire face and neck bright red. He had put a red skullcap on to cover his hair and painted dark black eyes on his temples. He was wearing a white long-sleeved T-shirt. He had cut some cardboard into the shape of a bird's wing, painted the whole thing black, and glued some white chicken feathers on the lower part of the wings in a roughly triangular shape. The wings were stuck to his shoulders somehow. He had apparently used heavy-duty wire, which he had fashioned into the four-toed claws of a woodpecker and wrapped the wire with pieces of a gray towel. Bits of wire stuck out from the ends of each claw to form talons. The claws were attached to his belt somehow. The elasticity of the wire caused the feet to jiggle forward and backward with each step to create a menacing effect. This effect, however, was somewhat mitigated by the pièce de résistance, the beak. He had somehow rolled up a sheet of white plastic into a narrow, sharp, pointed cone that he had tied to his nose with red string.

He entered the classroom and stopped, looking at his nonavian classmates. I'd say this for my classmates: they could have been worse. There was just a low tittering going on in the background. Jerry sat down in his front-row seat. At least he didn't have far to go. Miss Krueger must have been stunned. Mouth open, she just stood there with a piece of chalk in her hand and gawked with the rest of the class. After a long interval that seemed like an hour but was probably no longer than twenty or thirty seconds, she continued with her lesson, picking up where she had left off.

At noon, the Four Musketeers headed out of the classroom on the double to the girls' restroom across from room eight. It was important to beat Jerry out the door. As it turned out, we didn't really need to hurry. Jerry waited in the classroom for it to empty, then he set off down the hall. Charlie and Bill immediately began to shove Mack and me. We began to push back. Harsh words were said. Then harsher words. Next, yelling. Suddenly the door opened, almost hitting Bill, and a little girl exited. Before the door could close, Mack and I muscled Charlie and Bill inside, closed the door, and pushed on it to keep it closed. Charlie and Bill immediately began to pound on the door and leaned into it. They succeeded in moving it only about an inch. Then they started their pounding again.

"Let us out, you jerks."

Jerry ran up, holding his beak. "Can I help?" he asked, sounding hopeful.

"We've got Charlie and Bill trapped," I said. "Couple of jerks, if you ask me."

"I know," Jerry said, and once again asked, "Can I help?"

Mack said, "Yes. You can hold the door closed. Bob and I are going to go get Snake."

"Who's Snake?" Jerry added his weight to the door.

"That's what the kids call Vice Principal Hathaway," Mack said. "I'll bet he'll give them hell for being in the girls' restroom. He's in charge of discipline. If spankings are required, he's your man." We had no intentions of going to get Snake, of course. We just needed an excuse to leave. Meanwhile, Charlie and Bill had climbed out the window of the restroom, according to plan. We had figured Jerry would eventually get tired and just leave.

Mack and I left him to his task and walked down the hall toward the cafeteria. We looked up, and miracle of miracles, Snake was walking toward us.

"Let's go to the restroom, Mack," I said, and we ducked into the alcove to the boys' restroom. After a few seconds, I opened the door quietly and stuck my head around the corner. Snake had reached the girls' restroom. I was close enough to hear the whole encounter.

"What in the world are you doing, Jerry, and why are you dressed like that?"

"I'm a redheaded woodpecker. I was told it was Audubon's birthday and to dress up like a bird." He had relinquished his door-guard position.

"Whose birthday?"

"Audubon's."

"Audubon. The bird guy? I didn't know it was his birthday."

"Yessir. The bird guy. I'm beginning to wish he didn't even have a birthday."

"Well. Whatever. So what are you doing, Jerry? You know this is the girls' restroom, don't you?"

"Yessir. Charlie and Bill went inside, and I'm holding them there for you. I'm glad you're here."

"Charlie and Bill are in the girls' restroom?" He opened the door and yelled, "Charlie! Bill! Are you two in there?" No answer. "Charlie! Bill! Come out here right now!" Snake opened the door a bit wider and yelled, "Is anybody here?" No answer. He disappeared inside and a moment later reemerged, frowning. "Who put you up to this, Jerry?"

"Uh . . . It was my idea, sir."

There was a pause as Snake thought this over. "Okay, Jerry.

Okay. Why don't you go home and change out of your bird outfit? I'll tell Miss Krueger you'll be a little late. And what is that thing in your hand?"

"My beak."

As Snake walked by, I heard him say under his breath, "That was a dumb question, Hathaway."

***

Jerry's appearance put him at a distinct disadvantage, and I was sure he'd had difficulties wherever he'd gone to school in years past. I guessed he was hoping for better luck at our school. I'd give him that. He sure did try hard to fit in. At least before he gave up.

He wasn't dumb by any stretch, but he had some troubles in class. I think maybe it was because he got nervous.

One day, we were supposed to give speeches on an adventure we'd had. When Jerry's turn came, he got up and, with trembling hands, held his paper high to, at least partially, hide his face. Then he began to read with a quavering voice.

"My father and I like to go hunting. I once shot a twelve-point buck. My father was real proud of me. I have a picture at home. My mother made sausage out of the meat. It was real good. I have my own gun. It is a break-action gun. I like it. It is not too heavy. One day me and my father went hunting. We were out in the woods. It was cold. We heard a noise, and we looked around and about six wild whores were coming at us. There was a mother whore and some baby whores. She looked mean. She had big tusks. She was coming straight at us. We were close to our deer blind, and so we ran over to it. My father told me to get up fast. So I did. Then he started up after me. The mother whore grabbed him by the leg and pulled. It only had his pant leg and not his leg so he pulled it loose. It tore his pants. We got up in the blind. When we looked down, the whores were walking around at the bottom of the blind. I was scared but my father was not. They finally went away and we went home. When we got home my father told my mother all about being attacked by wild whores. The end."

Miss Krueger had a paper over her mouth. She managed to say, "Thank you, Jerry. You may sit down."

Before Jerry could move, Charlie piped up. "What was it that attacked you and your father, Jerry?"

"Whores. Wild whores," he said.

Miss Krueger said, "That's enough, Charlie. Sit down, Jerry."

***

A few weeks later, Jerry showed up at school lugging a complete drum set he had gotten for his birthday. His parents probably now had empty aspirin bottles scattered throughout the house. He had the whole setup—a snare drum and a bass drum with a foot pedal or whatever you call it. Attached to the bass drum were a couple of tom-toms and a cymbal. Finally, and worst of all, he had drumsticks. He looked like a one-man band guy who had forgotten all his instruments but one.

He staggered into homeroom with the whole shebang, accidentally hitting one or the other of the drums at random intervals. It looked like he and the drums were having a wrestling match—and the drum set was winning. As he neared his seat, the drum set gained the upper hand and threw him to the floor. Then, to further the humiliation, it pounced on him.

I'd give him this, he was undeterred. He fought off the fiendish drums and stowed them in the corner. He slid into his seat and sheepishly looked around at the twenty-five pairs of eyes peering at him.

Miss Krueger said, "Jerry. You have drums." It was a question. Jerry had a ready answer.

"Yes, ma'am."

"Why?" she asked, and it seemed like a good question to me.

"I thought maybe I could play a song. Or two. For the class. Today."

"Oh, I don't know, Jerry. We have a lot to do today."

"Oh, come on, Miss Krueger," Charlie said. "It won't take long. I, for one, would love a serenade."

I couldn't believe he said that. Serenade? Seriously?

And then Mack said, "Yeah. He went to a lot of trouble. And it was obviously dangerous to get them here."

So I said, "Please, Miss Krueger."

Then the rest of the class joined in. "Please, Miss Krueger. Please."

"Oh, all right," she relented. "At the end of the day. One serenade . . . uh, song." Everybody clapped and cheered. Jerry beamed his lopsided smile.

There was a lot of discussion at recess about the drum affair and the impending "serenade." Kids were wondering what the song was going to be. I couldn't imagine what song you could possibly sing with just drums as your accompaniment. Jerry wasn't talking. He seemed to be enjoying his day for once.

As the day wore on, Jerry seemed to be getting nervous. He couldn't sit still. He kept jiggling his leg and fiddling with his pencils. Finally, with ten minutes left in the day, Miss Krueger said, "Okay, Jerry. You're on."

Jerry took his drums to the front of the class and set them up. He borrowed Miss Krueger's chair and sat down. He got a soulful look on his face, stared at the ceiling, and began to sing.

"I'm always chasing rainbows." Blap, blap, boom.

"Watching clouds drifting by." Blappity, boom, boom.

"My schemes are just like all my dreams." Blap, blap, crash.

"Ending in the sky." Rat-a-tat-tat-tat.

It was like watching a car crash in slow motion. It was

excruciating yet fascinating. The decent part of you wanted it to stop. The sadistic part of you couldn't look away. I glanced around the room. Mouths were agape. Eyes were opening wide. At least no one was laughing.

Well, those were the first few lines. Hadn't we all suffered enough? Surely he would quit now. Surely he had had enough. Surely he could see that we had had enough. Surely he wouldn't sing the rest of it. He did.

"Some fellows look and find the sunshine." Crash, crash.

"I always look and find the rain." Boomity, boom, boom.

A little admiration crept into my thoughts.

"Some fellows make a winning sometime." Crash, bangity-bang.

"I never even make a gain, believe me." Crash, bangity-bang.

You had to hand it to the guy. That took guts.

"I'm always chasing rainbows." Rat-a-tat, boomity, blap.

"Waiting to find a little bluebird in vain." Blappity-blap, kaboom. Bam . . . Bam . . . Bam . . . Boom . . . *BOOM!*

It was mercifully over. There was a deafening silence. Jerry was sitting there still as a statue, still examining the ceiling.

Michael O'Grady, who did this all the time and on purpose, much to Miss Krueger's chagrin, rolled over on one butt cheek, bit his lower lip, and *BRAAT*—let out a mighty, teeth-rattling fart as his commentary on the performance.

The classroom exploded with laughter. It wouldn't stop. Not even with Miss Krueger clapping her hands and yelling, "That's enough, class. That's enough."

I was the only person in the class who was applauding. No one saw me. Thank God I was sitting in the back row.

✳✳✳

It was Saturday, the day after the soul-satisfying "Fwoggie" episode. The Four Musketeers had planned an excursion to Cole

Park. The park was right along the shoreline. There were tons of palm trees all in a row along Ocean Drive, the street that bordered this long and narrow park. Other trees were scattered here and there throughout the spacious open areas of the park. There were koi ponds in a wooded area. We called them goldfish ponds.

You could play baseball or football in the open areas. The chief attraction, however, was the water. We loved walking along the beach barefoot and looking for whatever we might find. You never knew what it might be.

I got up, and Momma had breakfast ready. On Saturdays, she always had a big spread of eggs, bacon, toast, fruit, and orange juice, and we were even allowed coffee milk. She let Frankie and me make it ourselves. We would pour a little of her Cajun coffee in a glass, fill the glass with milk, and, best of all, add as much sugar as we wanted. It was a once-a-week special treat.

But I wasn't hungry. I ate a little fruit, and that was all I wanted.

"What's the matter, Bob?" my mother asked.

"I don't know. I'm just not hungry," I said.

She came over and kissed my forehead. "You're hot," she said. "I need to check your temp."

She went and got the thermometer and placed it under my tongue. I hated that part. After the obligatory one-minute wait, she drew the thing out of my mouth and, while squinting, announced the result. "A hundred and one . . . point six. You're not going anywhere today."

"Oh, Momma. We're going to Cole Park."

"Not today, you're not. Do you feel bad in any other way?"

"No. I feel fine." In fact, I didn't feel fine. I felt like I was coming down with a cold. Also, I had a little pain in my left ear, and my neck felt a little stiff.

By Monday morning, I felt a little worse and still had a fever. Momma wouldn't let me go to school.

On the way to the doctor's office that afternoon, my left eye began to water and burn a little. We went in and sat down. While waiting to see the doctor, Momma said, "Bob, wipe your mouth," and handed me a Kleenex.

"Why?"

"You have some saliva at the corner of your mouth."

I reached up and touched the left corner of my mouth. It was wet. I wiped it off with the Kleenex and thought, *Oh my God! I'm drooling!*

The doctor said that although I was awfully young for it, I had Bell's palsy. He said the palsy usually went away in two or three months. He gave us a prescription and patted me on the head, and we left. He said I could go to school tomorrow. I didn't want to. In fact, I was terrified. I wanted to stay home in the worst way. For two or three months, in fact.

By Tuesday morning, I couldn't close my left eye. My mouth was drawn off to the right side. I looked in the mirror and smiled. It was lopsided. I tucked a handkerchief in my pocket for my drool.

On the walk to school, I told my friends about the diagnosis and what the doctor had said. I exaggerated a little and said it would last only one or two weeks.

Charlie said, "So, how long have you and Jerry been twins?"

Mack said, "Well, now I know what to get you for Christmas. Handkerchiefs."

"And I'll get him some goggles," Bill added.

"All right," I said. "But I want blue ones."

And so it was, on the walk. By the time we got to school, I was feeling a lot better. Then we got to homeroom, and as we neared the door, coming down the hallway from the other direction was Jerry. He looked at me and I at him, and then he ducked through the door.

The kids in my class didn't really bother me that day. However, as I walked to the back of the classroom to my seat, all eyes were on me. There were some wrinkled noses. Other kids stopped what they were doing, froze, and stared. No one smiled. Certainly not me. There was nothing to smile about.

At recess, my friends tried to protect me, but the older kids just brushed them aside. They had some serious tormenting to do, and I was the target.

"Hey, kid. Do us a favor and put a paper bag over your head."

"Isn't it time for you to go home? You're making us sick."

One of them acted like a monkey in front of me—dangling his arms, hopping around, and hooting.

Another pretended to walk by nonchalantly, suddenly noticed me, and pretended to vomit—just like Charlie had done on Jerry's first day.

At the end of school that day, I told my friends I wouldn't be walking home with them. They asked why, but I just told them I needed to go to the library for an assignment. I stopped by the library briefly, and then hung around outside and waited for Jerry to come out. He finally did and began his walk home in the usual way . . . with his head down. I followed him for a couple of blocks, then sprinted a little to catch up.

"Jerry, wait up. I want to talk to you." He kept right on walking.

"Jerry. Wait up. I *need* to talk to you. Please."

He stopped and turned around. "What?"

"Could we just talk for a minute? Maybe sit down."

"Where?"

"I don't know. Anywhere. Doesn't matter. The curb?" I sat down on the curb. After a moment's hesitation, he sat down about three feet away.

Again he said, "What?"

"I don't know. I just needed to talk to you. How was your day?"

"Fine. Same as always."

"Did you notice my face?"

"Yes."

"So how do you do it?"

"Do what?"

"I don't know. Just get by. Just live with it. I'm having problems. Not with my friends but with other kids. And I worry about what people think."

"At least you have friends. No one wants me around. I'm an embarrassment. I guess you could say my sister is a friend. She knows I'm just a normal kid here"—he touched his head—"and here"—he touched his heart.

I didn't know what to say about that. So I said, "I thought your drum performance was kind of cool. That took nerve. I couldn't have done it myself. Like I say, I thought it was cool."

"I know you did."

"Wait. How do you know?"

"I saw you applauding." He gave me a small, wry smile.

"Oh."

"That meant a lot to me. Someone who didn't laugh."

"Jerry, why didn't you rat on us when Snake caught you outside the girls' restroom in your woodpecker suit?"

"How do you know I didn't?"

"I was spying on you," I confessed. "So, why?"

"Simple. I wouldn't have liked me if I had."

I thought about that for a moment, then said, "Look. My friends and I go down to Cole Park on Saturdays a lot. Want to come?"

"No. I don't think so. But thanks for asking."

"Why not?"

"Your friends don't like me."

"My friends don't really know you. They just need to get to know you. They still like me, and I look like you now."

"Well, not really."

"Okay. Not exactly. But close enough now," I said.

He just shrugged.

"It might help if you didn't wear the goggles."

"I have to wear them. My eye dries out and hurts if I don't. And if it gets too dry, it starts watering. The doctor calls it reflex tearing. It waters because it gets too dry. Crazy, huh? I tried eye drops, but they don't help. They said they could sew my eyelids partially shut and it'd help, but my parents didn't want that and neither did I."

"Maybe you could get cool glasses instead? You know. The kind motorcycle riders use."

"I can't wear glasses."

"Why not?"

"In case you haven't noticed, I only have one ear. You need two to wear glasses. Otherwise the glasses wind up in your lap . . . or your mouth. Ask me how I know that."

"What happened? Why did this happen to you?"

"It wasn't my idea. I was just born with it. It's called Goldenhar Syndrome."

"Golden Heart Syndrome?"

"No. Goldenhar. Har. Like a laugh. You know . . . har, har. Only it's not funny."

"I like Golden Heart better. Jerry . . . answer me this. Is it true you have six toes on one foot?"

"Yep. On my left foot. I have two little piggies who went wee, wee, wee, wee all the way home. I have a lot of wee-wee in my left shoe."

I laughed. So did he.

***

Three weeks later, my Bell's palsy was gone. It was Saturday, and the five of us were at Cole Park. We were barefoot and walking in the surf, looking for hermit crabs or seashells or dead jellyfish to poke or whatever else little boys look for when they are trying to scrounge up an adventure.

There were some teenage girls walking our way. Bill saw them coming first. "Watch out, guys. Looks like some wild whores are headed our way. And it looks like they're headed right toward you." He punched Jerry on the shoulder.

"They're probably attracted to redheaded woodpeckers," Jerry said. Turned out he was good at not taking himself too seriously.

The girls strolled on by us. Jerry said, "False alarm. Thank God. I'm really not feeling up to fighting off whores today. My beak is tired." Turned out Jerry was very funny.

After the girls had passed us, Charlie sneaked up behind Jerry and pulled the strap on his goggles back, and then let it snap and pop him on the back of his head.

"Ow!" Jerry spun around, reached down, got a big handful of wet sand, and ran after a retreating Charlie. He caught Charlie, pulled his jeans back at the waist from behind with his free hand, and shoved the sand down the back of his pants. Charlie tripped and fell on his face, and Jerry tripped over Charlie. They both just sat in the surf laughing.

Charlie said, "Froggie, you are one cool guy."

Yeah, you heard me right. We called him Froggie. We were, after all, guys. Guys could do that with their friends. But no one else had better call him Froggie.

Chapter 5

Mrs. Moore

Backward

I didn't particularly like her. In fact, I hated seeing her. She seemed to have what psychiatrists call a flat affect. There was no expression in her voice. Just monotone. There was no expression in her face. No smile. No frown. No excitement. No nothing. She was hard of hearing. She seldom had anything to say. Certainly nothing that interested me. Her name was Mrs. Moore, and she was eighty-four. She had thin wispy gray hair plaited in pathetic little rows, which were always pinned to the top of her head with bobby pins. She always had a head full of bobby pins. Why she never took them out, I had no idea. And wrinkles, wrinkles, wrinkles. Fortunately, she wore no makeup since it would no doubt just collect in the crevices like grout in an old bathroom.

Today was my birthday, and I was anxious to get home. Joanne always had something fun planned for my birthday.

I sighed and opened the door, and there sat Mrs. Moore— hands clasped in her lap. As usual, there was absolutely no expression on her face. I smiled (as I always did). She didn't. I wondered if she even knew how. I looked her in the eye (as I always did) and repeated her name (as I always did). I got to do this quite often, as she had glaucoma, and I was her ophthalmologist. This meant I saw her on a regular basis—and would continue to see her on a regular basis until she died. This time was different.

She had developed cataracts, and I had operated on her the day before. The nurse had already removed the patch, and I asked her how she was doing. She said fine, as she should have, since her vision was perfect. I did my exam, told her everything looked great, and counseled her on what eye drops to use and all the usual things a doctor tells a routine post-op patient. I left the rest of it to my assistant, who had by then entered the room behind me, and headed for the door.

As I opened the door and was about to make my getaway, I heard her say in her usual flat voice, "Dr. Carson?"

"Yes, ma'am?"

"I want to ask you something."

"Yes, ma'am?"

"Yesterday, when you were finishing my operation, and you were putting the patch on my eye, did you say, 'I love you'?"

Well, that was unexpected. Of course I hadn't said "I love you." I didn't even like her. I needed to get home. I was tired. I opened my mouth and said, "No." I stepped out in the hall and closed the door.

Chapter 6

The Jetty

Forward

I felt pretty bad. Not awful. Just pretty bad. Diarrhea, or "dire rear" as my little cousin called it, will do that to you. But that was last night. Today I just felt bad and weak. Everything that needed to find an exit had already done so. My best friends and I were in my car on our way to Mustang Island and the jetties at Port Aransas. Mack, Charlie, Jerry, and Bill had been my best friends since elementary school. They were the family I had selected, and what was nice is that they had selected me too. The kind of people who knew all your faults and liked you in spite of yourself.

We would stop at the small tollbooth at the entrance to the causeway, pay our dollar, and cross over from the mainland at Corpus Christi to Padre Island. We could have driven the eighteen miles to the jetties at Port Aransas on a highway. Instead, we always drove on the beach. That way, we could use the fifty-foot section of rope and an old tire we kept in the trunk. The first thing we would do when we got to the beach was tie one end of the rope to the rear bumper and the other end to the tire. The driver would start the car up, and away we would go, pulling the tire behind us with the rider atop the tire being yanked back and forth from the sand to the surf and back again. There was a contest to see who could achieve the highest speed before falling off.

As we frequently did in the summer, we were going spear-fishing. We had everything you could possibly need: masks, fins, snorkels, spearguns, and inner tubes. All this equipment was of a quality one could afford on a teenager's income. In other words, crapola. To save a few bucks, we'd made our own spearguns. A pipe, some tape, a few odds and ends, some surgical tubing, and voilà!—you were a menace, or, in our case, five menaces. The last thing we had, and had in abundance, was an impressive lack of common sense.

There was a string of narrow barrier islands extending about two hundred miles along the Texas Gulf Coast. There were three cuts through this strip of sand forming four separate islands. They separated the Gulf of Mexico from the mainland of Texas with shallow bays between the islands and the mainland. Shortly after arriving on Padre Island from Corpus, you turned north, passed over a bridge, and were on Mustang Island. At the northern end of Mustang Island was Port Aransas and the South Jetty. There was a half-mile-wide cut there called the Ship Channel. On the other side of the channel was St. Joseph's Island and the North Jetty. The jetties were each about one mile long, and their fingers reached out into the Gulf. They were nothing more than jumbled masses of five-by-five-foot cubes of red Texas granite. In most areas, there were concrete or asphalt paved walkways that extended down the center of the jetties.

Our drill never varied. We walked out about halfway on the South Jetty; donned our masks, snorkels, and fins; cocked our spearguns, occasionally even remembering to put them on safety; climbed out over the granite blocks; and shoved off into the water. We would paddle around for a while, notice that the water wasn't as clear as we would like, and then someone would say, "I'll bet the water is clearer off the North Jetty." We would all agree with this idiotic statement even though it meant we would have to swim across the Ship Channel to a separate island. We would grab our inner tubes, and away we would go, across the channel to the North Jetty on St. Joseph's Island.

Today it was Mack. "I'll bet the water is clearer off the North Jetty," he opined.

I was thinking, *This is really dumb. I'm weak as a kitten. I ought to be home in bed. I'm not sure I can make it over there and back.* Therefore, I replied, "I'll bet you're right. Let's go."

That was when it got exciting. Four teenage boys, sitting in inner tubes, flippers on their feet, masks and snorkels on top of their heads, spearguns in their laps, kicking with their feet and paddling with their arms. The fifth boy, Jerry, thought inner tubes were for sissies, so he just swam across using the only stroke he knew, the backstroke. One of us had to carry his speargun. You may think I'm kidding, but I am not.

As we poked along across the channel, we found that avoiding the tankers was easiest. They were too big to sneak up on you, few in number, and generally traveling slower than the other boats. The shrimp boats were faster and more numerous, and the captains seemed to be decent-enough people to try to avoid running us over, but not decent-enough people to think they could completely ignore us. They would blow their horns and wave their arms and yell at us. I doubted it was words of encouragement. The worst were the pleasure boats. They were faster, far more numerous, and more maneuverable than the shrimp boats. Perhaps they weren't really trying to run us over, but occasionally it did seem that way. They would pass close by and ask if we were okay. When we said yes, they would curse us out and ask if our parents knew what we were doing. We assured them that they certainly did not. This invariably made them madder.

Today, Jerry, who was well ahead of us, was about halfway across the channel when he suddenly stopped, began treading water, and started to yell at the top of his lungs. Then he began to beat the water with his fists. Mack, Bill, Charlie, and I looked over and immediately saw the reason. About thirty feet away came three dorsal fins slicing through the water, heading in his direction. The fins all disappeared beneath the surface in unison and surfaced on the other side of Jerry and—*fwooshh*—made the characteristic sound a dolphin makes when it breathes. We saw the three fins again as they resurfaced. One of them had a curious semicircular piece missing from the back edge of his dorsal fin. Then they were gone. There was a moment of supreme quiet, and we were all motionless. Then the fun started. In other words, the ribbing.

"Hey, Jerry, you can uncross your legs now."

"Jerry, I didn't know you could scream so loud . . . and high. I thought for a second there you had turned into a girl."

"I'm impressed. Your mommy would be proud."

"So what were you thinking? That you were going to slug the sharks in the nose?"

To which Jerry replied, "Aw, I was just playing with them."

We all hooted again. Eventually, Jerry began to laugh too.

When we got across, we climbed out over the granite blocks and stowed our inner tubes. The South Jetty had been crowded and filled with fishermen and tourists. The North Jetty was deserted. Maybe that was one of its attractions.

Then we adjusted our masks and snorkels, cocked our spearguns, and went in. This was the moment I always loved. There was the Air World and there was the Water World. With your mask out of the water, you were in the Air World. Your world. It was bright. There was the sun. Colors were vivid with high contrast and sharp shadows. Things moved fast. You looked up and you could see forever. You could see eternity. If you looked far enough and squinted a bit, you could see where Heaven was sure to be. If you tilted your face down six inches, that world disappeared . . . in an instant. Water World was dimmer. More mysterious. Foreign. Colors were muted. Pastels. Things in the distance faded away. More strikingly, movements were slow, languid. Vegetation moved gently. And it was quiet. That was the big thing. A quiet you never got in Air World. The only thing you could hear was your own breathing. Heaven was nowhere to be seen.

As many times as we had done this, I had never actually killed a fish. None of my friends could make such a claim. I cruised around a bit, admiring the scenery. Then I took a deep breath and went down to look under a rocky ledge, but nothing was there. On the way up, I accidentally bumped my elbow, my fingers tightened, and I discharged my speargun, which I had forgotten to put on safety. The four-foot aluminum rod with its barbed tip shot off into the haze. I could barely see the near end of it. I swam over to retrieve it and found to my astonishment that I had skewered a mullet right in the middle. The mullet looked a little sad. I was not. My first kill! I couldn't wait to show him to the guys and tell them at least some of the story. As you might know, "the truth" is different from "the whole truth." In my opinion, he was a magnificent, if rather stunted, member of his species. He measured about nine inches in length. I had no idea what I was going to do with him, but for now, I only knew that I would in some way be keeping him forever. I swam over to the jetty, climbed out, and sat on a granite block. The rest of the guys were still in the water. The sun was out, and I just sat there and experienced one of those moments where all was right with the world. They were rare but they were real. I was young. I was healthy. I was happy. I had friends. I relaxed and sat there and enjoyed it for about half an hour. I wasn't in the mood to break the spell.

Then Mack clambered out, sat on a nearby block of granite just out of the water, reached down, pulled a four-foot tarpon out, and laid it on the block. My rare feeling went away. The tarpon was stunning. Mack was so proud. I tried to hide my mullet under my leg. Bill and Charlie emerged from the water about then, and we all oohed and aahed over the tarpon. It deserved every ooh and every aah.

Jerry surfaced, swam over, and said, "Hey, Bob, I never noticed this before, but you seem to have a fish head growing out of your leg."

I was busted. I pulled him out from under my leg and held him up by the tail. "Behold! Moby Dick!"

This was greeted by a chorus of laughter. Charlie said, "He's a real cutie!"

"Watch out, Bob," Bill said. "If he's playing possum, he could come to and do some serious damage to your cuticle."

Mack saved the day. "Considering his size, that was an excellent shot."

I went with that. "Damn right. And I got him from about fifteen feet." Now I had to keep him. I put him on my stringer, and we all glanced across the channel to the South Jetty. The tide was going out. That meant that all the water in Corpus Christi Bay was trying to get out to the Gulf through one narrow channel, and we had to cross that channel. It was time to go.

We could see a few folks on the South Jetty, fishing and sitting and walking around, and one large group of people standing in a circle at the foot of the jetty next to a little restaurant called the Three Bees. I'd bet they were having fun. I wished I were there with them. There were a lot fewer boats in the channel now. The shrimp boats were still out in the Gulf, and the pleasure boats were heading to the boat basin. There was not a tanker in sight. I threw a piece of driftwood in the water and tried to keep up with it by walking. I couldn't. We retrieved our inner tubes, walked as far down to the base of the jetty as we could, and jumped in, Mack and I trailing bleeding fish on stringers.

Jerry, doing his backstroke, was soon in the lead. The rest of us sat in our inner tubes and began paddling. We seemed to be making nice progress, but all you had to do was look at the South Jetty and see that we were also being pushed seaward at a distressingly rapid rate. About halfway across, I began to flag. Mack, Charlie, and Bill hadn't noticed—we were all just concentrating on our own situation. As the gap widened, Bill looked around, saw where I was, and yelled, "Come on, Bob. You've got to catch up."

"Sorry. This is as fast as I can go. Y'all go ahead. I'll make it."

Ten minutes later, I could see that they were going to make it but that I had a problem. Since sitting in the inner tube wasn't working well, I squirmed out of the tube, dropping my speargun in the process. Then I pushed the tube ahead of me while kicking as hard as I could with my flippers. This worked better, and I could tell I was making progress. I noticed I wasn't tired anymore. I was too scared to be tired. But, by God, I still had my mullet. As I looked up, I could see Jerry already on the jetty, running toward where Mack, Charlie, and Bill were just climbing onto the granite about thirty yards from the end.

And then there was no doubt. I wasn't going to make it. I quit paddling and was able to climb back in the inner tube. By the time I passed the tip of the jetty, all four friends were standing at the end, yelling and waving. I watched as they continued to wave and wave and get smaller and smaller. I looked up at the sun and guessed it would be going down in an hour or two. I tried to calm down, but it didn't work well. Any rational thought always came back to the fact that I was in real trouble. There was nothing to do but sit in the inner tube and hope for the best. The worst seemed much more likely. My heart was beating so furiously I could see my chest pulsating, and I began to feel nauseated.

At least the Gulf was fairly quiet, and I knew my friends were going to try to get some help somehow. The guys would probably call my parents, and that was a bad thought. I looked around and saw not a single boat.

I began to pray. First, for deliverance. Then I began to tell God I was sorry for all the bad things I had ever done and that I would be a better person if He would just get me out of this fix. Immediately after this insincere pledge, I began to see who I could blame for this. First, and most importantly, it wasn't my fault. However, let's not forget that Mack shouldn't have suggested we swim over to the North Jetty in the first place. And, come to think of it, Bill, Jerry, and Charlie shouldn't have agreed to go along with him. And God. Let's not forget about God. If He hadn't given me that diarrhea, I would have had the strength to make it across just like the other four guys.

All the while, I was getting more and more panicky. Trying to calm down wasn't working. I tried to think of pleasant thoughts, but the only thought I had was a couple of lines from some poem we had been studying in English class:

> Alone, alone, all, all alone
> Alone on a wide, wide sea

Not comforting. And, worse, it wouldn't go away. Like a song that gets stuck in your head.

I began to yell, "Help! Help!" Then I waited, but no help came. So I tried again. "Help! Help! Help!" Still nothing. So I just tried to think of nothing. I bobbed a bit and sank deeper in the inner tube. "Oh God. Oh God. Oh God. Why me? What did I ever do to anybody?" There was no reply.

Then I looked up and saw a most dreadful thing. There was

a large gray dorsal fin slowly moving toward me about thirty feet away. And this fin was not breathing like a dolphin. I held myself as far out of the tube as I could to try to get a better look and also, irrationally, to try to get completely out of the water. It just kept coming. Although I was by then in full panic mode, I began to concentrate on the situation and consider what I could do. I sure wished I still had my speargun, but that was pointless. The only weapons I had were my mask, my snorkel, and my flippers. I thought perhaps I could stick one of my flippers out and let him bite that. Perhaps he would conclude I wasn't good to eat. Failing that, I was going to hit him on the nose with my fist. Or my snorkel. Or something. I was going to do something.

He was twenty feet away. Then ten feet away. Suddenly his dorsal fin jerked sideways about a foot. His fin slowly turned away from me at ninety degrees. He moved toward my left a few feet. His fin jerked sideways another foot or so. Finally he turned around and swam slowly away from me. As he did, his fin jerked sideways another foot before disappearing beneath the surface. I was bewildered. *What the hell? I mean, what the hell?*

Fwooshh. I whirled around and saw a dolphin surface about six feet away. He had his head out of the water and was eyeing me. And I mean eyeing me. He was looking me over. I sat there motionless and then smiled slightly. I know it sounds absurd, but he sure seemed to smile back at me. I whispered, "Thank you. Thank you so much. You are very brave. I owe you my life. But you know that, don't you? What I don't know is why. I wish you could tell me why."

He moved forward until he was about two feet from me. I reached over slowly and, with my fingertips, hesitantly stroked the side of his face. He leaned into my hand a little. A powerful feeling surged through my being, and I felt a bond with him . . . like we both knew something no one else did. I reached over, slipped my mullet off the stringer, and offered it to him. He took it gently and held it for a moment in his mouth, then swallowed it whole, turned, and swam out to sea. As he did, I saw a curious semicircular scar on his dorsal fin. I became perfectly calm. I was okay and I would stay okay. Of that I was certain. Someone was watching over me.

I was picked up about thirty minutes later by a couple of teenagers fishing in a twelve-foot aluminum johnboat with an eighteen-horse Mercury outboard on the transom. What two teenagers were doing three miles out in the Gulf in a boat that size with no life jackets and the sun about to go down, I did not know. I doubted their parents knew either.

We had taken my car, but I let Mack drive home. They asked me all about it on the drive back. I told them about everything except the dolphin. I don't exactly know why, but some things just can't be shared. Not even with your best friends. They did ask me what happened to my mullet. I just said, "Oh, I gave him to a friend."

Chapter 7

The Vacation

Backward

Ever notice when you ask someone what they did the past year, they always tell you where they went on vacation? Vacations are life on steroids. You see things you've never seen before. You eat things you've never eaten before. You meet people you've never met before—and will never see again. You buy things you don't need. Things are strange and different. You never know what to expect. If you don't let the inevitable hiccups ruin your day, you will have the time of your life. And we all crave, and more importantly need, to have fun. Sometimes life is just fun. Joanne and I decided to go to Italy.

***

We dropped Salty, our dog, off at my cousin David's house and drove to the airport in Austin. Once there, we waited in line for our opportunity to go through the security line and all that fun stuff. Not wanting to lug around a big container of

Benefiber, I had sealed the powdered laxative in some Ziploc bags and put them with my other meds in my carry-on. My bag went into the "suspicious" line after going through the new X-ray machine they had just started using. It thought I might be secreting some coffee in my Ziplocs. Apparently coffee can be a serious threat to an aircraft. When they opened my bag, they found the bags containing white powder but no evidence of any dangerous coffee. Undeterred, they decided to test the laxative to see if it was cocaine. Imagine my surprise when their electronic gadget determined that several of the bags contained cocaine. Maybe that was why my laxative always made me feel better. So they patted me down and concluded that, yes, I was a male. I was so relieved. They also discovered I was ticklish. Then they called a cocaine specialist, who had to come over from headquarters to deal with the emergency.

I looked over and Joanne was encountering some difficulties as well. The X-ray machine didn't like her either. I could hear the whole thing. They then brought out the metal detector, and it (the metal detector—not Joanne) went berserk (Joanne would go berserk later). Her carry-on made it through with no issue. Its owner was shuffled off to one side, where she was allowed to wait for what she later conservatively estimated to be four and a half hours. I would have put it more like five to ten minutes. She was then whisked off for a proper interrogation. Joanne tried to tell them that she'd recently had a knee replacement, so why didn't they just "wand" her knee, or whatever they called it, but they didn't seem too interested in her opinion. She was given the option of public humiliation (patting down of her crotchal and boobal areas in full view of shocked passersby) or private humiliation (patting down of her privatal and hooteral areas in a special room). She chose the former. As the young, serious, wide-bodied, no-nonsense matriarch went through her paces, Joanne said, "Usually by this time, they're throwing money at me." I was so proud of her, though I was concerned they would ask her to explain the smoke coming out of her ears at the end of her encounter. She then came over to watch my ordeal.

To kill time while we waited for the cocaine specialist, they confiscated my tweezers. I guessed they thought I might try to hijack the aircraft. I can see it now, me standing at the front of the plane brandishing my tweezers and saying, "Everyone do as I say and nobody gets plucked." After about fifteen minutes, the cocaine specialist arrived with his two burly assistants. I supposed they thought their thugs might be needed to pummel me into submission if I showed any signs of resistance. He got out his little vials and conducted his own tests. After about five minutes, they discovered, much to their chagrin, that I was innocent. I put on my belt, watch, shoes, and dignity, and we flew to Rome.

We got off in a rainstorm, did all the customs stuff, and went to the rental car window. In view of my desire to avoid litigation, let me just refer to the rental car company as Himtz. Why I decided to drive in Italy, I had no idea. After signing my life away, refusing all the great gas and insurance deals they had to offer, and learning such important things as how to open the gas cap, the gal behind the desk gave me the keys. I left Joanne to guard the luggage and went in search of the vehicle.

It proved to be parked outside a quarter of a mile away. I then figured out the basics of the car, such as how to start it, adjusted the mirrors and seat position, put 'er in reverse, looked in the rearview mirror, released the clutch, depressed the accelerator, and jerked forward into a fence. My head snapped backward, since I had been expecting to go backward, and then snapped forward, and my head hit the steering wheel as the car hit the fence. I depressed the clutch, let it roll back a little bit, and tried again. Same damn thing. Ran into the fence. I reexamined the little picture on the gearshift knob and discovered you were supposed to move the gearshift lever up and to the left, just like I had done.

Again and again I tried the same thing, and again and again I lurched forward into the fence. I tried depressing the knob, lifting up on the knob, twisting the knob, cursing at the knob, and finally, complimenting the knob. Then I opened the door in the rainstorm, put my left foot on the pavement, and pushed the car back so as to have more room for error. I closed the door, put the thing in reverse, and drove into the fence again. At this point, I was wishing I had taken out the insurance. I realized I had no choice but to walk back in the rain and face the Grand Inquisitor. It was awful.

Joanne: "What took so long?"

Me: "The car was a quarter mile away."

Joanne: "Why are you wet?"

Me: "It's raining."

Joanne: "Why didn't you wear your raincoat?"

Me (huffily): "I didn't want to."

Joanne: "Well, where's the car?"

Me: "In the parking spot."

Joanne: "Why?"

Me: "I couldn't get it in reverse."

Joanne: "Huh?"

This could be a first in the long history of the rental car company. The CEO would be saying, "He totaled the car and didn't even *leave* the parking spot!"

I went back to the lady at the counter and explained the problem. "Oh yes. You have to pull up on the ring at the base of the gearshift knob, or it won't work at all. And by the way, it needs diesel."

I stood there with my wet hair plastered to my skull, a pool of water collecting at my feet, and thought, *Well, thanks for the intelligence, lady.* I turned around and walked back in the rain to our "full-size" car, a pint-size Fiat. I guessed over there, anything larger than a skateboard was properly called "full-size."

When we finally got to our four-star hotel, we found out you couldn't actually park at or even near the hotel. We had to park at the bottom of a hill and climb about thirty steps while dragging our refrigerator-size suitcases behind us. From there, we followed a cobblestone sidewalk to our hotel. The only sign was a three-by-five-inch brass plate on the door. The place was spectacular, aside from the size of our room, which was about ten by ten feet.

We were really tired, but it was too early to go to sleep. We were close to the Roman Forum and Colosseum so decided to walk around. To tour the Forum, you needed a great imagination. Almost all of it was in ruins, just rubble lying around with signs and pictures telling you what it used to look like (or so they say). Joanne set a personal record by taking 172 steps without actually taking a picture. We walked to the Colosseum and got an audio guide for our self-guided tour. Turned out that place was old. And I mean really old. I thought it had been built in 1964. I might have been thinking of the Astrodome.

We stopped at a restaurant for dinner on the way back, and I went to the restroom. I walked in, closed the door, and was faced with a unique problem. There were two porcelain facilities, which were quite attractive and looked like those porcelain figures Delft makes. The problem was I couldn't tell which one was the sink and which one was the urinal. After studying the problem for a minute or two, I made my choice. Then I went back to our table, got our Polaroid camera, returned to the restroom, took photos of the mystery facilities, and went back to our table. I showed them to Joanne and asked her which one she thought was the sink and which one was the urinal. She studied the situation for a minute or two and made her choice, and wouldn't you know it, her choice was different from mine. So . . . I either peed in the urinal and washed my hands in the sink, or I peed in the sink and washed my hands in the urinal.

We went back to the room and climbed gratefully into bed. Another long day.

***

At breakfast on the roof of our hotel, I asked Joanne if she had ever seen the famous scene from the 1960s movie *La Dolce Vita* starring Marcello Mastroianni and Anita Ekberg. She replied, "I know of a poodle name Dolce."

We went down to the small enclosed lobby of the boutique hotel ten minutes before our scheduled pickup time for our overview tour of Rome. About forty-five minutes later, we were still waiting, so Joanne decided to make herself some coffee from the espresso machine there in the lobby. I was reading in my guidebook but heard her putzing around next to me and then *BANG!* There was an almighty explosion. My first thought, of course, was *Nuclear attack!* But then I regained my composure and more calmly reasoned, *Meteor from space!* But no. It was only Joanne, who had tried to make coffee in the espresso contraption by inserting a container of cream in the coffee slot and pulling the handle down hard. The resultant explosion blew milk all over the lobby, on the wall, on the counter, on the floor, all over the machine itself, me, the front-desk clerk, and Joanne's hair (I discreetly failed to mention this last factoid to her). She immediately began to flap her arms and apologize profusely, as two additional employees were summoned and sprang into action with towels and mopping thingies. Joanne decided to help out by increasing the frequency of her flapping and the volume of her chorus of regrets as they mopped away.

Finally, the employees decided to at least partially rectify the situation by sending Joanne to the restroom, or *toilette* (pronounced twah-*let*-tuh), to compose herself. I still kept quiet about the dairy product in her hair. She reappeared in a few minutes and began to apologize again as the last vestiges of her crime were eliminated by the staff.

Finally our guide showed up about an hour or so late. His first words were "I am Francisco. This is not my fault." He claimed he had gotten caught in traffic. He was fluent in three languages: French, Italian, and Spanish. English, not so much. He was hard to understand when you could hear him, which was seldom. He didn't use the microphone in his little bus, since he was trying to keep us all from being killed by other crazy drivers. This was a "semiprivate" tour but was probably better termed a "not-very-private" tour. There were eight tourists including Joanne and me.

We went first to the Trevi Fountain. We were treated to a sight few tourists ever see. The fountain had no water in it. It did, however, contain a squadron of white-clad sanitation workers scrubbing the fountain with long-handled brushes and then hosing it down. I threw a few coins at them just for the hell of it. Our "guide" had stayed back with the bus to guard the vehicle.

Next we went to the Pantheon for another unguided guided tour. There Joanne was bumped in the butt by a guy trying to take a photo while looking at the hole in the roof. Apparently he was on a mission, and that mission was to bump Joanne Carson in the butt. Well, he picked the wrong American to try that tactic on. She bumped him back just as another tourist bumped her butt from the other side. She went after him too, took out her camera, looked at the hole in the ceiling, and bumped him back. It was the Battle of the Butts. She walked over to me and, by way of commentary on the encounters, said, "Hah!"

Then it was back on the bus, as our next stop was to be the Spanish Steps. On the way, our driver pointed out other interesting things, but we had no idea what because we couldn't understand him. Once at the Spanish Steps, we were told there were 136 of them. We walked all the way to the top, and I counted them. There were only 135. Liars! At the top, Joanne was approached by the nicest young man carrying three roses. He offered one to Joanne simply because he wanted her to "have good luck."

"Well, how nice." Joanne took it from him. I was thinking, *No, Joanne, no "free" roses. And we've got all the luck we need.* I stepped in front of Joanne and gave her the *Give him the damn rose back. This is not going to be free, and we don't need no stinking roses* look. Instead she handed me the rose and gave me the *All right, Mr. Big Shot, you give him the rose back* look. So I handed him the rose and gave him the *Take your rose back or you'll wish you had. We don't want any of your damn luck* look. He refused. I insisted. He refused. I stuck it in his belt and he walked away.

"You're my hero," Joanne said. "The way you made him take his rose back was masterful."

"That would mean a lot more to me if you'd stop giggling."

We had lunch back at the hotel. On the way to our room afterward, I noticed that they had removed the espresso machine from the lobby. I moved our passports to the hotel-room safe. The only thing already in the safe was Joanne's lip gloss.

"What is your lip gloss doing in our safe?"

"No wonder I couldn't freaking find it."

That afternoon, we went to the Vatican and St. Peter's. Of course, we stopped by the Sistine Chapel. The place was packed. There were employees there whose only apparent job was to go *SSSHHHHH* every time the noise level rose above what I would call "chapel level"—which was quite often. I called them the Shushers. What a way to make a living. Telling people like Joanne Carson to shut up.

When I asked her where she wanted to eat that night, she

naturally said, since we were in the capital city of Italy, that she was in the mood for Chinese food. I know. I didn't understand it either.

***

At 6:15 our first morning in Florence, we were awakened by a little bird on our patio. He sounded like a chickadee with the hiccups who had just found a bullhorn.

We walked to the Academy to see Michelangelo's statue of *David*. David's hands were too big. Why did no one ever point that out? I was more impressed with his *Prisoners*, men who were trapped in blocks of granite and appeared to be trying to escape.

After lunch, we walked over to the Uffizi Gallery, a huge place containing the private collection of the Medici family. One of the paintings was of Lorenzo the Magnificent. I told Joanne that when I was in high school, I was known as Bob the Magnificent. I didn't think she believed me. There were a lot of Nativity scenes. In one of them, the three kings had brought along some leopards and monkeys. I just remembered the part about oxen and asses and sheep. Guessed I missed the monkeys. Now we'd have to go buy monkeys for all our Nativity sets.

The place was packed. It was also freezing. Joanne had a problem with cold hands. She opened her purse and pulled on her mittens. In one room, we encountered a large group of tourists moving en masse. They were all wearing red baseball caps on which "I Love Jesus" was embroidered. The I Love Jesus group was really obnoxious. They may have loved Jesus, but they sure as hell didn't like the rest of us. One of them, who weighed about three hundred pounds, was taking a photo and backed into Joanne with his butt. *Here we go again,* I thought. Sure enough, Joanne butted him back. And then he butted her back. And then she butted him back. It was the Battle of the Butts Part II. I dragged her away by her purse. She turned around and shot the Jesus lover the finger. The effect was minimized somewhat by her mittens.

On the way back to our hotel, I reminded her, "You said earlier you forgot some things to put on our trip list. What were they?" We had lists for our trips of anything we might possibly need. If we found ourselves on a trip and realized we didn't have something we needed, we added it to the list.

Joanne: "I don't know. I forgot."

Me: "But you remembered the things you forgot."

Joanne: "I know. But I forgot again."

***

The alarm went off at seven the next morning. Joanne went across the room and began to fiddle with the coffee maker. There were no written directions—just pictures. "You better hope I figure this thing out pretty soon, since you have to spend the rest of the day with me." She soon discovered that you needed to add water to make coffee. Well, who knew? After ten or so minutes of trials and errors, accompanied by a constant stream of verbal abuse directed (mainly) at the coffee maker, she discovered you had to push the "On" button.

She got dressed while the coffee brewed. She had a pair of socks that were actually labeled "right" and "left." That day, she was putting on her socks and said all of a sudden, "Oh my God. I have my left sock on my right foot." She took it off and was putting it on her left foot and then said, "Oh my God. This is my *right* sock."

Before we left the room, Joanne put her lip gloss in the room safe again. Amazing woman, my wife. I said not a word. I was learning. It had taken a long time.

At breakfast, we were eating our meal when, out of no-where, Joanne squealed, "Oh my God!"

"What?"

"That boy over there is eating an omelet, and he picks up the whole omelet on his fork and takes a bite out of it and then puts it back on his plate. And the amazing thing is his mother is sitting right there."

I was stunned to my very core. I began to shake so uncontrollably my omelet fell off my fork.

We decided to spend the morning climbing to the top of the Duomo, all 463 steps. It turns out they were all in the *up* direction. We bought tickets, and the reservations were for 10 a.m. Our tickets gave us no special privileges. We had to stand in line with all the rabble. So we went rabble hunting and found them in a long line outside the tower. Ahead of us was a couple wearing top hats. The only logical explanation was that there was a chimney-sweep convention in town.

Joanne went to walk around the square while we waited, and then I did the same. There were caricaturists around the square, and one of them had a sign saying "Caricatura simpatica in 3 minutes." I guessed he forgot his Italian halfway through the sign. Judging by his display, the "simpatica" part meant that he could give a woman big boobs.

On the way up to the top, we discovered that the stairway was fine if you were an Olympic gymnast. The "handrail" in spots being the ceiling. For another thing, the stairs were of different heights. For yet another thing, there was only one dim light at the bottom of each section. The best part was the spiral sections, where you met people coming down and someone had to stop and flatten themselves against the wall. If it was your lane that was moving and your lane was the one on the inside, then you had to figure out how to go up using stairs that were about three inches deep. The view at the top was very nice. Whether it was nice enough to risk a skull fracture was another matter.

After a quick lunch, we got in our car and headed out for our big leather excursion. Joanne had been hankering to get at least one fine-leather purse, which Florence is famous for. We set out for the Florence Leather Market across town with me driving and Joanne as my navigatress.

It started to rain soon after we set out. I turned on the windshield wipers, and the knob came off in my hand after I had rotated it to the "Slow" position. I could slightly improve my visibility if I moved my head back and forth to follow the wiper. I was following, or trying to follow, Joanne's navigation instructions when she said the following: "Oh. You should have turned back there."

It soon became obvious that she was right. I should indeed have "turned back there." We found ourselves on a narrow street with slick cobblestones as pavement and a few shops and restaurants here and there. There were no other cars on the road and no cars parked along the street. There were ruts on either side of the street for drainage. The ruts were now filled with water. It was really coming down. We were descending, and the road got steeper and narrower. I decided to back up to the top of the hill. I had stopped right in front of a restaurant, and a guy was sitting at a table not two feet away. I rolled the window down and said, "Leather market?" and pointed straight ahead and then behind me. The gentleman pointed straight ahead, and so I canceled my escape plan. A few feet farther, the wheels on both sides of the car slipped off into the ruts. I pushed on the brake pedal, but the thing just kept sliding forward. The car came to a satisfying halt right after both side mirrors got torn off and both front fenders hit buildings on either side. I decided to try to reverse. At least I could do that now. No go. We were stuck. Then it stopped raining. I looked up and thought, *Really, God! Now? Your timing is horrible.*

Joanne was no help at all. She had begun with her hyena imitation again. We couldn't get out of either door. Fortunately the car was a hatchback. I opened it, and we both climbed out and hopped to the ground. People came out of stores and restaurants, and every single one of them was laughing. At that point, I had no choice. I joined in. While we waited on the wrecker, we went back to the restaurant and had a nice dinner with the guy who'd pointed out where the leather market was. His name was Carlo. He was a college professor. He spoke perfect English. We decided to send him a Christmas card. Good times.

***

Our hotel in Venice was very close to Piazza San Marco, and we walked there first. We were lucky, and there was no flooding of the square that day. The pigeons were out in full force. We heard a band playing on one side of the square, and so, being attracted by the magical pull of music like most humans, we sauntered over. As we got close, one of the pigeons that was watching things from a lookout atop a building dive-bombed us. Joanne squealed. Sadistic bastard. Or bitch. Probably bitch. She flew back up to her perch. She looked right at us and made some pigeon sounds. Probably some form of avian trash-talking. Then she launched again. This time she made a lower pass and released her ordnance. She got me right on the left loafer. Then she flew off to her perch again. We decided to retreat, so we walked to the other side of this huge, beautiful square. We heard another competing band. This one was playing Mozart's *Eine kleine Nachtmusik*. I told Joanne that they had recently discovered that Mozart was not his real last name.

"Really?" she said.

"Yes. They found out his real last name was Zart. His first

name was Moe." I didn't think she believed me, judging by the look on her face and the sudden pain in my nether regions.

After lunch, we walked around a little more and found an art gallery. Unfortunately, it was mainly modern art—not my favorite. There were several small rooms. The first was a room full of shovels. The next room had a big pile of corn on the cob on the floor. The walls were covered with rugs. This art critic identified them as shag. Next was a room with about a hundred beer bottles suspended by ropes. Sadly they were all empty. By then, I was about ready to chugalug me some art.

I supposed the purpose of great art was to make you think. When we got to the napkins room (or maybe they were hand-kerchiefs), I thought, *Are you kidding me?* We began to look for an exit. This was about all the culture we could stand. Instead we got the bricks-hanging-by-ropes room. That place had a thing for ropes. The last room had an actual painting. At last! Something to look at. It was an oil painting about four feet by four feet. It was a whole bunch of sperm swimming around, all pointed in different directions. This prompted one Joanne Carson to opine, "They're all going in different directions be-cause none of them will ask for directions—and only one in a million gets there."

***

We had an interesting last night in Venice. There was no ther-mostat in the room. That apparently was controlled at the hotel's command headquarters somewhere deep in a bun-ker under the building. The previous night, it had obviously been set to "Boil." That meant you had to open the door to the balcony in order to survive, and that resulted in the room apparently thinking it was cooling off to inhabitable levels (a situation clearly not to be tolerated in the bunker), so the heat came on with a vengeance. There were gale-force winds in the room the whole night—some hot and some cold. I'm surprised it didn't snow in the room sometime during the night. On the bright side, there were no flies.

We woke late, but before we could leave the room, Joanne had to straighten it up because "the maid will be coming." The previous night, while we were out, the maid came and folded Joanne's dirty underwear, and this obviously could not be allowed to occur again. On our way out, she opened the hotel safe and deposited her toothpicks in it. I didn't ask.

I wanted to take a gondola ride but had trouble persuading Joanne. I thought maybe she was afraid she would fall in the canal. But no. She was afraid the gondolier would start singing—and what was she supposed to do then? She finally relented as long as I made the gondolier promise not to sing. Surprisingly, the canals did not smell at all. Each gondola was decorated according to its owner's taste. Ours was all dolled up to resemble a floating bordello. Red velvet everywhere. I made him promise not to sing, and Joanne and I got in. Some other gondolas we passed had singers, so we got to listen to someone else being embarrassed.

When we got back to the hotel, we sat on a terrace, had some wine, and watched the world go by on the Grand Canal. One of the powerboats that went by was a jet boat of some kind. It had a large flange-like thing extending from the side of the craft. Joanne asked me what it was, and I told her it was an "aquitudinal lateral stabilizer." It was so cute the way she looked at me and then shot me the bird. They then lowered the flanges, and the craft really took off. She had to admit the aquitudinal lateral stabilizers appeared to be worth every penny they'd cost.

We walked back to our room, got dressed, and went out to dinner. Surprisingly, she wanted Italian food.

After dinner, as we walked along the Grand Canal, we heard strains of Vivaldi's *The Four Seasons*. We followed our ears to a church. The doors were open on that fine night, and for unknown reasons there was only a table in the way at the door. We could look in and see the musicians. As we stood there, they performed the last four movements of the piece. One of those was my favorite. It was a magical, unexpected moment in my life..

We went back to the hotel and stopped at the bar. The place was crowded, and just after we ordered, the lights dimmed, and spotlights illuminated a small stage. A magician, the Amazing Antonio, came out. He had four people come up onstage, one of whom was Joanne. He took a set of cards, handed them to Joanne, and had her put them in whatever order she wanted. Then he was able to "read her mind," as he called it, and told her what order she had put them in. If he did indeed "read her mind," I'll bet he went home with a bad headache that night. Better him than me.

Back at our room, we found some info by British Airways on the floor about our flight to New York in the morning. One of the papers had the following advice: "In an effort to eliminate any unfortunate incidents at the airport, guests are kindly reminded not to pack the following items in their carry-on luggage: box cutters, ice axes, ice picks, knives, meat cleavers, razor blades, sabers, scissors, swords, metal with pointed tips, mace, pepper spray, or aerosol spray." So, we couldn't take ice axes *or* hair spray onto the airplane, or we might have an "unfortunate incident."

***

We arrived in New York after an uneventful overnight flight from Rome. The only thing worth mentioning was that we flew business class. Those seats had a feature that Joanne loved. Our two seats were basically all one module. Side by side, but Joanne faced one way and I another. Separating our two seats was a window-like affair that either one of us could raise or lower. It was opaque, and so isolated her from me. The appealing thing to her was that she could push a button, and I just went away—even midsentence. Saved her the trouble of shooting the bird.

We checked into our hotel and got a map of Central Park. The desk clerk said to just walk around and forget about the pedicabs and buggies. He did advise us, no matter what, to avoid an area called the Ramble. You could get lost in there. So we walked to Central Park.

Joanne took some photos of the tall, narrow buildings adjacent to the park and began to worry that they would "just topple over." The first attraction we came to was the Central Park Carousel with its annoying music. That was where one of the final scenes of *The Catcher in the Rye* occurred. Holden Caulfield winds up sitting there, watching his little sister, Phoebe, going round and round. Going nowhere—presumably not getting any older. It was the only time in the book he was happy. It made me happy too. Poor Holden.

At the Bow Bridge, a couple was having wedding photos taken. The prospective bride looked none too pleased. She was saying loud, uncomplimentary, profane things to the photographer and the prospective groom. Maybe he would luck out and get some noise-canceling headphones as a wedding present. We elbowed our way across the bridge and immediately got lost for a couple of hours in the dreaded Ramble—or Bramble, as I came to think of it. At one point, you could not see any of the skyscrapers of New York. Kind of nice, actually.

We eventually came to Tavern on the Green. It was much nicer than I had expected. We sat down and each had a beer. The waitress was named Princess. At least it was memorable. She was quite chatty and smiled a lot—don't tell me New Yorkers aren't nice. I gave her a nice tip and, I hope, a nice smile as we got ready to leave.

We left and began the hike to our hotel. We had gone about a quarter of a mile, maybe less, when we heard some running footsteps coming up behind us. We stepped to one side. Dang runners anyway. They can be as bad as snowboarders—just without the snowboard. The footsteps stopped, and their owner tapped me on the shoulder. I spun around, and there stood Princess, puffing like a locomotive.

"Sorry to startle you." She reached into her pocket and handed me my credit card. "You left this on the table."

"Oh. My gosh. Thank you so much. This could have spoiled our day—and then some." I extracted my wallet and pulled out a twenty.

"No. No, thank you. I don't want that. That's not why I did it."

"Well, okay." She walked off without another word. After we got home from our trip, I sent a letter to the manager of the bar. Like I said, don't tell me New Yorkers aren't nice.

On the way back to the hotel, we decided to walk through the Plaza Hotel. We were turned away at the door because we were not "residents." I thought it might have really been because I was wearing my Herbert's Taco Hut T-shirt.

That afternoon, we got on a ferry and went to see Ellis Island. Joanne and I had parents who went through Ellis Island. My father came over as a two-year-old from Ireland in 1907, and Joanne's mother as an infant from Poland in 1908. Immigration officials labeled with chalk the clothes of immigrants who were suspected of having medical problems, and family lore had it that my grandfather had been labeled with a big *G* for goiter. He had taken off the sweater they had labeled, turned it inside out, and was able to pass the inspection. Joanne's family lore had it that her grandfather had been asked how much money he had, and he had seventeen dollars. At that time, you were supposed to have at least eighteen dollars, so the official gave him a dollar, and he got in. We found my grandfather's name on a wall they had there. There were oral histories, and I listened to one of the short ones. It was from an Italian woman who came over in her teens. She had an eye disease called trachoma and had to be hospitalized for one year to treat it. When she was finally released, she was reunited with her aunts. When she got to New York City, she said, "I couldn't stop crying. There was all that relief came out of me." The best thing was the collection of photos. My favorite was of a family of four as seen from behind. The father held the hand of a little boy of about two, and the mother held the hand of a girl of about five. They were standing there, looking at the skyline of New York City in the background. The father would probably have become someone's grandfather. What if he had become my grandfather? What did he see? Even if he didn't know it, he was seeing me.

That evening, we elected to do a super touristy thing and take an evening cruise, complete with dinner. I fully expected it to be cheesy and the food to be atrocious. When we got there, we stood in line at the boat so that the guy there could tell us to stand in line on the other side of the huge parking garage to get our boarding passes, so we could return to stand in line at the boat. It was icy cold inside the boat. Joanne immediately began to complain. I had been unreasonably prodding her to leave our hotel, and this egregious attitude caused her to forget her wrap. She began to drape napkins over herself to survive. I had to surrender my napkin and then request five more from our waiter. One for me and another for Joanne to use during our meal, and three to complete Joanne's ensemble. We cruised by the World Trade Center around dusk and decided to go outside for a better view. I left my wine inside so that I could hold on to Joanne on the wet and unstable decking. She took her wine with her and then, as soon as we got out on the deck, handed it to me to hold so she could get some really professional-looking photographs with her Polaroid camera. People from all over the ship came to watch me lurch around, trying not to pitch overboard without spilling any of her Chardonnay.

We glided by the Brooklyn and Manhattan Bridges and then out to the Statue of Liberty. It was all lit up, and we both stood out on deck, looked at her, and felt the tears roll down our cheeks. It made me proud. I thought of my country as being this rambunctious, energetic, well-meaning, good-hearted, optimistic, bright-eyed, confident teenager. We charged around the world, trying at least to do what was right. Making mistakes and sometimes acting unwisely but at least trying to make the world a better place—not just complaining about what other countries were doing. Ours was a country with a conscience. For Americans, complaining about her was an option. Loving her was a given.

Chapter 8

The Light

Forward

I was feeling good. Real good. Could not have been better, in fact. I had just left the wedding reception of my favorite cousin, David, who grew up in San Marcos. I had been a groomsman, and that was why I was in a tux. I was in my Mustang convertible, the top was down, and one of my favorite songs was playing on my brand-new portable cassette player. It was seventy degrees, the sky was clear, and there was a full moon. The summers were hot in Texas, but the springs were glorious, and it was late April.

It was about nine o'clock on a Saturday evening. I was nearing the courthouse square in San Marcos. David and I had spent a lot of time in the square—both as young kids and even as adults. Little had changed. I found that comforting. It was nice to have an enduring link between two chapters of your life. Valentino's, our favorite pizza place, was still there. Sweetie's, the ice cream parlor, was still there. All the aluminum siding was now gone, thank God. The statue of Texas

Ranger Jack C. Hays, after whom the county was named, still stood guard over all square-related activities. Lucky's, my least favorite bar, was, unfortunately, still in business.

As I neared the square and the red light at Hopkins Street, the light turned yellow at just that precise moment when you didn't know what to do. A little earlier and you were going to stop. A little later and you'd just sail on through. The Cadillac ahead of me sailed on through. It was going to be close for me, but I made that split-second decision and gunned it. I probably ran a red light—just a little bit. Lot of good it did me though. The light at Hutchison Street, the next intersection, was red. I stopped alongside the Cadillac.

"Woo woo. Hey, good looking. Nice tux," came a voice out of the Cadillac. I looked over, and a girl stuck her head out of the rear window. "We're going to Lucky's. Why don't you join us?"

She was really attractive. But it all seemed a little pushy and unexpectedly direct, so I said, "No, thanks. But I appreciate the invitation."

"There are five of us in here. You're bound to like one of us, although I'd bet on me."

"No, thanks."

"Chicken!" The light turned green, and the Cadillac went across the intersection and pulled into an open parking spot down the street from Lucky's.

I drove by and then thought, *She was kind of cute. Maybe I am chicken. What do I have to lose anyway? Why not?* So I circled the block and pulled into an empty spot next to the Cadillac. I got out and walked over to Lucky's. It was one of the biggest, loudest bars in San Marcos. I walked in and looked around but didn't see Cadillac Girl anywhere, so I climbed the stairs to the rooftop section. The five of them were all at a table. They each had a Shiner Bock in front of them.

She looked up and yelled, "Hey, Tux Man. Over here."

I walked over and pulled up another chair. "I decided not to be a chicken," I announced.

"Glad to hear it," Cadillac Girl said. "I'm Suzanne." She pointed around the table. "And there's Caroline and Reese and Nola and Evelyn. Got it?"

"Yeah. Got it. Suzanne, Caroline, Reese, Nola, and Evelyn. I see you all like Shiner Bock."

"We do. And I see you have a good memory."

The waitress walked by, and I stopped her and ordered a Bud. Just to show I was my own man.

Suzanne said, "So why are you in a tux, was it to impress me, and what's your name?"

"I'm Bob. I'm in a tux 'cause I just came from a cousin's wedding. I was a groomsman."

Suzanne looked me over. "You're kinda cute. Maybe it's just the tux. Take it off and let's see what you really look like."

The other four laughed and in unison began to chant, "Take it off. Take it off. Take it all off."

"No, I think not." My Bud arrived, and I took a sip. All at once, I was wishing I had been a chicken. Sometimes you just want to be someplace else.

Caroline said, "So what do you do, Bob?"

"I'm a resident at Parkland Hospital in Dallas. I spent a lot of time here when I was a kid. I just came back for the wedding."

"A doctor, eh? I have these two big bumps on my chest. Perhaps you could look at them?"

I got up, and I could hear them hooting at me as I walked down the stairs and out onto the street. I stood there for a minute and took a few breaths. The night didn't seem so special anymore. Funny how a few words could really screw something up.

The door opened behind me, and a girl walked out. I glanced at her, and we made eye contact for a moment, and all of a sudden I couldn't breathe right. She skipped a step, then walked briskly down the street. I stood there like a statue. She was almost to the corner when I began to run after her to catch up. She must have heard me coming because she stopped and whirled around. Her long, dark hair whipped around her face and then settled back into position. Her green eyes looked scared. And gorgeous. My heart was pierced. And pounding.

I skidded to a halt in front of her and said, "Sorry. Sorry. I . . . uh . . . didn't know what to do. I had a choice. One I've never had before. I could have just stood there and watched you walk away, or I could take a chance. I had to take a chance. I know it doesn't make any sense, but there it is. Look. I just need to talk to you for a minute. Okay?"

"Uh . . . I don't think so. I just had one bad encounter. I'm not really ready for another. It's been a bad evening."

"But the bad encounter wasn't with me." I looked around, desperate for some inspiration or help. We were standing right in front of Sweetie's.

"Look." I pointed to my left. "I love ice cream, don't you? Everybody loves ice cream, right? I'd love to buy you an ice cream cone. Any flavor. I'll even pay for two scoops."

"Uh . . . I don't know."

"Okay. Okay. You drive a hard bargain. Three scoops."

She smiled a little. After a brief pause, she said, "One scoop is enough."

I went over and held the door open. She walked in ahead of me. As she stepped by, I caught her scent—faint but fresh and natural. There were a few small round tables with chairs and one employee, an earnest-looking teenage boy with acne and one of those goofy poufy hats. Curly red hair shot off in all directions around the hat.

"Can I help you?" His voice cracked when he said "help."

"What would you like?" I asked.

"I'm a plain vanilla girl. And just one scoop, please."

"Me too. I'm a plain vanilla guy." I turned to the boy and said, "Two single-scoop vanilla cones, please."

He scooped them up, and I handed her the first gift I would ever give her. I took my cone and paid him. We sat down at one of the tables, she on one side and I on the other, wondering how my palm could possibly be sweaty holding an ice cream cone.

"You're wearing a tux. Why are you wearing a tux?"

"I was in a wedding. A groomsman. I was driving to my grandparents' home, where I'm spending the night, and a car full of girls stopped at the same red light as me and asked me to go to Lucky's with them. It was a mistake. Look, I know that at this moment you probably think I'm crazy, and I'm having trouble thinking of what to say to convince you I'm not. I am *really* nervous right now. So that doesn't help. Here, let me show you." I took out my wallet and opened it. "Here's my driver's license with my photo. See, my name is Robert Carson. I go by Bob. And here, here's my ID card for Parkland. I'm a doctor. A resident in ophthalmology. Here's my library card, which suggests I am probably literate. And here's my AAA card. Which, I admit, doesn't prove much other than that I can afford the twenty-five-dollars-a-year dues. And here's a photo of my dog. His name is Toby. I know I'm scraping the bottom of the barrel here, but I was totally unprepared for this. I'm sorry to have started with myself, but I felt I first needed to try to convince you I'm not a psychopath."

She smiled a little and encouraged me greatly by saying, "You're doing okay so far. Also, Toby is cute. I'm a dog person too."

"I'm hoping okay is better than scaring you to death."

She laughed a little. "Yes. I have to admit I'm no longer scared to death. Ice cream's good. Yours is starting to melt, by the way."

She was right. "I guess I was preoccupied." I took a small

bite, then said, "Is there anything you would feel comfortable telling me about yourself?"

"I'm a senior at Southwest Texas State here in San Marcos. I graduate next month with a degree in interior design. I start my first job in Fort Worth in July. I'm really excited. My favorite color is yellow. My name is Anita. How's that?"

"Anita. I love that name. My favorite color is blue. Blue and yellow go together well, don't you think?"

"Yes. I think so. I think about colors a lot. I have to."

"What led you to interior design?"

"It's the way it makes you feel. You know when you walk into some rooms, and they just feel right and comfortable. Like people can be happy there. And it excites me to think I can help people be happy. Plus, it's not just about color. It's like art in a way. You have to piece so many things together. It's like art that you can change and interact with. And you see it every day. And appreciate it every day. You know when you walk into a space, and it's all wrong. It's hard to be comfortable. It may feel cold. You feel distracted. But a room that's right? That's so different. I don't know. It seems like more than just a job. So now it's my turn. Why did you choose ophthalmology?"

"It's beautiful. The human eye is beautiful. It's so precise. The surgery is so precise. I guess I'm kind of obsessive-compulsive, and maybe that's why it's so appealing to me. And you can take people who can't see and make them see again. It is a special feeling to be able to do that."

The employee broke in. "Sorry. I gotta close up now. It's ten o'clock."

We finished our cones and walked out. We stood there on the sidewalk, looking at each other for a long, awkward moment. Finally I said, "So what do we do now?"

"I don't know."

"Okay. How about this? I'll drive over to the parking lot of Long's Steak House by the waterfall, and, if you want, you could follow me in your own car. We could sit in the park there and talk some more. Please say yes."

There was a pause, then a small "Yes."

"Great. Okay. I'm leaving now. See you in a few minutes." I turned and walked toward my car. After a few steps, I looked back. She was already walking in the other direction. She looked good from that angle too.

I drove over to Long's. They were closed, but there were still a few cars there. I guessed employees cleaning up and getting ready for tomorrow. I parked at the far end where there was a light. I thought it might seem less spooky to her. Since the entrance to the parking lot was back toward Sessom Drive where I'd turned in, I walked back there to wait for her. I had a hard time keeping still. I put my hands in my pockets and jiggled my keys. I should have been thinking about what to say to her, but I couldn't. Besides, we didn't seem to be having any trouble talking to each other. I leaned my head back and looked at the moon. All of a sudden, nothing seemed real. This was all too perfect. I started looking at each car that drove by, waiting for the car that would turn in. The rest of the lot began to empty as one employee after another came out, got in their car, and drove off.

I started to get a little worried. I had been there for ten minutes—or was it fifteen? The doubts came as the minutes went by. It slowly began to dawn on me that she wasn't coming. So, if she didn't, then what? Would that be it, or did I know enough about her to try to find her? But what a dumb idea that would be. If she didn't come, that would obviously mean she wasn't interested. She didn't get lost. She lived there, for crying out loud. I looked at my watch. I had been here thirty minutes. Standing in a parking lot for thirty minutes. Making a fool of myself. Okay. Five more minutes.

The five minutes came and went, so I turned around and walked back to my car. Upset and depressed and angry. Then I heard footsteps behind me. Running footsteps. I stopped and turned around, and she stopped right in front of me, arms dangling at her sides. She was out of breath, and her cheeks were flushed.

"I'm so sorry. I got stopped by a cop. One taillight was out. He took his time giving me a ticket and a lecture. Then there was a wreck around the corner, and I had to park across the street on campus, and then I had to run. I thought you would be gone. But I had to take a chance. I had to. Seems like I heard that already tonight."

"I was worried. I thought you weren't going to come."

We walked over to the park adjacent to the restaurant and sat on a bench for a few minutes until she caught her breath. Then I said, "See that big flat rock across the river to the right of the waterfall?"

"Yes."

"When I visited my grandparents here in the summer, my cousin, the one who just got married, and I would go over there and sit on that rock and talk and watch the world go by. Or, more honestly, watch the girls go by. We could go sit on it now, if you like."

"I don't think so. I'm wearing a nice dress, and my shoes would get ruined."

"Well, I'm wearing a tux. We could take our shoes off. It's only about calf-to-knee deep there. I could roll my pants up, and you could hold your dress up if you needed to. And anyway, it's only water. I took a bath in some this morning, and I even drank some earlier tonight."

She looked at me, smiled, and said, "Okay. You're sure talking me into a lot tonight."

We took our shoes off and held them in one of our hands, and I rolled up my pants and she held up her dress a bit. The water was clear and cold. It always was. The San Marcos River was spring fed.

It was mainly a gravel bottom there, but there were a few big, slippery rocks. It was hard to see them at night. Halfway across, Anita stumbled a little. She shot her hand out, and I grabbed it. We held hands the rest of the way across. When we got to the rock, we stopped, and I held our interlocked hands up to eye level and said, "Guess what?"

"What?" she said.

"They fit together perfectly. Like two puzzle pieces."

She smiled. "Yes, they do, don't they?"

I helped her up on the rock, and we looked across this pretty little river at the huge cypress trees on the far side and the lights of the university beyond the trees and the moon beyond the university. It was a small waterfall, and you could hear the pleasing swishing sound off to our right.

"Beautiful, isn't it?" she said.

"Yes, you are," I said.

She gave me a gentle punch on the arm and said, "You know what I mean."

"I do. Worth a slightly wet dress and a slightly wet pair of pants, huh?"

"Yes."

Then we lapsed into silence for a few minutes and just enjoyed the moment. Strangely, it was a perfectly comfortable silence. Not awkward at all. I think she felt the same.

After a few minutes, she said, "This is scary, isn't it?"

"What do you mean?"

"It's so fast."

"Fast is good."

"I know, but fast is scary."

"I'd have to say, I'm very much in favor of tonight. Except for the part when I thought you weren't coming. That was awful."

"Sorry."

"I know. I guess I'll have to forgive you. But I'm not so sure

I can say the same thing about the cop." She smiled. I held out my hand palm up, and she put her hand in mine and squeezed.

I said, "Are you looking forward to getting out of school?"

"I was, but the closer it gets, the more anxious I get."

"Why?"

"I don't know. I guess the real world is going to be different. A lot of things to figure out. I'm not really afraid. Maybe anxious was the wrong word."

"Being at the bottom rung of the ladder again, right? I know that feeling. Freshman in high school. Freshman in college. First year of medical school. Internship. Army. First year of residency. A lot of ladders to be at the bottom of. You climb one ladder, and the reward is another ladder."

"Yeah. That's it. Another ladder. Sometimes I think maybe I ought to stay in school and get a master's. But then I wonder if that's just being a chicken."

"That's why I went in that bar and sat down with those girls. They called me a chicken. Isn't that pathetic? They were pretty obnoxious. And crude. So I had a snit and got up and left. I was trying to cool off a bit when you walked out."

"Really? That's pretty much what happened to me. I had a snit too."

"So there's something else we have in common. We both have snits. I'll bet my snit was better than your snit."

She laughed and again punched my arm lightly.

"You enjoy punching guys in the arm?"

"Just you, apparently. It's a new experience for me."

I punched her lightly on the arm. "Take that."

She laughed. "This is fun." She unfolded her legs, dropped them into the water, and kicked her feet back and forth. I did the same. "I'm going to miss San Marcos. It's such a pretty little town. This school was the perfect place for me."

"I always loved coming here all those summers. Hanging out with my cousin David. Riding our bikes around. Playing in the river. Great memories. It was David's wedding tonight. He lived just down the street from my grandparents." There was a brief pause, and I said, "How would you like to play Two Heads on a Trunk?"

"Two Heads on a Trunk?"

"Yeah. It's fun. It's a game."

"Never heard of it."

"That's 'cause I just made it up."

"How do you play?"

"Come on. I'll show you."

We hopped down in the water and walked back across the river. I said, "Wait here. I'll be right back."

I walked quickly to my car and got my portable cassette player, took out the tape I had been listening to, and popped in another one. I walked back to where she was standing under a huge cypress tree.

I asked, "Do you like opera music?"

"Some, I guess. I don't know much about it though. I saw an opera once in Dallas."

"Ever hear of *La Bohème*?"

"Yes, that's the one I saw! It was in Italian, so I had to look at the subtitles all the time. I liked the start anyway. It got sad later on."

"This is from the first part. It's where the guy meets the girl when she comes to his apartment looking for a match to re-light her candle. His candle goes out too, and they touch hands in the dark—kind of like we did. In English it's called 'Your Tiny Hand Is Frozen.' Remember that part?"

"Yes."

I put the tape player on the ground between us, rolled down my pant legs, and said, "Okay. This is how you play. You stand about two feet from the trunk and place your feet about two feet apart. Then you lean forward and press your forehead to the trunk, put your hands behind your back, and close your eyes. I'll do the same. Then I turn on the cassette player. Next comes the important part—you are only allowed to think about the music. You just stand there and let the music wash over you, and you just feel it and surrender to it. It's a new way to listen to music. That's it. Simple as that. I've never played before. It should be fun."

She got into position. I leaned over, adjusted the volume so it was low, hit the "Play" button, and got into position too. The music started. I usually preferred country or pop, but to my ear this was the most beautiful music I had ever heard. It made my heart ache. The lyrics were in Italian, but I knew what they meant.

> When it comes to dreams and visions and
>   castles in the air,
> I've the soul of a millionaire.
> From time to time two thieves steal all the
>   jewels out of my safe,
> Two pretty eyes.
> They came in with you just now,
> And my customary dreams
> My lovely dreams
> Melted at once into thin air.
> But the theft doesn't anger me,
> For their place has been taken by hope.

After it was over, I reached down and hit the "Stop" button. She seemed embarrassed to have to wipe away a few tears from her eyes.

"Sorry. I didn't mean for that to happen," I said.

"Don't be sorry. That was amazing. What does it mean?"

"I'll tell you later." And I did.

"This has been the most perfect night of my life. I'd like to end it now if that's all right with you."

"I think the same."

We sat on a bench and put our shoes back on. We walked to her car. On the way, I said, "Would you give me your phone number?"

"Sure. But you don't have a way to write it down."

"Believe me. I don't need to."

"Are you sure?"

"Yes. I'm sure. I have a good memory."

She recited the number, and I repeated it back. It was burned into my brain.

"Anita. I do love that name. What's your last name?"

"Thompson."

She got in the car and closed the door. She looked down and started the car. I tapped on the glass, and she turned to face me. I mouthed one word. *Wow!*

She smiled, and as she turned her face back, I saw her mouth one word. *Wow!*

Sometimes you just gotta take a chance. Love could know reasons that reasoning couldn't know.

We got married three months later.

Chapter 9

Christmas

Backward

My favorite holiday was Thanksgiving. Unfortunately, it was Christmas. There were just so many other things going on at Christmas that made that season too busy, too crazy, too emotional, too everything. Now, Christmas Eve and Christmas Day were okay—unless you were too exhausted or got too sick from all the Christmas "too" stuff.

This Christmas season, Joanne and I were both feeling sorry for ourselves. Our Christmases were usually pretty calm and orderly. We normally put a tree up but hadn't bothered this year. With no kids, we didn't have most of the craziness our friends had to deal with. No kiddie presents or cookies for Santa or school programs or pageants at church.

The problem was this year we had no dog. It was our first Christmas ever without at least one dog. Our Pepper had died two months ago. Joanne had decided she could never bear to go through losing a dog again, and so here we were. Dogless.

***

Pepper had been a little black (surprise, surprise) terrier-mix mutt. We'd gotten her as a puppy. We already had an old dog named Barney. I was in the front yard one day when a little girl of about ten stopped on the sidewalk in front of our house. I was kneeling down as I worked on a sprinkler head near the sidewalk. I looked up and smiled at her.

"Hey, mister, wanna see something?"

"Sure," I said. "Whatcha got?"

"This." She shrugged out of her backpack, put it down, reached in, and pulled out a black puppy. She put it down, and the puppy ran right over to me, pulled on my shoelaces, licked my hand, looked me in the eye, and yipped twice.

"Do you want her? She's only ten dollars."

"No. Thank you, though. She seems like a fine dog."

"Are you sure you don't want her? My daddy says if I can't sell her, we have to take her to the pound, and they'll kill her. So I'm trying really hard to sell her. How about five dollars?"

"Uh . . . ," I said, standing up. The puppy tried to climb up my leg and, in the process, got a death grip on my ankle. Joanne and I *had* talked about getting another dog. "Uh . . . ," I said again. "Wait here. I'll be right back."

I scooped the puppy up and went in the house. "Joanne. Joanne. Where are you?"

"In the kitchen."

I went into the kitchen, held the puppy up, and said, "Ta-da! Look what I just got. And she was only twenty dollars."

"Oh, Bob. What have you done? You know we talked about getting a Yorkie."

"I know. But the salesman was very persuasive. Come meet her."

"What are you talking about?"

"Just come out front."

We walked out to the front yard. She was sitting on the curb with her backpack on. Her back was to us.

"Sweetheart," I said. She stood up and turned around. "Could you please tell Joanne here about the puppy?"

"My daddy says if I can't get rid of her, we have to take her to the pound, and they'll kill her. She needs a home. She's only five dollars. She's cute."

Joanne said, "She is cute. But we were planning on getting another kind of dog."

"How much was the other kind of dog gonna cost?"

"About four hundred dollars."

"Well, she's only five dollars, and she's here right now. And I saw your other dog in the window a minute ago, and I'll bet he would like someone to play with. She needs a home."

Joanne took the puppy from me and held her up to her face, nose to nose. The puppy licked Joanne's nose and wagged her tail. "Bob," she said, "give the young lady forty dollars. I just saved you three hundred and sixty bucks."

***

She was Joanne's dog from the start. There was no doubt about that. She tolerated me well, but I was an afterthought. Just like poor Barney. Pepper's star, moon, and sun were Joanne. Joanne couldn't go to the bathroom without her companion on her heels. When Joanne was in the bathroom, Pepper would sit there and get what Joanne termed her "potty scratches."

She began by sleeping in a crate in a corner of our bedroom. Joanne thought she looked kind of forlorn, so she moved the crate about three feet from our bed. When she was potty trained, we opened the door to the crate, and Pepper began to sleep nestled against the bed.

I had no intention whatsoever of sleeping with a dog in my bed, and I didn't like the direction this "sleep creep" was taking. I voiced my sincere concerns. My sincere concerns were sincerely ignored. Next, Pepper jumped onto the bench at the foot of our bed. To prevent any further encroachments, I glowered at her every night before turning off the lights.

One morning, I woke up and saw a furry black mass curled up in the crook of Joanne's knees. Joanne opened her eyes, looked at me, and smiled an *I told you so* smile. I was a beaten man and I knew it.

***

Pepper was a brave little thing. Probably the terrier blood in her. When Joanne was outside, Pepper would patrol the perimeter of the yard and keep herself between Joanne and the woods beyond with all their mainly imagined dangers. I used to tease Joanne about this, but one day Pepper began barking furiously at something on the ground. Joanne called her, but she wouldn't come. Joanne went over to see what she was barking at when Pepper gave a terrific yelp and jumped backward. Joanne scooped her up and then saw the rattlesnake. She rushed her to the vet. It must have been a dry bite because she never got sick or even swelled up. The vet said that happened fairly often.

In the winter, Joanne dressed her up in baby T-shirts. She claimed it was to keep her warm, but she spent almost all her time indoors and Central Texas winters aren't much anyway. Pepper eventually had quite a wardrobe. After a few years, she had outfits for every season except summer. That would have just been too cruel. Of course, the Fourth of July was an exception.

It had always been funny to me how quickly a good dog could feel the rhythms of the family and the moods of its owners. Pepper seemed to know what we were going to do even before we knew. When we came home, we would open the door and always be greeted by a black nose attached to a wriggling body with a wagging tail bringing up the rear. However, when I brought Joanne home after a breast biopsy, the nose was there, but the wriggles and wags were not. She immediately sensed somehow that there was a problem. There was no sign of joy. She followed us to the bedroom, jumped up onto the bed, and lay down quietly next to Joanne.

✳✳✳

It wasn't long after we got Pepper that a most amazing thing happened. Joanne had epilepsy, and the seizures came on unpredictably. It was a problem. Joanne seldom hurt herself during her episodes, but sometimes she did, and it was a real worry and a social problem as well. The meds she was taking then helped but did not eliminate the seizures. One day, I was watching TV in the den, and Joanne was in the bedroom with Pepper. Suddenly Pepper came running into the den, barking vigorously, ran back to the bedroom, then ran back to the den, still barking. She simply would not quit. I yelled to Joanne to make Pepper shut up, but there was no answer. I finally got up and went to the bedroom and asked, "What in the world is wrong with your dog?"

"My dog. My dog. My . . ." Then she got that faraway look in her eyes that I was so familiar with and dreaded so much. I raced over and got her to lie down on the bed just before her grand mal seizure began. It was rare but it was real. Some dogs could somehow sense that an owner was going to have a seizure. That was like a miracle. Now Joanne had a chance to possibly abort her seizures with her meds or at least get in a safe spot.

We lost Barney a couple of years after we got Pepper. He had been a good dog, and Pepper seemed to miss him too. But Barney was not a shadow. Barney led his own life and had his own priorities and interests. Pepper's only interest was Joanne. Pepper's life was Joanne's life.

***

Dogs are very effective communicators. Of course, there was the bark. But there were all kinds of barks. The volume and timbre and urgency could all be varied. Pepper had a specific bark that meant "Barney is at the door, and he wants to come in right now." There were whines, yips, moans, cries, whimpers, growls, and combinations of all those. Pepper also had a whine-growl-moan that unmistakably meant "Oh c'mon, people, let's go already." Add body language, tail language, and eye expressions to all that, and you had a talk show host. Pepper's vocabulary was huge. Joanne and I learned to read her, and she learned to read us.

Elvis learned to read her too. Elvis was a squirrel who came to visit Pepper regularly, beginning about a year before she died. I wasn't sure what Elvis's friends called him, but he obviously needed a name and that was the name I gave him. He looked like an Elvis. Cool, confident, even cocky.

We had a big pecan tree in the backyard, and he would climb down, scurry over to the sliding glass door of the den, and look at Pepper. Pepper would run up to the glass and go nuts with growls and barks and whines and yips. Elvis would sit there with his little squirrel barks and chirps, and flick his tail. Joanne and I would enjoy the show from the sofa. Eventually I began to realize that they were talking to one another. I thought Joanne would be interested in what they were talking about, so I began to translate—Pepper in one voice and what I thought the King of Rock and Roll would have sounded like if he had been a squirrel.

One of their early conversations went like this:

Elvis: "Betcha can't get me."

Pepper: "I hate you. I hate you. I hate you."

Elvis: "Oooh. I'm so scared. By the way, you're missing some teeth."

Pepper: "I hate you. I hate you. I hate you."

Elvis: "Wanna see me flick my tail?"

Pepper: "I'm gonna kill you. You look like a rat."

Elvis: "My mommy says I'm handsome."

Pepper: "You still look like a rat. You'd better watch out, or I'll slobber on the glass."

The visits continued and the tone eventually changed a bit.

Elvis: "Here I am again."

Pepper: "So I see. See if I care."

Elvis: "I found a nut today."

Pepper: "Poo poo pee doo."

Elvis: "Your manners are worse than your breath."

Pepper: "Your manners are worse than your butt."

Elvis: "Is that supposed to make sense?"

Pepper: "Go away. I hate you."

Elvis was persistent. I'd give him that. He kept coming back for more discussions, and they actually got more civil. I was getting better at interpreting them. At least that was my stance. Joanne seemed less impressed with my translating abilities. However, she did seem to enjoy Elvis's visits and my efforts.

Elvis (scratching on the glass): "Pepper. You in there?"

Pepper: "Yes. Where have you been? You're late."

Elvis: "I lost a nut. Couldn't remember where I put it."

Pepper: "Why didn't you ask me? There's one over by the rosebush."

Elvis: "Oh yeah. I remember now. Thanks."

Then, one day there was this:

Elvis (scratching on the glass again): "Hey, Pep. It's me."

Pepper: "Do you mean, 'It is I'?"

Elvis: "Yeah. Whatever. Say, how's your new kibble?"

Pepper: "Awful. It tastes like dog food."

Elvis: "Tell 'em you want some pecans."

Pepper: "Watch out! There's a cat behind you! Run! Run for your life! Now! Now! Now!"

Elvis whirled around and took off like a shot. The cat did too and ran to cut off Elvis's angle of escape. Elvis spun around in the other direction toward the nearest tree as the cat flashed by. He leaped and hit the tree three feet off the ground, and just as he was tearing around to the other side, the cat hit the tree where he had been milliseconds before. Elvis sped up the tree to the top and, looking down, let the cat have it.

Elvis: "You sorry SOB. You unconscionable piece of excrement. Your mother should have kept the stork and thrown you out."

And on and on he went. Elvis could be quite eloquent when the occasion arose.

One morning a few weeks later, I was pouring my morning coffee when I heard the garbage truck coming down the street. Well, crap! I'd forgotten to take the trash out the night before. Again. I might still have time. I opened the sliding glass door and ran out, sliding it closed behind me. I got the garbage can and ran as I pushed it to the front curb. I made it! Then I walked to the back of the house. As I reached the door, I saw that I had not completely closed it. It was open a couple of inches. As I prepared to pull it open and go inside, I saw that Elvis had gotten into the den. He was sitting up in front of Pepper flicking his tail. Pepper was sitting down in front of him. Her tail was swishing back and forth furiously. She had pricked up her ears. I caught a movement in my peripheral vision and looked over to see Joanne watching the scene from the kitchen.

Pepper whined and, standing up, dropped her head and forepaws down, put her rump in the air, and wagged her tail. Elvis dropped down on all fours and reached over and scratched Pepper gently on the nose. I went quickly around to the front door and opened it, making a lot of noise. I walked into the den just in time to see Elvis scamper through the crack in the door.

I turned to Joanne and said, "Did you see that?"

"Yes. I saw the whole thing."

"Amazing."

"What did they say, O Great White Squirrel Whisperer?"

"Elvis said, 'I love you, Pepper,' and Pepper said, 'I love you too, Elvis.'"

***

Two months before Christmas that year, Joanne had taken Pepper for a walk. Just like she did every day. There was a leash law in our city, but Joanne looked up and saw a large, unleashed pit-bull mix walking down the street, looking right at Pepper. Pepper began to growl and pull at the leash. Joanne pulled back, trying to reel her in. The pit bull began to run at Pepper. Joanne screamed and grabbed Pepper by her haunches. As she was pulling Pepper to safety, the pit bull grabbed Pepper by the throat and wrenched her from Joanne's grasp. Then he began to shake her like a rag doll. Pepper wriggled free, but the pit bull seized her chest in his mouth. Joanne could hear the ribs cracking. Joanne continued to scream and began to kick the pit bull. It didn't seem to feel a thing. And then, for some reason, it released Pepper and walked off. Joanne picked up her dog, cradled her, rocked her, and cried.

Joanne called me at work from the vet's office. I canceled the rest of my appointments and left. When I got there, Joanne was in a room with Pepper and the vet. She was bent over Pepper, whispering to her—so low I couldn't hear her, though I could read her lips. They were saying, *My sweet baby. My beautiful little girl.* But Pepper couldn't hear her—she was gone.

***

Now it was the Christmas season. Joanne had gone shopping to get me something. I didn't care what. Neither did she. I was walking by her desk in our bedroom. The middle drawer was open a bit, and I noticed a leather notebook I had never seen before. I pulled it out and opened it. It was one of those notebooks filled with blank lined pages. On the first page, Joanne had written, "Things My Pepper Did." I rapidly flipped through the book. There were about thirty pages filled with Joanne's handwriting. I flipped back to the start and began to read:

She knew when I was getting ready to leave—by changing shoes or the way I walked or the sound of keys—and would listen attentively for the words "Pepper want to go?" If she was told "Pepper, stay," she would just droop.

She could sit up indefinitely. Her tricks were sit, speak, sneeze, shake, and down. She would often go straight to down to avoid doing the other tricks.

She would watch the deer but chase them away only if one of us came outside.

She liked to go boating. She would whimper and whine if anyone was in the water.

We took her to Garner State Park once. She had heartworms at the time and was not supposed to run. We chained her to a lawn chair to go to the dance. She chased us, dragging the chair behind her.

She would yip and bark loudly all the way home after being boarded—to fuss at us for leaving her.

She would sleep on her side with her legs crossed. She often snored.

She was missing one afternoon. When we went out calling for her, we could hear her barking in the distance. She was caught in a raccoon trap behind a neighbor's house.

We took her to the ranch, and she chased a goat.

She didn't like baths.

I slammed the car door on her tail, and it was always kinked after that.

She loved to have the wind blow in her face from the car window and "sniff the dangerous air," as Bob called it.

If there was something dead around, she would roll in it.

She would walk underneath the edge of the fireplace ledge to scratch her back.

She would get very nervous if we stared at her directly for a few seconds. She would then sit up, wagging her tail vigorously, and snort and wiggle. Sometimes she would grin.

Bob would say, "Wag your tail, Pepper." And she would.

She was a nester in dirty clothes or bed coverings that were on the floor or on afghans. She would use one paw to push up the kitchen throw rug, then turn around several times and lie down. It often took several tries before the rug was right.

She hated to go to the vet. She would start shaking and whining as soon as we got inside. She would keep running to the door, hoping to go home.

She loved Halloween and all the children. Sometimes Bob would hide behind the front door and "talk" so that the children thought Pepper was talking.

She would go to the fridge for ice cubes and had to have two. She could count and waited for the second piece.

As a puppy, she loved balloons and stuffed animals. She would worry them until they were "dead."

When we scratched her tummy, she would cross her front paws in the air and wave them while wriggling her back.

Over the years, she had eleven precious puppies and was a wonderful mother.

She had soft and gentle and expressive eyes.

She had feathery kisses.

The house seems so empty without her.

I didn't hear the back door close. Then Joanne was standing in the doorway of the bedroom. She screamed at me, "Those are *my memories*! You had no right!"

I looked up, startled. Then I screamed back, "These are *my* memories too! They're not just yours. If it had been a child, would you have said, 'Let's not have another child. It hurt too much to lose this one'?"

"We *don't* have a child. We'll *never* have a child. We couldn't even adopt one because of my epilepsy. We tried to have a child. We tried. I tried. It just didn't happen. I'm barren. What a word to describe a human being. Like I'm a desert. Deserts can be barren. Why do people have to be barren? Barren." And then, in a whisper, "I'm barren."

I went over to her and folded my arms around her. "And you're loved. And capable of loving. We *need* a dog. We need something, someone to love. By not wanting another dog, you are saying that the pain of Pepper's death was more powerful than the joy her life gave us."

***

On Christmas Eve, we were driving home from an early church service. It was unseasonably warm. There was a little girl sitting in a lawn chair with a ski cap and a jacket on next to a cardboard box with the words "Puppies 4 Sale" scrawled on it. I slowed down. Joanne didn't say anything. I stopped. Joanne didn't say anything. I opened my car door. Joanne opened hers.

We walked over, and the little girl said, "Hi, mister. Need a dog?"

"Maybe," I said. "What's your name?"

"Jenny." I sat down on the grass. "I only have one left. He's white. Mom says he's some kind of terrier."

She reached into the box to grab him and put him down. He ran right up to me and pulled on my shoelaces, licked my hand, looked me in the eye, and yipped twice. I handed him to Joanne, and she held him up to her face, nose to nose. The puppy licked her nose and wagged his tail.

"We'll take him," she said.

"Don't you wanna know how much he costs?" she said.

"We really don't care," I said.

Joanne named him Salty. We went home with our prize and put up our Christmas tree, pausing on occasion to mop up puppy pee. Dogs meant home. We had a home again. Joanne had big plans for T-shirts.

Chapter 10

Christmas

Forward

My favorite holiday was Thanksgiving. Unfortunately, it was Christmas. There were just so many other things going on at Christmas that made that season too busy, too crazy, too emotional, too everything. Now Christmas Eve and Christmas Day were okay—unless you were too exhausted or got too sick from all the Christmas "too" stuff.

We had been doing okay with all the gift buying and had already bought a present for each of Jerry and Lisa's two kids, Mindy and Geronimo (not his real name, thank God). Now all we had to do to finish that little project was to wrap them and decorate them and get cards for them and box them up and have Anita take them to the post office and stand in line for an hour and mail them. There was some pleasure in knowing they had to do the same for our two kids, Rebecca and Cole. Jerry and Lisa were our best friends. Jerry was a plastic surgeon, and he and Lisa were now living in Dallas.

They always left their shopping and wrapping to the last

possible moment. That meant the only way for us to receive our presents on time was if they shipped them by bus. We always had to go down to the Greyhound bus station in San Marcos to get them on Christmas Eve. It had become one of our Christmas traditions and one that, strangely enough, Rebecca and Cole had come to look forward to. It was our annual yuletide Trip to the Bus Station. I think the attraction was the grittiness of the bus station. The place was dirty, the lighting was bad, and the employees were diffident. They tended to slouch a lot. There was a garish pinball machine. I let both Rebecca and Cole play it. The place just had a lot of personality. I think it was like a walk on the wild side to them.

The presents were always nice and gave each of them something new to shake, poke, heft, and try to peel the Scotch tape off of. When we got home, I got out my trusty Swiss Army knife and slit open the packing tape.

There were several gifts in the box. More than two. Now this was dirty pool. We had sent them only two. One for each kid. That was the deal, the unspoken deal. I had to admit I was a little upset with them. I took the first present out and handed it to Cole to put under the tree.

"Daddy, who's Ken?"

"What do you mean, 'Who's Ken?'"

"It says 'To Ken, Love Grandma.'"

"What? Let me see that." Sure enough, the card read "To Ken. Love Grandma." So I turned to Cole and said, "Who's Ken?"

"I dunno. I asked you first. Which one is my present?"

We pulled the next present out. It also read "To Ken, Love Grandma."

In fact, all five of the presents were labeled "To Ken, Love Grandma."

I looked at the label on the box: it was addressed to us, the return address was Jerry and Lisa's, and, to top it off, the handwriting was Jerry's.

Well, Ken might have been happy but Cole and Rebecca, not so much. They lost interest immediately and wandered off. I put all the gifts back in the box and set it in the corner of the room.

That evening at dinner, I told Anita about the "To Ken, Love Grandma" conundrum. "Well, you'll just have to call Jerry or Lisa about it. Maybe they'll know what happened."

After dinner, I called their home number. Jerry answered, and I explained about the box.

"Any idea what happened?" I said.

"No. None. That's so strange. We did mail Rebecca's and Cole's presents in a new box. What did the box look like? Did it have some red stripes on it?"

"No. It looked kind of beat up. No red stripes. Do you know a Ken who has a grandma named Grandma?"

"Nope. I'll tell you what. I'll go down to the bus station the day after Christmas and get to the bottom of this."

"Well, all right, but lots of luck on that. What are you going to tell them? 'Hey, remember that cardboard box with the shipping label on it? You remember, the one with tape on it. What did you guys do to it? And, by the way, who are Ken and Grandma?'"

"Thanks for the vote of confidence. I'm going to try anyway."

He called back the day after Christmas and thanked us for our presents to their kids. I said, "On behalf of Ken and Grandma, we thank you too. How did it go at the bus station?"

"Not well. They thought I was crazy. We'll send Rebecca and Cole other presents."

"That's nice but really not necessary. We're going to have to rent a storage shed for their presents as it is. You know how their uncle Frankie is about presents."

I put the box with the Ken-Grandma presents in the hall closet, and then we forgot about them.

On Valentine's Day, Anita and I were sitting on the couch in the den, drinking a glass of wine. Anita said, "You know those Ken-Grandma presents we got at Christmas? What do you think we ought to do with them? I saw them in the closet yesterday, and I've been thinking about them ever since."

"I don't know. Maybe there's something good in some of them. Maybe Grandma was rich."

"You're so bad. I mean really. What do you think we should do? Because I know what I think we ought to do."

"Then that was one of them there Rhetorical Questions, wasn't it?"

"Yes. And as I said, you're so bad."

"Okay. What are we going to do with them?"

"Well, first, we need to open them. They can't just continue to sit in a closet unopened. Next, we can't keep any of them. I mean, they're not ours. Maybe give them to that police program for underprivileged kids. What's it called?"

"Blue Santa."

"Yeah. That's it. Maybe we could give them to Blue Santa."

"Okay."

"'Okay' what?"

"Uh . . . Okay, I'll go get them? Do I mean I'll go get them later, or do I mean I'll go get them now?"

"You mean now."

"Oh. Nice to be married, so I don't have to be confused about what I think I might mean."

I went to the closet, got the box, and put it on the floor next to the coffee table in front of the sofa. I took the presents out of the box and placed them on the table. "So, which one do we open first?" I said.

"Let's just do them in order of size. Starting with the smallest."

"Okay. Who is the designated opener?"

"You are. I'll be the designated opinion giver."

I chose the smallest one. Grandma wasn't much for decorating her presents. She just tied white yarn around the boxes. All the boxes were wrapped with the same red paper with images of Rudolph. Where the paper was wrapped around the box, those Rudolphs were upside down. "Do I open them like a girl or a boy?"

"Like a man, sweetheart."

I cut the yarn with the scissors on my trusty Swiss Army knife and tore the paper off. Then I opened the small white box and plucked out a Christmas tree ornament by the loop of fishing-line-like material threaded through the eyelet on the top. It was a white plastic sphere and was painted haphazardly with alternating red and green stripes. Not exactly a thing of beauty. "I hate to tell you this, but I don't think Blue Santa's gonna want this. Blind Santa, maybe."

"Yeah, you're right. Maybe we should just keep that one, after all, and put it on our tree every year. You know, as a reminder of Grandma."

"And Ken. Let's not forget poor little Ken just because he's male." I considered pointing out that she had just said we couldn't keep anything, but then my sanity returned. I dutifully set the thing aside and made a mental note to place it on the tree myself next year—in the back . . . way in the back. The next present was wrapped in a flat shirt box. I opened this one and took out a pair of pajamas. They were blue and covered with teddy bears.

"Hey, look," I said. "These will probably fit Cole in a couple of years."

"No way. Those will be fine for Blue Santa. But don't you think that's kind of sad? Ken could have had those pj's from his grandmother."

I unwrapped the third one and revealed a box about twelve inches on each side. The writing on the box announced that it contained "One 10X Lighted Makeup Mirror."

"Maybe Ken's kinda kinky," I said. Anita punched me lightly on the shoulder. I opened the box and peeked in. "It appears this makeup mirror has fuzzy ears." I pinched an ear and pulled a brown teddy bear out of his nest of paper. "Now this is kinda cute," I said editorially.

"Oh, it is, isn't it? Oh dear. Just think. A grandmother got that for her grandson. She went to a store and looked over all their teddy bears and chose that particular one for Kenny."

"You mean Ken."

"Okay, Ken. But you know what I mean."

I started unwrapping the fourth present. With each present, I noticed I was opening them a bit slower. I was not enjoying this as much as I thought I would. It was, in fact, kind of sad. I peeled off the last of the paper and pulled out a nice sweater about the right size for a seven- or eight-year-old.

Anita said, "Oh, it's so pretty. What size is it?"

I looked. "I don't know. There's no tag."

"Oh *no*! That's terrible!"

"Why is that terrible?"

"It means it was knitted by hand. Grandma knitted that by hand for Ken. It must have taken her weeks and weeks. We need to find Ken, Bob."

I thought, *Wife of mine. Woman I love, you're crazy!* What I said was "How are we going to do that? It's impossible." There was no reply. Anita was getting a nice start on being distraught.

I picked up the last and largest present and put it in my lap. I looked at it, sighed, cut the yarn, and began to slowly peel the paper away. I was faced with a plain white box and a lid that lifted off. I removed the lid, and its contents were covered with white tissue paper. On top of the tissue paper was an envelope. I opened it and read the note out loud.

Dearest Ken,

I made this quilt for your father, my only

child, many years ago. Just as it covered and protected him when he was a little boy, now it will cover and protect you, my only grandchild.

All the love in my heart,
Grandma

I removed the tissue paper, then pulled out and unfolded a slightly faded quilt.

Anita, now tearing up, said, "Oh my God. Little Ken didn't even get his quilt. Bob, we *have* to find Ken."

"But that's impossible." Great. Now I was tearing up.

She only said, "You're confusing impossible with difficult."

"But the only clues we have are Ken and Grandma. Forgive me for pointing this out, but that's not a lot to go on."

Anita said, "I know, but we have to try."

"How do we try?"

"I don't know. Let's look at the box. Maybe see what the postmark says."

"There is no postmark. It was sent on a bus."

I picked the box up and put it on the table. "Look at this, Anita. I didn't notice this before. There's a place next to Jerry and Lisa's label with the remnants of what I'll bet was another label. Look." There was a rectangle of tape surrounding an empty center. "It looks like someone used a razor blade or box cutter to cut out a label. I'll bet some bored bus station employee just cut out the proper labels and switched them around; that way, two families would get the wrong presents. Someone else got Rebecca's and Cole's presents, and we got Ken's presents from Grandma. Probably thought it would be a fun thing to do."

Anita looked at the box and said, "I'll bet you're right, sweetie. Kind of makes you sad, doesn't it?"

There was no other clue on the box.

"Okay. Let's look at the presents again." I started with the quilt. "It's handmade. Let's look at the design." The design gave no clues. No pattern. No special squares. "I don't see how this could help."

"Let's look at the sweater."

The sweater was no help either. So the teddy bear was next. His box obviously didn't help. There was a small tag on him with the word "GUND." I announced this to Anita.

"That's no help," Anita said. "They make about a million of them every year."

I took the pajamas from their box and spread them out. They were covered with teddy bears. "Maybe she knew he had a thing for teddy bears. Or maybe he was just teddy bear age." I looked at the top. There was a label with the size. "It says 'Small.' Well at least we know the size of pajamas he wears. He's obviously not large or medium."

"Let me see those." Anita looked at them for a few seconds, read the label I had just examined, then folded them back up and held them to her cheek.

"Here's Exhibit E." I retrieved the ornament from its box. "Oh. I didn't notice this before." There was a tiny label pinched around the filament that formed the loop. "It just says 'Keystone.'"

"Let me see that," Anita said. "Keystone. I wonder what that is."

"Well, Pennsylvania is the Keystone State. It has to have something to do with a business in Pennsylvania. Right? But what kind?"

"Maybe they make ornaments."

"If so, they can't sell very many. This thing is pretty crappy. Who would buy one anyway?"

"Yeah. I agree. But still, that seems to be our only clue. I'll bet it's a business in Pennsylvania."

The next day, I called information and asked for the number for the Philadelphia Chamber of Commerce. I dialed it and a pleasant young lady answered. I asked for the number of the Pennsylvania State Chamber of Commerce. They were in Harrisburg. I called there, and another nice young woman answered. I asked if she knew of any members who manufactured Christmas ornaments. She said no, but she could ask the director when he came in. I asked if she could send me a list of all the businesses in their organization whose name started with the word "Keystone." She said she would, and she would be sure to ask the director about Christmas ornament manufacturers. I thanked her and made my report to Anita.

Ten days later, I got a letter saying the director was not aware of any Christmas ornament manufacturers in Pennsylvania. She also enclosed a list of businesses beginning with "Keystone." It was seven pages long and listed 273 businesses. Of course, it did not include those Pennsylvania businesses starting with "Keystone" that were not members of the statewide Chamber of Commerce.

"Want to look at the only clue we have?" I handed her the reply.

"Doesn't look too promising, does it?"

"No. What do you suggest?"

"We can't write letters to all of them. Let's go through the list and see if we can determine if the full name suggests they might make ornaments."

Anita decided to take on the job. She was able to eliminate a lot that way—like insurance companies, gyms, and auto parts dealers. She wound up with a list of thirty-three possibilities.

My job was to write the letter.

> Dear Sir,
>
> I am curious whether your company manufactures Christmas ornaments. We have come into possession of an ornament and are

anxious to talk to the manufacturer of this item for compelling sentimental reasons.

If you manufacture ornaments, please simply indicate so at the bottom of this letter and return it to us in the enclosed self-addressed stamped envelope.

Sincerely,

Bob Carson

In the next six weeks, we got a handful of replies—all of them negative. I was ready to give up. Anita was not.

One day, she walked into the den holding the pajamas and said, "Look at this, Bob. I got to wondering if there was something on the reverse side of the size tag. And there is." She held up the pajamas and turned the size tag over, and in tiny letters were the words "Sunshine Duds."

"What do you make of that?" she asked.

"Probably the manufacturer."

"That's what I think."

"Well, we have the manufacturer, but I'm not sure how that will help us. Any ideas?"

"No. I'll think about it."

I thought about it too. I remembered the "GUND" tag on the teddy bear. I went to the closet and got the makeup mirror box. I took it to the breakfast table where the light was good, sat down, and opened the box. I lifted the teddy bear out of his nest by his ears. I found the "GUND" tag and flipped it over. Blank. Not a thing. I sighed and began to put him back in the box. In his little nest. In his nest of wadded-up newspapers. Newspapers! I pulled one out and smoothed it on the tabletop. It was an ad for a furniture store. On the other side was an ad for a Chevy dealer. At the top were the words *Gainesville Sun.*

"Hey, Anita! Come here! Quick!"

She hurried in with a worried look on her face. "What? Are you okay?"

"Yes. Look what I found in the teddy bear's box!" I handed the paper to her.

"*Gainesville Sun*. We've been looking in the wrong state, I bet."

"Me too. Question is, what do we do now?"

"Quit looking in Pennsylvania, for one."

"Remember, we do know someone in Florida."

"Mack."

"Yeah, Mack. I'm not sure how that will help, but maybe he knows of a business there called Keystone. There can't be that many in Florida, for crying out loud."

I gave my childhood friend Mack a call that night. We stayed in touch regularly, so my call was no surprise. After the preliminaries, I told him the Ken-Grandma story and asked if he knew of any businesses named Keystone. He said no but that there was a town called Keystone Heights between Jacksonville, where he lived, and Gainesville. It was closer to Gainesville. He had clients there and drove by the turnoff sign all the time but had never been there. He thought it was possible there could be some businesses there using "Keystone" in their name. He would be driving there in a couple of weeks, and he would leave a little early, take the turnoff, and stop by and look in a phone book.

Two weeks later, he called with his report. He said it was a nice little town. He stopped and got gas and asked to borrow a phone book. There were three businesses starting with the word "Keystone": Keystone Gardens, Keystone Services, and Keystone Retirement Home. He gave me their phone numbers, and I thanked him profusely. Good ole Mack. Helping me out since the third grade.

At last things were looking up—especially the retirement home. Retirement homes contained grandmas.

I called them first. The line was busy. I called Keystone Gardens. A man answered.

"Keystone Gardens. Top o' the morning to ya. This is Chuck. Who do I have the pleasure of speaking to?"

"I'm Bob. Listen, Chuck. I know this is going to sound a little strange, but do you or any of your employees have a child or a grandchild named Ken?"

"Ken? Not that I know of."

"Does your firm make Christmas ornaments?"

"What? Christmas ornaments?"

"Yes."

"No. Why would we make Christmas ornaments? We sell homes. Right here in beautiful Florida. Right now, we're offering a great deal. Five percent down, and we take care of getting the loan for you. Twenty years. The interest rate is low, low, low. Believe me."

"Chuck?"

"Where do you live now?"

"Texas, but—"

"Texas. Too hot. Hot, hot. I've been there. Not hot here. Warm. Nice and warm. That's what we've got."

"Chuck?" I began to lean forward to try to get the handset closer to the base so I could hang up.

"I gotta tell ya, these homes are just gorgeous; all of 'em have a back porch. We even throw in two rocking chairs. Not one. Two!"

I leaned in a little closer, my nose three inches from the base. I tried again. "Chuck? Chuck?"

"Yes, sir."

"I gotta go." I hung up.

I tried the retirement home again. The line was still busy, so I dialed Keystone Services.

"Hello," the voice said over a loud banging sound.

"Yes. Is this Keystone Services?"

"Huh?" It was hard to hear him over the background noise.

"My name is Bob Carson."

"Huh?"

I decided yelling might be a good idea. *"I'm trying to find out if anyone who works there has a kid or a grandchild named Ken."* There was no reply, so I added, *"Or, if by any chance, your company makes Christmas ornaments."*

"Hello?" he yelled.

"Hello," I said, thereby clarifying the situation. *"By any chance, do you—"* The noise stopped. "Ah good. Hello. I'm Bob Carson, and I wonder if anyone who works there has a kid or a grandchild named Ken."

"No."

"No one there has a kid or grandchild named Ken?"

"Yes."

"Yes, no one does, or no, no one does?"

"Yes. No one does."

I took that as a no. I moved on. "Do you make Christmas tree ornaments?"

"No. We clean out septic tanks. 'We Scoop Your Poop.' That's our motto."

"Thank you." I hung up. I thought, *I sure am glad there are people who like that line of work.* I was even gladder I wasn't one of them.

I tried Keystone Retirement Home a third time. This time it rang. "Hello. Keystone Retirement Home. May I help you?"

"Yes. My name is Bob Carson, and I am trying to locate an individual. I believe I have some items that belong to them. I have reason to believe they might reside there. Could you tell me if any of your residents have a child or grandchild named Ken?"

"Not that I know of, but I'm the receptionist. Let me put you through to administration."

I waited a few seconds, got a second hello, and gave my

spiel to someone named Allen. He said, "I'd like to help, but we can't give out personal information on our residents. If you like, I could put a notice on our bulletin board. We have about a hundred residents here, most of them women, and most of those are grandmothers. Why should I say you want to know about Ken?"

"We received some Christmas presents by bus addressed to Ken from Grandma, and they are not ours. We think someone switched the labels as a joke. We are trying to return them to whoever Grandma is so she can forward them to Ken. I believe they have significant sentimental value to them both."

"Nice of you to try. I hope this helps. But why do you think she might live here?"

"One of the things Grandma gave to Ken was a Christmas ornament with a small sticker on it that said only 'Keystone.'"

"That makes sense. For several years, we have been buying some plain white plastic ornaments and letting the residents decorate them any way they want. Some of them put a little Keystone sticker on them. You may be onto something."

I was really excited now. This had to be the place. I couldn't wait to tell Anita.

"Thanks so much. I'll send you a letter to put on the bulletin board. You'll give me a call if something turns up?"

"I sure will." I gave him my number.

I told Anita that night. She wanted to write the letter and went right to her desk.

> Dear residents and family members of Keystone Retirement Home,
>
> Our family received Christmas presents this year that were not intended for us. We feel certain they were intended for a child or grandchild of a woman residing in your facility. We

feel strongly they have great sentimental value to the intended recipient.

The resident of Keystone would have a son or, more likely, a grandson named Ken, and the resident of Keystone would be known to her family as Grandma.

If anyone knows who this person might be, please contact the administrator.

Sincerely,

Anita and Bob Carson

And then we waited. One month later, we had no reply. I called Allen again. He said he was sorry, but they had had no bites. I had an idea. "Is there a newspaper in your community? Even a weekly one."

"Yes. It's weekly. The *Keystone Heights Sentinel.* Do you want their phone number?"

I said yes and also asked for the address. Anita had been standing by for this conversation and asked, "Why do you want to know about a newspaper?"

"Newspapers are great big bulletin boards."

I decided to write a letter first.

It wound up being a long letter. I addressed it to the editor of the newspaper and outlined the whole story. Again I enclosed a self-addressed stamped envelope. In conclusion, I asked him if he could run a human interest story, hoping that someone in the area would be able to help.

Two weeks later, I opened my return envelope and read this scribbled at the bottom of my letter:

"Not interested."

It was signed "A. H."

"Probably stands for Ass Hole," Anita said.

"All right. Now I'm mad."

I picked up the phone and called the *Sentinel.* A nice young woman answered the phone, and I asked if I could talk to a reporter. She said, "Yes, sir. I'm a reporter. In fact, I'm the only reporter. I'm Aly Thompson. May I help you?"

I spent the next twenty minutes relaying the whole story to her. Then I asked the big question. "Would you be willing to write a story about this? Perhaps someone in the Keystone Heights area will know who these people are."

"I would love to."

I said, "I have to tell you, I sent a letter to your editor about this, and he or she turned me down."

"Oh, don't worry about that. He's my uncle Albert. I'll write it and pat his bald head, and he'll run it."

A week later, I got a copy of her article in the mail. The headline was "Mystery Grandma and Grandson Missing." It was well written. The last sentence was "If anyone knows who Grandma or Ken is, please notify the *Sentinel*."

I was thinking, *Great! This is just perfect.*

But it wasn't. On a Saturday morning one month later, I was sitting at the breakfast table, reading the mail, while Anita was reading the paper. The letter from the *Sentinel* was on the bottom. I opened it and saw that I had gotten a short note from Aly: "No response to the story. So sorry."

"Read this." I shoved the note over to Anita.

"Well crap" was all she said.

"Yeah. Couldn't agree more," I said.

The phone rang. I picked it up and a voice said, "Mr. Carson, this is Aly Thompson from the *Sentinel*."

"Oh yes. We just this minute opened your note. Too bad. Thanks so much for trying."

"I did better than try, Mr. Carson. I found Ken."

"What? You found Ken. Are you sure?"

Now it was Anita's turn. "What? She found Ken?"

"All I have is the contact information I got in a short note I received. Do you have a pen?"

"Yes."

"His name is William Burns. His address is 113 Chatten Street in Austin, Texas. That's all I have."

"That's enough. Wow! My wife is right here. We are going crazy. Thank you so much, Aly. You're amazing. We'll be sure to let you know how it turns out."

"Great. I wish you would. I'd like to run a short follow-up story."

I went down to the library and found an Austin phone book. I found two William Burnses, and one did live on Chatten Street.

I called him up that night. "Mr. Burns, this is Bob Carson in San Marcos, and I think I have some presents that belong to your family. They are all for Ken from Grandma."

"Oh my God! That's fantastic. Can we come by sometime soon and pick them up? I don't want to risk them being shipped again."

"Sure. Anytime. We're not going anywhere this evening. You could stop by about eight if you wish."

"Perfect."

I gave him our address and directions to the house. I got the presents and stacked them neatly in a corner of the living room, which was adjacent to the playroom.

Precisely at eight the doorbell rang, and Anita and I both went to the door. We opened it, and there stood the two of them. The man was holding a bag. We introduced ourselves and had them come in. Ken was a bright, blue-eyed little guy with a perfect part in his brown hair. He was wearing a sweater. So, Grandma knew her man. Anita put her hand on his shoulder and steered him toward the living room and his presents. Mr. Burns grabbed my arm and pulled me aside as they walked off. He began speaking in a low voice choked with emotion.

"Mr. Carson, you have absolutely no idea how much this means to our family. When the presents disappeared, we were frantic. We were just sick to our stomachs. You see, my mother, Grandma, died last December twenty-third. At the funeral, a relative of mine was telling a guest about the disappearance of the presents, and another guest overheard the conversation. This lady was throwing away some old newspapers recently when she saw the headline, got curious, read that one story, and realized who the people were." He threw his arms around me and gave me a big hug.

We walked down the hall and into the living room. The presents were still stacked neatly in the corner. Ken was on the floor of the playroom, ignoring the presents. Anita was watching him play with Cole's electric train. Rebecca wandered into the living room, and I said, "Mr. Burns, this is our daughter, Rebecca."

"Nice to meet you, Rebecca. Where is Cole?"

I was puzzled. "How do you know about Cole?"

He reached in the bag he was carrying, pulled out two presents, handed one to Rebecca, and, handing the second one to her, said, "Will you give this one to Cole?"

I went over and picked up the stack of presents to hand to Mr. Burns. The ornament was on top, and it fell off and hit the floor. It rolled a few feet, and I could see that some of the paint had been chipped off by the accident.

"Oh my gosh. I am so sorry," I said.

Mr. Burns said, "Don't worry. She made dozens every year and gave us six every Christmas. We have about forty at home and don't need another one."

"Can I have it?" I asked.

"You want it?"

"Yes. Very much."

The Burnses took us out to dinner once a few months later.

We still exchange Christmas cards every year. Grandma's ornament is the first one to go on our tree each year. Anita and I alternate. On even years, I get to put it on, and on odd years, Anita gets to put it on. It goes on the front. Near the top.

I just love Christmas.

Chapter 11

The Light

Backward

I was feeling good. Real good. Couldn't be better, in fact. I had just left the wedding of my cousin David—who was also a good friend. He lived there in San Marcos. The wedding had been at the local Baptist church and the reception at what passed for a country club there. I was in my car, driving back to my grandparents' home, where I would be spending the night.

I found myself thinking about the wedding and the newlyweds' prospects for happiness. He had married a society girl from Houston. His family was blue collar. The girl, Cindy, was a real sweetheart, and her family was nice but didn't have much in common with David's family. The rehearsal dinner had been held at the local VFW hall. The entertainment for that evening had been a one-man band who billed himself as Billy Bob the Pretty Good. He had been off by himself with his cowboy hat sitting on the back of his head. He had set up his equipment in a dark corner of the VFW and was doing his thing and being completely ignored by the entire assembly.

He would play a song, then say something into his mic, all of which was unintelligible. At the end of his monologues, he would laugh and then play another song. I had wandered over to see what he was saying. Turned out he was telling jokes and then laughing at his own witticism. He was obviously of the opinion that he was hilarious. It was so bad that he was actually kind of funny—in a pathetic sort of way. At any rate, I was pensive. David and I had shared a childhood and I really wanted him to be happy. But I could see potential problems.

It was about nine o'clock on Saturday night, and I was driving my Mustang convertible down LBJ Street in San Marcos toward the courthouse square with the Hays County Courthouse in the center and its statue of Jack C. Hays out front. I loved that statue. Jack Hays was the real deal as a Texas Ranger. He was on his horse at full gallop, and he had his trusty six-shooter drawn. I was not in favor of guns and didn't even own one, but history was history and the guy on horseback was who he was. They kept him illuminated at night.

As I neared the square and the red light at Hopkins Street, the light turned yellow at just that precise moment when you didn't know what to do. A little earlier and you were going to stop. A little later and you'd just sail on through. The Cadillac ahead of me just sailed on through. It was going to be close, but I made that split-second decision and hit the brakes. I came to a head-snapping halt a bit farther into the intersection than usual. The song on my cassette player ended, so I reached over and hit the "Stop" button. I wanted to enjoy this gorgeous night with no distractions. The light turned green, and I immediately accelerated into the intersection.

Suddenly, I was spinning. Flashes of images passed rapidly in front of me like a crazy montage in a movie. Cadillac, Sweetie's, Cafe on the Square, courthouse, Jack C. Hays, Lucky's, Cadillac . . . then nothing.

I was conscious, but I couldn't see. I put my hands in my

lap because it was wet. I found glass. Why was there glass in my lap? Why was my lap wet? Why couldn't I see?

"Are you okay? Hey, buddy! Can you hear me?" Someone was talking to me. He sounded upset. "Hey, fella! Can you talk? Are you okay?" I wished he would leave me alone. I didn't feel good. I heard him trying to open my car door. But apparently it wouldn't open. Maybe he didn't know how to open a car door. Strange. Maybe I could teach him later. But not now. I didn't feel up to it.

I woke up when I heard the sirens. Way off. Way, way off. It sounded like the sirens were at the far end of a long tunnel but getting closer and closer. Did someone get hurt?

Then "Hey Buddy" started up again, only with a different voice—calmer, more assertive. "Hey, buddy. Can you hear me?"

This time, I answered. "Yes. I hear you."

"We're going to get you out of there and take you to the hospital. Okay?"

"Okay. I don't feel good. My lap is all wet. Why is my lap wet? I can't see."

"We'll take good care of you. We've done all this before. You're gonna be all right."

"Thank you, sir," I said. And I meant it. I was glad to hear I was going to be all right. I thanked him again. They eventually got me out of my car and put me on a stretcher of some kind, and then I started hearing sirens again, and we were moving. I realized my left arm and left leg hurt. I thought I might throw up. And then I did.

It felt funny to be riding along on a bed on wheels on my back and seeing lights flash by. Hey! I could see something! So that was good. Then I stopped moving, and there was a bunch of people around me. Poking and prodding. One of the voices said, "What is your name, please?" I told him. "Do you know where you are?" I told him I wasn't sure, but I guessed I was in a hospital. "Do you know what month and year it is?" I told him. I guessed I got it right. He didn't correct me. "Do you hurt anywhere?" I told him my left arm and left leg hurt and my stomach was beginning to hurt too. And, by the way, I said, I couldn't see. I hoped he would be interested in that last tidbit too.

"You've got a scalp wound. The blood is all in your eyes. We'll clean it and stitch it up and get some X-rays."

They cleaned the blood off my face. Even though I was still not myself, I was greatly relieved to find I could see again. I was a resident in ophthalmology. That vision stuff would likely come in handy. Then the X-rays. My grandparents showed up. There were papers and more questions. Then the same questions all over again. Didn't those folks ever talk to one another? And me, a doctor. Being a doctor was good. Being a patient was awful.

"Mr. Carson?"

"Yes. Although, actually, I am a doctor." I don't usually play the Doctor Card thing, but I thought this was a good time. I was beginning to think more clearly.

"Oh yeah? What kind?"

"I'm a resident in ophthalmology at Parkland in Dallas."

"Okay. Well that'll make this a bit easier." He told me I had a fracture of my humerus and a fracture of my femur, and, most importantly, they were concerned I was bleeding into my abdomen. They had to explore my abdomen. They would fix the fractures at the same time. Also, they would fix my scalp laceration. My eyes seemed to be okay.

My grandmother kissed me, my grandfather squeezed my right shoulder, and they told me they would call my parents, and away I went for another ride and more lights.

When I woke up again, I was in a bed. They had me cranked up a little. More bright lights. A nurse stopped by and took my blood pressure. When she was through, I asked, "How am I doing? What did they find?"

"You're fine. They stopped the bleeding in your tummy."

I was glad to hear that, but I was thinking, *For crying out loud, I'm a doctor. You can use a bigger word than "tummy."* I kept quiet though. It was *never* a good idea to piss off your nurse. As any doctor will tell you, they are the most important people in the hospital.

I got yet another ride down the hospital corridor and its now-familiar flashing light show.

***

The next few days were spent trying not to get too bored. I had what felt like two pounds of gauze on my head, a cast on my left arm and left leg, and a bandage covering my abdomen. I didn't look in the mirror for the first two days. When I did, I was relieved to see that the scalp wound was in my hair and not on my face. My family came to visit frequently. I kept telling them to go home.

On the third day, I heard a timid knock on the door.

"Come in." A young woman entered. Her right eye was black and swollen. She was carrying a shopping bag.

"Hi," she said. "I hope I'm not disturbing you. I can come back later if I am."

"No. No. It's okay." She was cute and also sexy. I had never seen anyone so striking. She had long, dark hair. Her eyes were green with light-brown flecks. "Are you selling something? Cookies, perhaps?"

She laughed a little. "No. I'm not selling anything. But it's funny you should mention cookies." She reached into her bag and put a tin on my bedside table. As she did so, she said so softly I could scarcely hear her, "Cookies. I made them myself."

She smelled good. "Thanks. What did I do to deserve cookies? Are you sure you're not selling them?"

"It's not what you did. It's what I did."

"What do you mean? What did you do?"

"I was driving. I was the one who hit you."

I had spent some time wondering who had done this to me. None of my thoughts had been in the least bit charitable. And there was no way in hell this could have been my fault. I had imagined telling my tale of woe to a sympathetic jury. The driver had probably been drunk. I hoped they would lock up whoever it was. They had damn near killed me. They could have ruined my life. And yet here was this beautiful, apparently sweet and contrite young woman, standing there with an empty shopping bag in her hand, who had placed a tin of cookies on my bedside table. I should have been civil. I was not.

"You could have *killed* me."

"I know. I'm sorry."

"I was lucky the six-inch cut was in my hair and not across my face."

"I know. I'm sorry."

"I won't be able to walk normally for months."

"I'm so sorry." Her eyes were getting moist.

"I thought I was *blind* at first."

"I'm sorry." She had dropped her bag and was literally wringing her hands.

I just kept at it. "I won't be able to use my arm for weeks. And I'm a surgeon."

"I know. I'm so dreadfully sorry."

"Wait a minute. You know I won't be able to use my arm for weeks, or you know I'm a surgeon?"

"Both."

"How did you find out I'm a surgeon?"

"I asked around."

"Tell me this. How in the hell did you manage to run that red light?"

"I shouldn't have. I know I shouldn't have. I'll never do it again. It changed to yellow at just that instant when you don't know what to do. I thought it would be okay. I thought I had enough time. I didn't . . . obviously. I'm so sorry. I hope you can forgive me."

She stooped over, picked up her bag, turned around, and headed for the door. As she reached for the handle, I said, "These cookies. They aren't poisonous, are they?"

She turned and said, "Maybe. Maybe not. Eat a few, and see for yourself." She smiled a little, spun on her heels, and was gone.

I reached over and opened the tin. Chocolate chip. My favorite. I picked out a cookie and took a bite. It was delicious—with a capital *D*. I ate four. Then I sat back and thought about what had just happened. I ate two more. I hated to admit it, but she could really bake a mean cookie. She was cute too. Did I mention that? I began to wish I had been nicer.

***

I was discharged two days later. I had called the director of my residency program and told him what had happened. I thought I should just stay in San Marcos for a while. I couldn't drive anyway. And I didn't have a car anymore. My grandparents were glad to have me, so I moved in with them. Just like old times. It was nice to live with someone who loved you so completely.

My grandfather took me around, and I picked out a brand-new used car. This time, I got a more sensible car, a Chevy Nova. It had an automatic transmission, so I didn't need a clutch leg or whatever you should call a leg that you use to depress a clutch. I figured I was ready to drive again. My grandmother wasn't so sure, but my grandfather and I outvoted her. She finally surrendered when I said I would get one of those doorknob shaped handles you clamp on your steering wheel. Granddad drove us to an auto supply place in a big strip center in town and got one. He attached it to the steering wheel, and I got in and took the wheel. We were in a big parking lot. I backed out of the spot carefully and drove toward the exit. There was one car ahead of me, waiting to enter the street. I was going slow, and as I moved to slow down further, I took my foot off the accelerator and depressed the brake pedal. The car wasn't stopping for some inexplicable reason.

"You gonna stop?" Granddad asked with an urgent tone in his voice.

"I'm trying!" I pushed harder on the brake. The dang thing just kept going and going and *BANG*, I rear-ended the car ahead of me.

"You okay?" I asked Granddad.

"Fine. You?"

I nodded. Then I just sat there. I couldn't believe it. I had never had a wreck in my entire life, and there was my second in a few days. The first one serious and not my fault, and this one a fender bender and all my fault. I looked down to where my foot was still firmly pressed . . . on the floorboard between the accelerator and the brake, where the brake in my old car had been.

The driver's door of the car ahead of me opened and an irate young lady got out and began to march toward me. She was gorgeous and had long, dark hair and green eyes with light-brown flecks. It was the cookie lady. I rolled my window down, and she walked over, bent down, and looked at me. "My God! You again? I want my cookies back!"

"I'm sorry. You can't have them back. I ate them all. They were great. Really great!" I noticed a goose egg forming above her left eye already. I thought it was the better part of valor to keep quiet about that at this point. Her right eye was still black. "My foot slipped or something. I put it on the floorboard and pushed. It's a new car. I missed the brake, I think."

"That sounds pretty lame."

"Yeah. I know. It is pretty lame. Granddad, this is the cute young woman who T-boned me a few days ago. Cute young woman who T-boned me, this is my grandfather."

"Nice to meet you," Granddad said.

"And I'm Joanne. Shall we inspect your handiwork?"

Granddad and I got out of the car—he a lot faster than I. Crutches slowed you down, and I wasn't very good with them yet.

We stood in a line and surveyed the damage. Both my headlights and both her taillights were broken. There was red and white glass all over the pavement. No scratches or dents. Just that.

"Looks like I poked both your eyes out," she said.

"And looks like I goosed you twice," I said.

Not understanding, Granddad said, "Are you talking about the goose egg above her left eye?"

"What goose egg?" Joanne reached up, touched her eye, and winced. "Well, looks like I'll have a matching pair. I think I'm gonna need some cookies for this. Is it turning blue yet?"

"Yes. Afraid so. Listen. I have insurance, but why don't we just drive to the Ford place, and I'll pay to have them fix your taillights. Again, I'm sorry." Then, for some weird reason, I stuck my hand out. She looked a little surprised but stuck hers out, and we shook hands. I'm not sure what that was supposed to accomplish but, strangely enough, it helped. She actually smiled.

"Okay. That sounds fine. You can follow me."

We drove over to the Ford place, and an hour later, the three of us were standing beside her car—now with two intact taillights. "Good as new," she said. "Thanks. For the taillights. Not for rear-ending me."

"You're welcome. Listen. I've actually been thinking about when you came to see me in the hospital. I'm afraid I behaved like a jerk. What you did was very sweet. I felt bad as soon as you left. In a way, I'm glad this happened—other than your acquiring that new black eye. I've run a few red lights too."

"You hurt my feelings."

"I'm sorry. We seem to be saying 'I'm sorry' a lot, don't we?"

"Yeah."

"I'd like to buy you dinner sometime," I blurted out. It seemed like the wrong time to say that, but it was too late now—and better late than never. She just stood there. Granddad coughed and shuffled his feet. No one said anything. "Wherever you like," I added helpfully. More silence. Granddad coughed again.

"Long's Steak House," she said. "Friday at seven? I'll meet you there."

I beamed like an idiot. "Great! See you there." She got in her car and drove off. I realized I didn't even know her last name.

"Well, you never know, do you," Granddad said. "Ain't life funny. Just like a train switch. Once you choose a track, there's no going back."

***

Joanne and I began to date as regularly as time and distance would allow. When she eventually moved to Dallas, we both knew it was getting serious. One evening, two years after we met, I was getting spiffed up for our date. I was normally very relaxed around her, but tonight I was nervous. Although I didn't know it at the time, I was about to screw up and do one of the dumbest things I had ever done in my life. And, in any event, you tended to be nervous when you were planning to propose to a woman. I took one last look in the mirror and patted the small box in my pocket, which contained the ring. Even though it was just a simple gold band, I had to borrow the money to buy it. Later on, when I could afford it, I would buy her whatever she wanted.

My plan was to go out to eat at a nice Italian restaurant and then suggest a walk by Turtle Creek. There was a bench right by the water, just off the pathway. It was as pretty a spot as you could find in Dallas.

I picked her up, and as we drove to the restaurant, she turned to me and said, "Bob, are you okay?"

"Fine. Just fine. Why do you ask?"

"Because you haven't said a word to me since I got in the car."

"Oh, sorry. I guess I'm just preoccupied."

"What about? Anything you can tell me?"

"Not now. Maybe later." Then I smiled at her and said again, "Sorry. I promise to do better."

When we arrived at the restaurant, I got out of the car and opened her door, as I always did. She seemed to like that. The restaurant was a new one for us, but I had scouted it out that afternoon and had reserved a table I liked in the corner. Joanne was delighted and seemed in a great mood. In other words, her usual self.

When the waiter came over and handed us the menus, I realized then that perhaps I should have looked at it earlier on my scouting expedition. I didn't know what a quarter of it was. I eventually ordered an unknown dish that ended in "ini" and sounded like it was something I might like. After we had gotten our entrées, I had the idiotic notion that you knew you were in a fine restaurant when you had no idea what you were eating.

Joanne looked up from her meal and said, "Did you ever do this when you were a kid?" She had sensibly ordered a spaghetti dish. She picked up a single strand with sauce dripping from it, held it up in front of her face, opened her mouth, tilted her head back, dropped the dangling end of the strand into her mouth, let go of the other end, and slurped. The loose end whipped around and slapped her on the cheek, depositing its load of sauce on her face. Then she laughed. A man at the next table looked over, frowned, and shook his head before looking away. Joanne stuck her tongue out at him. I laughed. And then she laughed. I reached over, took a strand off her plate, held it up, and slurped. It would not be honest of me if I didn't report that my slurp was a lot manlier than hers. The woman sitting with the guy at the next table looked over at me, frowned, shook her head, then looked away. This time I stuck my tongue out at her. Joanne laughed. Then I laughed.

I thought, *What a wonderful woman. How lucky can a guy get?*

We finished our meal and got back in the car. Turtle Creek wasn't far, and we were there in a few minutes.

"What's this?" Joanne asked as I pulled over.

"I just thought a walk would be nice." I reached in the back and got a picnic basket in which I had stowed a bottle of wine and a couple of glasses.

"What a great idea. What's in the basket?"

"You'll see," I said. She looked surprised but didn't say anything.

We walked through the park and saw not a single other person. We turned a corner in the path, and I stopped right in front of the bench where I was to propose. It was perfect. We sat down, and I opened the picnic basket and took the wine out. I was not a wine lover and seldom drank a glass, but I thought it was a nice touch. I congratulated myself on remembering a corkscrew. I got it out, and after fumbling around, I finally got it started and screwed it all the way in. However, I couldn't get the cork out. I pulled and pulled. Finally, Joanne said, "Uh, Bob. You're never going to get the cork out. That's a screw cap." Then she laughed so hard she had to bend over. I failed to see the humor in the situation.

I yanked the corkscrew out and looked down at my handiwork. I had created a small hole in the middle of the cap with jagged metal strips sticking up like a flower's petals. A moth landed on the opening, and I peevishly swatted at it with my left hand and cut my thumb. I succeeded only in knocking one of its wings off. The remaining half of the moth fluttered around trying to make a getaway. Blood spurted from the cut. I threw down the corkscrew, retrieved my handkerchief, and tried to stanch the flow. I felt dizzy and decided to sit on the ground for a while. Joanne somehow managed to avoid laughing at this point.

She eventually picked up the basket, and we got up and walked toward the car. I left the wine with its malicious fangs behind on the bench. A monument to my stupidity. I began to think, *Bad omen. In fact, four bad omens. First the corkscrew, then the moth, then the blood, and finally the dizziness. Maybe this is a mistake. Maybe this won't work. Maybe I ought to wait. This is a huge decision. One of the biggest decisions I'll ever make. This is a big, big deal. Maybe I need to think about it a little more.* And, lastly, *What if she says no?*

I took her home and then I went home. I went to the bathroom and looked in the mirror. There I was, looking back at myself. I didn't look very good. I said to myself, "You, sir, are an ass and a coward. Of all the dumb things you have ever done, this was the dumbest."

I took her back to Turtle Creek the next night. I forgot about the wine. That wasn't me anyway. We were all alone. I got down on my knee and got it right this time. Simple and sincere. That was who I was. I guessed that was what she wanted anyway. She said, "Yes." And then she said it six more times. It's a wonder she did. Maybe the dumbest thing she ever did. But, in my defense, I still opened the car door for her.

Chapter 12

The Vacation

Forward

We were leaving on our big annual "nice" trip tomorrow morning. We were going to Alaska as a family. Anita, Rebecca, Cole, and I. It was humid outside, and we had the air-conditioning cranked way down. The windows to the patio were covered halfway down with condensation. It was time for bed, but Cole began to draw a smiley face on the glass. Rebecca saw him and did the same. I got in the mood and drew one too. I announced that mine was the best to a chorus of boos. One of the best times in a person's life was the start of a vacation. It's true.

After the alarm went off, Anita soon discovered she had lost her gold ring, which she had carefully placed in a particular spot on her dresser. Its disappearance was a complete mystery. "This is crazy" was her only comment. I was commanded to aid with the hunt. The first place I was commanded to look was in the bathroom wastebasket. I pawed through used Q-tips and used dental floss and other moist detritus. No ring. It was not under the bed. It was not in Rebecca's or Cole's bedrooms or the kitchen. We both began to despair. As the catastrophe reached a crescendo, it unexpectedly took a turn for the worse. Anita suddenly realized she had also lost her watch. We finally just had to give up. If this weren't enough, as we got ready to walk out, Anita had trouble putting on her shoe. Her dang foot just wouldn't go in. At least this part of our problem got better when she took her gold ring and watch out of the shoe. Clever way to remember to take them with her.

We loaded up the car, drove to the airport, got our bags out, and walked into the Building Where You Lose All Control Over Your Life. Our ticket agent was moving so slowly that I thought perhaps he was completely encased in transparent goo. I put my big bag on the scales and waited for the goo to loosen up. Thank God we were early. He put the bag on the conveyor belt behind him, and it disappeared into the bowels of the airport. Unfortunately, it was then he realized he had forgotten to put the destination sticker on it. So the airline had lost my bag before we'd even checked in. I was standing there, thinking, *This has* got *to be a world record.*

We went to the gate and sat down in the waiting area. Two minutes later, the gate agent made an announcement: "Your 10:40 a.m. flight to Dallas is delayed due to awaiting aircraft. Flight 1282 now departs Austin at 3:02 p.m. and arrives in Dallas at 4:06 p.m." In other words, we just missed our connecting flight to Anchorage. I looked out the window, and there stood our plane. It was just sitting there. It was just awaiting. Five minutes later, she came on again with another announcement: "Update. Flight 1282 to Dallas now departs at 1:02 p.m. and arrives in Dallas at 2:02 p.m." In other words, if we ran through the airport, we still had a chance. Then, and I swear this was true, one minute later, she came on again with this jewel: "Update. Flight 1282 to Dallas now departs at 10:40 a.m. and arrives in Dallas at 11:42 a.m." I could swear I saw her laugh after she put the phone back on its hook. They of course let the first-class snoots board first, and by the time our big group of peons was allowed to board, the elitists were adjusting their blankets, fluffing up their pillows, and sipping champagne. As we walked through their compartment, I farted three times. Nice SBDs. We took our seats and spent the next five minutes entertaining ourselves by watching the first classers holding their noses and waving their arms in front of their faces. Anita got the window seat, and I had the middle seat. A nice gentleman had the aisle seat and immediately took out his handkerchief and went to work trying to saturate it with nasal secretions punctuated by sniffs, sneezes, and coughs, all the while apparently trying to hawk up a newborn water buffalo chunk by chunk, which obviously had gotten lodged in his throat. Across the aisle, Cole lost the earphones to his Walkman.

Once we landed in Dallas, we were told to see a gate agent for connecting-flight information. Sure enough, at the end of the Jetway, there he was. We walked up to him and asked where we needed to go for our flight to Anchorage. He was obviously a very important gate agent because he was staring at his official clipboard, and we could tell we were interfering with this extremely important task. He spared us a moment and looked up long enough to say he didn't think they had a flight to Anchorage. Then he got back to his clipboard-staring duties. We thanked him, and as we walked off, I glanced at his name tag. I mean, who in the world would name a kid Asshole McPrig?

We eventually arrived in Anchorage, and our bags were almost the first to come down the carousel. I was always petrified mine would be the first ones off because I was afraid I would have a stroke if they were. I was shocked and pleased to see that my bag that hadn't gotten a destination sticker was on the carousel. Unfortunately, they'd lost Anita's. We got to go to the lost-luggage office, where we met Asshole McPrig's brother.

After checking into our hotel, we took a walk in downtown Anchorage. A lot of the shops there had huge stuffed animals. Cole was in a goofy mood, and we got photos of him by a moose on all fours (the moose, not Cole), Cole howling with a wolf, Cole with a bear on his hind legs, Cole with a bear on all fours, Cole with bear cubs, and Cole with a moose on his hind legs. I know that sounds a little weird, but we have photographic proof. Rebecca was laughing at all her little brother's antics, and this prompted her observation: "My laugh cracks me up."

We got on a bus to Whittier and boarded our cruise ship. They took our pictures getting on so that we could have the privilege of buying them later. Then they gave us free peanuts and allowed us to listen to a lengthy pitch about some coupons they had for sodas while we were on board. I guessed the peanuts were to make us thirsty. We were also given the opportunity to buy coupon books for hot cocoa, coupon books for coffee, wine tasting coupons, and plain old coupon books. We went up to our room, stepped out on our balcony, and watched our departure. We went down to eat and then straight to bed. We were tired.

****

In the middle of the night, we felt the ship begin to pitch up and down. Each time it fell, it created a long, loud boom. Kind of pleasing, really. At least it was until the pleasant boom was replaced by a loud banging. It sounded like an elf with an attitude and a hammer was loose in our cabin. I hated elves. Especially elves with hammers. I got up three times to look for the dang elf so I could strangle him but never found him. Finally our alarm went off, and it was off to the shower and perhaps the worst bathing experience of my life. A pitiful little stream of water dribbled out of the showerhead. Both a blessing and a curse, as the temperature of the water wildly, unpredictably, and with distressing suddenness changed from arctic cold to thermonuclear. As bad as my shower was, Anita's was even worse—at least according to her. It was the loudest shower I ever heard. It was heartrending. Cries of scalding pain followed by shrieks of surprised cold. I thought I would never stop laughing. She vowed to find the chief engineer to rectify this abomination.

We went down to eat breakfast at the big buffet restaurant. The rest of the family went through the line, but I wanted eggs and went to the omelet station, where I stepped in front of the "Place Your Order Here" sign. Without looking up, a guy behind the counter said, "What do you want on it?"

"What are the choices?"

He looked peeved. He turned his head to the right and pointed to a display of colorful whatevers off to the left.

"What are they?"

"I don't know."

I found an order sheet lying off to the side of the counter and pointed to my choices. "What's your table number?"

"I don't have a table number."

"You need a table number."

I left to find a table. Anita and the kids were still in the buffet line, so I was on my own. I found a rare vacant table and rumpled up some napkins to try to stake my claim and returned to the "Place Your Order Here" counter just in time to hear him tell his helper to cancel my order.

"I haven't left. I got table number fifteen, and I still want my omelet." I went back to my table and almost had a fistfight with the couple who had commandeered my table. I finally sat down and tried not to doze off while waiting for my food to arrive and for the drink attendant to saunter by so I could order coffee. The rest of the family finally came and sat down. Cole had scrambled eggs, fried eggs, hash browns, and Tater Tots. Anita and I kept quiet. It was his vacation too.

The big event of the day was an ice-carving demonstration. We all went to the lido deck, and it seemed like the whole ship was there. We were fortunate enough to get good seats. There in the middle of the deck was a big block of ice. Promptly at two, the announcer tapped his mic and the hype began. He apparently was to be the chunk-by-chunk announcer for the proceedings. Did we know that Indonesians are the best ice carvers in the entire world? Well, he had me there. I didn't know that. I guessed I missed the latest ice-carver ratings. Did we know the block of ice weighed three hundred pounds? He had me again. I would have guessed one hundred fifty. Did we know that the block of ice would weigh one hundred fifty pounds when our ice carver was through with it? Well, dang. I missed another one. Did we know that your average ice carver took two hours to do a carving such as the one we were about to witness, but that ours would take only twenty minutes? Okay. Now I was beginning to feel really stupid.

Our hype guy raised his voice and said, "And now, ladies and gentlemen, please give a big hand for the greatest ice carver in the Pacific, Bruce Sukarno." He got out his tools, and the ice began to fly. Our chunk-by-chunk announcer chattered away through the whole performance. After a while, he began to repeat himself. I mean, there was not really a whole lot to say about it. After about ten minutes, he began to ask if anybody knew what it was going to be. At one point, I was pretty sure the burgeoning creature's nose fell off. Something fell off. That was for sure. Bruce got a distressed look on his face and paused for about thirty seconds and then started up again. Five minutes later, the announcer again asked what we thought it was going to be. Rebecca thought it was a sailfish. Cole thought it was a moose. I thought it was either a swan or a grizzly bear.

Anita had no clue. In another five minutes, he was through and there it stood. His twenty-minute masterpiece. According to the announcer, it was a dolphin. So I guessed Rebecca won. At least it was some kind of sea creature. I still thought it was a swan or a grizzly bear.

We opted next for a little class, so we went to high tea. We ambled over to the restaurant and sat down. The waiter came by and offered us some hot tea and scones. It was delightful until the music started. They had a violinist accompanied by an accordion player. Why didn't they just bring out a blackboard and someone could scratch their fingernails on it? I threw some scones at the accordion player. Or at least I thought about it. I can imagine the headline: "Accordion Player Sconed to Death on Cruise Ship." We spent the afternoon up on deck, looking at whales, birds, otters, and orcas. After dinner, we went to the show. It was a stand-up comedian. He was not so hot. At the end of the show, he said, "You've been a great audience. I wish I had a better act." Back to the room, where Anita lost her nightie. Rebecca found it. Then Anita lost her toothbrush. Lying in bed, in the dark, Rebecca and Cole kept yapping away. Eventually the subject turned to the fact that they were having trouble going to sleep. I told them it was a scientific fact that it was much easier to go to sleep if you weren't talking.

✳✳✳

We were awakened in the morning by long, low-pitched, mournful blasts from a horn of some kind. It almost sounded like a foghorn. I got up, threw open the curtains, and was greeted by . . . fog. And lots of it. Rebecca stepped out on the balcony and reported that it was "pitch-white" out there. We went down to breakfast and sat silently at our table, chomping away, trying to wake up and become something resembling human beings. None of us were sparklers early in the morning—especially Anita.

A guy came by and asked if we minded if he sat with us. Well, what could you say? He told us his name was Ferdinand and immediately began jabbering away. We were glad to let him take the lead, which allowed us to just sit there and chomp, swallow, and burp. He explained that he was the environmental leader for the cruise, and how were we doing and where were we from? It soon became obvious that it was one of those deals where someone asks you a question not because they have the slightest interest in your response but because they want to answer their own question.

He began to tell us all about the subject that fascinated him most in all the world . . . himself. We learned that one of his uncles made $250,000 a year, and he did not. He seemed to think this was quite unfair. Then he told us all how to live our lives and be better people. We were all so grateful. He was obviously wise beyond his years. I tried to kick him under the table, but he was out of range. According to him, he was an extremely impressive fellow. He explained how he had skipped his TV remote into the sea and dumped his TV set in the trash in order to become a better father. I bet he earned himself a lot of "Dad! You did *whats?*" over that.

He must have liked the way that sounded because we sat at an adjacent table for lunch, and he used the exact same words to enthrall that table. He also expounded to those poor souls about nouns, adjectives, and, I kid you not, participles. When was the last time anyone talked to you about participles? I don't know about you, but I had very little interest in participles and no interest whatsoever in someone who did have an interest in participles.

When the captain announced our arrival at Margerie Glacier in Glacier Bay, we went out on our balcony to witness the majesty of this huge hunk of ice. We couldn't see the dang thing. It was, as was earlier reported, "pitch-white." Each side of the ship had thirty minutes to view the fog. When our thirty minutes of fog viewing were over, the ship spun one hundred eighty degrees so that the other side could have an equal opportunity to see absolutely nothing. We did, however, hear a seagull. Then it was on to Lamplugh Glacier. Much more impressive. For one thing, you could see it. The scene was spectacular. We saw several icebergs calve. Loud cracks and then big waves as the thing crashed into the sea. We saw otters and whales. A memorable day.

We spent the evening watching a magician with the unlikely name of Duck Wizniewski. I told Cole I was not sure if his name was Duck or if he was an actual duck. I had hoped he was an actual duck. I could just imagine a duck waddling onto the stage and sawing a pig in half. He was actually pretty good. For his grand finale, he changed his three lovely assistants into two motorcycles. Not sure what happened to the third lovely assistant. Maybe there was a problem during the transmogrification process. At any rate, the motorcycles just stood there. No zooming or vrooming. A huge disappointment.

***

I woke up in the middle of the night, and I was freezing. No wonder. My duvet was gone! I looked over and saw that my much-loved wife had stolen mine. She was lying there warm as toast, acting innocent. I reached over and stole it back. This caused her to wake up in a fury, and she stole my cover from me again. This forced me to search for life-sustaining warmth elsewhere, and so I looked on the floor on my side of the bed, and what did you know, someone had put one on the floor right beside the bed. Unfortunately, when I put it back on the bed, I put it on at a ninety-degree angle, so when I stuck my feet down, they stuck out of the bottom. So I rotated it a hundred eighty degrees and tried again. Those of you who have ever taken geometry would know that didn't solve the problem. So I woke up enough to realize another ninety-degree rotation might produce a better result. It did, but then the top part of the duvet was down at my feet. That meant the bottom part where the opening resided was now at the top. That probably explained why my arm got stuck in the opening. And that probably explained why I had a dream in which I was being swallowed by a great white shark. I was fighting it off valiantly when my lovely bride saved me by grumbling, "*What* are you doing? You've been jerking around all night."

I had trouble going back to sleep because (a) I was too upset due to my near-death experience with the shark, and (b) Anita was snoring (a fact that she had been denying for years). Although how one could deny that one was snoring when one actually was snoring and therefore was asleep the whole time one was accused of snoring was beyond me.

After all of us were awake, we went out on the balcony to examine the day. We were in Juneau, a pretty little city. There were large white foamy areas on the surface of the water. Rebecca asked me what they were, and I told her they were whale farts. She liked the explanation and pretended to believe me. Cole just laughed and said, "Good one, Dad. Whale farts."

We had two adventures scheduled for the day. The first was a boat ride to an adjacent island for a nature walk in the woods. When we got to the island and got off the rubberized raft deal, we discovered that our guide was to be none other than the ubiquitous Ferdinand. Fortunately, he had left his participles back on board. We took off down a kind of logging road, and Ferdinand began his nonstop explanation of the flora, the fauna, and the Ferdinand. When we'd had about all we could stand of the latter, we put on a burst of speed and got far enough ahead to get a little peace.

We hadn't gone far when we saw a nice pile of what we

feared might be bear poop. We decided to wait until Ferdinand showed up to ask him what it was. After assiduously studying the specimen, he proclaimed it to, in fact, be bear poop. Someone asked him if he had any bear spray, and he said yes and added that he was prepared. Suddenly Ferdinand and the Carsons became best buddies. Another few yards away was another pile of bear poop. That one was still fragrant and steaming. I guessed he (the bear) had had some bad Tex-Mex the night before. Someone in our group heard some rustling in the woods off to our right. As they reported this, they stepped to their left behind their neighbor, a fact that the neighbor apparently noted, since the neighbor said, "Hey! What are you doing?" The rustling faded away. Ferdinand said that he had wanted to walk along the beach but his boss told him no. So the bear scare wasn't his fault at all. We were all exhilarated. Nothing can quite match the thrill of not being eaten by a bear.

We went back to the ship for lunch and then got on another boat and went to a nearby cove. We wound up in a pretty cove and anchored. They had some two-person kayaks on the boat, and Anita and I got in one, and Rebecca and Cole got in another, and we began to paddle around the cove. We were about thirty feet from the boat when Cole made the astute observation, "I gotta pee." I solved the problem by saying, "Sorry, buddy." Anita was sitting in the back (or to use the correct nautical term, the buttocks) of the craft, so I couldn't tell if she was actually paddling. She began to offer numerous helpful suggestions to help the captain of the vessel (me) perform his duties better. We hadn't been out long when we heard the characteristic spewing sound of a whale. We looked around and saw him just lying on the surface, this huge gray glob. Turned out whales sleep, and this guy was taking a nap. We paddled over, and Anita took some great photos of him, and of Rebecca and Cole and the whale, and I took some great photos of my thumb. I told Cole and Rebecca to paddle over and poke him with a paddle to see if they could wake him up, but Anita vetoed that plan. We then paddled over to a small, rocky island in the middle of the cove, since we saw a group of harbor seals hanging out there and swimming around. They were very curious and startled us a time or two when they got real close and then made a great splash and disappeared beneath the surface. The boat blew a horn, and we paddled back to the boat, and they took us back to the ship. We had a nice evening. And so to bed.

***

After breakfast the following day, we returned to our room only to discover that the maid had not left us clean paper cups for Anita's third cup of coffee. She decided to call down to the front desk and give a full report on this outrageous, intolerable situation. She went right over to her bedside table and picked up the TV remote, turned the TV on, held the remote to her ear, and waited impatiently for someone at the front desk to answer the phone call she was attempting to make on the TV remote. Her efforts at communicating her dire situation were doomed to failure, however, because even if they did answer, they probably wouldn't be able to hear her with all the noise *The Price Is Right* was suddenly making.

Today we were going on a rail trip on the White Pass and Yukon Railway. After breakfast, we went back to the room, and I was then ordered back down to the buffet to get supplies for our trip. We would be gone all day and needed to pick up some sandwiches and chips to eat for lunch. I was late, and so the selection of sandwiches was rather limited when I got there. They had lots of cucumber-and-tongue sandwiches and one ham-and-cheese. Tongue of what, they didn't say. None of us were vegetarians, so I got the ham-and-cheese and three tongues, put them in a paper bag, and went back to the room with my prizes. When Anita asked what they were, I told her I wasn't going to tell her. She grabbed the bag, and I edged to the far side of the room. She peered between the slices of bread.

"*What* is this, may I ask?"

"Tongue."

"Of what?"

"I didn't ask. I didn't want to know."

Rebecca and Cole started making gagging sounds and actually began to boo.

On our way out to the bus, we stopped by the buffet and picked up some apples and Froot Loops. We donated two of the tongues.

After a short bus ride, we got to the train terminal. It was a short railway line built for the Yukon gold rush in the nineteenth century. The scenery was absolutely spectacular. The best yet. Waterfalls and deep gorges and high snowcapped mountains and tunnels and clear rushing rivers and beautiful lakes. We stopped and ate our lunches at the summit. I had water and a tongue sandwich. It had a pleasant texture. Sort of like Play-Doh. The other three got the good stuff. Or at least the not-quite-so-bad stuff. We spent almost the whole trip on the back platform. You could see a little better there. Rebecca and I both got cold. Fortunately, I had remembered to bring along an extra sweater, so at least Rebecca was warm. Next time, I'd bring two sweaters.

When we got back, we walked through Skagway. We found ourselves in a big crowd, walking right behind a family from another cruise ship. There were two lively teenage daughters walking along, one on either side of their mother. All three of them had their arms around each other's waists. The father was off to the right. They were laughing and having the greatest time. They were speaking what sounded like Italian. The wife was in her midforties and had a nice tan. There was a fly on her left shoulder—I could see it now, decades later, so vividly. Only it wasn't a fly. It was a melanoma with an uncanny resemblance to a fly. Many years earlier, I had taken a dermatology elective, and this "fly" had all the characteristics of a melanoma. What to do?

It seemed unconscionable to tap her on the shoulder in front of her entire family, in the midst of a vacation, and say, in essence, "Pardon me, but you have a potentially deadly cancer. You need to see a doctor soon, or you could die. And by the way, have a nice day." And what if she didn't speak English? I hesitated.

Just then, Cole yanked on my arm and told me to make Rebecca quit poking him with her fingers. When I looked back, the woman had disappeared in the crowd. I tried to run after her, but we were in the middle of a huge crowd of tourists, and some were turning right, some left, and some were going straight. I guessed straight and spent a frantic hour looking for her. I never found her.

At dinner, we sat at a table with a nice couple from New York and a personal injury attorney from New Jersey. According to him, he and everyone in his family were geniuses. Everyone else in the world was an idiot. We ignored him, and the New Yorkers began to tease Cole. Cole got in a silly mood, and at the end of the meal, he made a smiley face on his plate out of his shrimp carcasses, brussels sprouts, sausages, and asparagus. As the pièce de résistance, he placed the handles of a row of forks under his plate so that the tines stuck out beyond the edge of the plate for the hair. For some reason, it was so silly we and the New Yorkers just screamed and made fools of ourselves, according to the attorney. To hell with him. We had fun.

***

Today was the highlight of the entire trip—according to the kids. It was to be the first zip line adventure for either of them.

At the zip line place, they had a bald eagle named Simon in a cage out front. He was a rescue eagle. There was some problem with his talons and one wing. There was a zip line employee standing nearby. I asked her how they were able to find out his name was Simon. She looked at me like I had crabs crawling out of my nostrils. We suited up and piled into a van for the ride up a hill to the starting place. The ride up the hill was a real treat. Bumps and ruts and tree stumps. The only apparent shock absorbers on that thing were our spines. Up at the first station, Rebecca and Cole crowded their way up to the front in case a meteor destroyed the planet before they had their chance to zip-line. They gave us neophyte zip liners detailed instructions on how to zip-line properly. Apparently, you just jump off a platform into space, gravity takes over, and away you go. That was about it. Those things had a kind of brake you could apply if it looked like you were coming into the landing platform too fast. The first section was pretty tame. We all survived. Hey! This could be fun. The next one was longer, and being the gentleman that I was, I went last. My zip line equipment was obviously faulty; something was just too slippery, and I achieved what I estimated to be Mach speed in the first ten yards. Thank God for those brakes. In other words, I stopped about a hundred yards from the platform, about forty feet in the air, gently bouncing up and down, going nowhere. Somehow, through sheer force of will, I was able to maintain total control of my sphincters. I was, however, getting dizzy. And nauseous. Rusty, our leader, zip-lined back down and somehow crawled back up the line to the platform, dragging me behind him. Anita seemed to enjoy my situation. She pulled out her camera to immortalize the moment. Rebecca and Cole immediately left for the next section. We didn't catch up to them until the very end. There, we stopped on another platform. Instead of simply having some stairs to descend to get to the ground, they had rigged up a kind of rappelling rope affair. They hooked you onto your zip line harness, and you leaned over the edge of the platform, and they lowered you slowly to the ground. I was last. Again. There was a thick rubber mat at the edge of the platform, and as they began to lower me, my shoe got caught in the mat, and I rotated slowly as I descended so that it looked like I was performing a swan dive off the platform in super-slow motion. Halfway down, I began to rotate again so that I landed flat on my back. It could have been worse. I could have landed on my head. I sat up to weak applause from my adoring family. Rusty unhooked me and said, "Nice job!" I think he was lying. They then actually placed gold (colored) medals around our necks. Mine said "For Conspicuous Stupidity."

That was to be our last evening on board. At dinner, Anita let me choose the wine so she could, as she put it, "complain if it's no good." Rebecca ordered her usual dessert, a big bowl of whipped cream. It was her vacation too, and vacations were the perfect time to do something you, by God, just wanted to do. It probably didn't need to be, or perhaps even shouldn't be, sensible. I was of the firm opinion that that was a good thing.

Back in our room, we began to pack, which was no fun. Anita had some peanuts and began to throw them at Cole. He was catching them in his mouth like a seal. They were laughing and having such a great time that they decided to take the game outside on the upper deck to get more room. Cole, Rebecca, and I had a lot of fun laughing at Anita's girlie-girl throwing motion. I showed her how to throw like a man, but she wasn't interested. She half emptied a big can of peanuts down Cole's gullet. We went back down to our room, got a couple of glasses of wine, and went out on the balcony. Cole and Rebecca joined us. Anita and I sat there in silence and looked at the spectacular, ever-changing scene. The kids were quiet. Anita and I looked around after a few minutes and saw that they were both sitting in chairs on our balcony with their knees drawn up under their chins and covered with blankets. They looked happy. Cole said, "Great trip, Dad." Rebecca nodded her agreement. Anita and I were so blessed. God knew what He was doing when He made Alaska.

***

"May you experience each day as a sacred gift woven around the heart of wonder." An Irish priest once said that. I wished I had. Rebecca and Cole would forget most of the details of that trip, but they would remember some of them. And they would know it was a gift to them and that they were wanted and loved. After all, what you saw was not nearly as important as what you experienced. Anita leaned her head on my shoulder, and I leaned my head on hers. I thought that, one day, when our children were in their sixties and had a get-together, they would look at one another and say, "Remember when we went to Alaska . . . ?"

Chapter 13

The Jetty

Backward

I was on my way to Mustang Island and Port Aransas, or Port A, as we called it. It was one of the smallest cities in Texas (although I doubted it deserved that rather lofty designation). It made up for it by having a big personality. And I loved it. It made "laid back" seem like a synonym for "frenzied."

I had been dating Dolly for nearly a year, and things were going well—not mercurial, just smooth. She had been visiting a sick grandparent in McAllen and was on her way back to Corpus. I had suggested we meet up in Port A for a walk on the beach and a trip to our favorite seafood restaurant on the island, and she jumped at it. I'd had an upset stomach the night before and hoped that wouldn't ruin our plans. We were to meet at three o'clock outside the Three Bees, a burger joint at the foot of the South Jetty. I was right on time, parked the car, and waited. Three thirty came and went, and no Dolly. She was always on time, and I started to worry a bit. At four, still no Dolly, so I ducked inside the Three Bees to use the pay phone in the corner and called her home. Her mother answered and said Dolly had called and said she would be two or three hours late. She'd had some car trouble. She was still heading to Port Aransas for dinner.

Well, hell. There went our walk on the beach. I was relieved, but now I had some time to kill. I walked out on the jetty and sat on a granite block. It was a beautiful day. I just enjoyed being there, watching the seagulls and the shrimp boats, tankers, and pleasure crafts go by in the Ship Channel. It was hard to stay awake. I thought I dozed off a couple of times.

As I was struggling to keep my eyes open, some classmates walked by, carrying inner tubes and spearguns.

"Hi, Bob," Mack said. Mack was there with Bill, Charlie, and Jerry. Jerry had some kind of congenital problem with his face, but it didn't seem to stop him from doing anything. The four of them were really tight. I had individual friends, but we didn't hang out together like those four did. I'm ashamed to admit it, but I was a little jealous. Mack was in my physics class and was real smart and real nice. I thought that under different circumstances, he and I could have been good friends.

"Here by yourself?" Bill asked.

"Not really. Well, I am right now. I'm waiting on Dolly. She's late, so I'm killing time. We're going to eat at the Gulf Stream when she gets here."

"Great place. Have a shrimp for me," Jerry said. They walked on by, and I resumed my reverie. Eventually I got bored with that and remembered I had my rod and reel in my trunk, and I figured I could go fishing. I changed that plan almost immediately when I realized I didn't really want to have to deal with dead fish that day. I figured I would just get some bait and go sit on the jetty and dangle a line in the water and watch the sheepshead nibble at the bait.

I went back to the Three Bees. Underneath their mysterious name was the explanation in bold letters: "BAIT, BREW,

BURGERS." It was a popular place and, as was typical of so many Port Aransas businesses, extremely informal. The front door was a screen door with a rusty waist-high horizontal metal band advertising "Lone Star Beer—The National Beer of Texas." You pulled on this as you entered and then listened to the spring of the door bang it shut behind you. It was basically a screened-in covered structure with ceiling fans and no air-conditioning.

I was too young for the "brew" part of their signage, and my stomach was not ready for the "burger" part. I was there for the "bait." I was also hopeful that Brenda would be there. She was the unadvertised fourth and fifth *B*. In her case, the fourth *B* stood for Brenda, and the fifth *B* stood for boobs. As I walked across the squeaky wooden floor, I saw that I was in luck. I sat on a stool at the end of the counter, and she came over. I was the only customer at the moment. Why she didn't just pitch forward on her face was a mystery my friends and I often discussed. She always wore tight white T-shirts and no bra.

"Hiya, sailor. What can I do ya for?"

For some reason, I thought that was hilarious and so made a fool out of myself by cackling in a nervous, high-pitched way.

"Easily amused, I see," she said.

"Yeah. I guess. I view it as one of my many virtues."

It was her turn to laugh. Her boobs jiggled. *Okay. I need to remember this,* I thought.

"I need a box of your finest dead shrimp. Well, actually, I don't really *need* a box. I just *want* a box. You know. Of your finest dead shrimp." What was wrong with me? I sounded like an imbecile.

"You're cute. Kind of weird. But cute."

"Thank you, I guess."

I paid her and left, thinking that the next time I came in, I was going to be armed with some really great jokes.

I got my fishing pole and tackle box and took my bait out on the jetty. I found my original flat chunk of granite and sat down. I put some bait on my hook, dangled it in the water, and watched as these pretty little fish came up and began to enjoy their free meal. If I happened to hook any of them, I would take my pliers, remove the hook, and throw them back in. I looked at the channel and saw Mack, Jerry, Bill, and Charlie swimming across on their inner tubes. At least I think it was them. They were about halfway across. One of them was beating the water with his fists. It was one of those tranquil times when it was nice to be alive, nice to be sitting in the sun, listening to the waves, nice to be feeling the breeze on your face, and nice to be alone with your thoughts.

Then this old geezer came and sat down on the very next chunk of granite. He had only about ten thousand others to choose from. He had a beard, flip-flops, and one of those baseball caps with the long, long bills. To be fair, I should probably have mentioned that his beard was short and neatly trimmed. He had sunglasses, but they were perched on top of his hat. He had big pouches under his eyes. He was a squinty-eyed guy, but, even so, you could see his eyes were wise and sad and tired and kind. A person's eyes could make you like them before you knew anything else about them. He wanted to talk. I didn't, but there was one thing about fishing. It was the most democratic of all sports. You could and would meet folks from all walks of life, and you would have something in common.

"Hi," he said.

"Hi," I said.

"How ya doing?"

"Fine. How are you doing?"

"Fine."

I'm sure Oscar Wilde would have been green with envy had he heard our discourse. Or maybe Oscar would have been green due to nausea.

"Nice day, huh?" I said.

"Gorgeous day. Just gorgeous."

"Nice rod."

"Thanks. Catching anything?"

At this point, I was thinking, *A chimpanzee could be having this conversation. Maybe I should go find one, so I can get back to feeding fish.* Instead, I said, "Well, actually, I'm not really fishing. I'm just feeding the sheepshead some shrimp."

"That so? I haven't heard that one before."

"I know. I'm a rebel. It's the first time I've ever tried it. I was bored. My girlfriend is late for a date, so I'm just killing time. Do you fish a lot?"

"I do now. I didn't until about six months ago."

"What happened? Did you realize you were bored?"

"No. Not really. Well, maybe that was a little of it. I just needed to get out."

"Oh. I'm Bob, by the way."

"Nice to meet you, Bob. I'm Scott. What grade are you in?"

"I'll be a senior next September."

"What are you going to do after high school?"

"Go to college."

"Where?"

"No idea. I also have no idea what I want to do."

"It'll come to you sometime when you least expect it. Don't worry about it."

"Okay. I'll try."

He lapsed into silence, and I was content to let him lapse. I returned my attention to the sheepshead.

"Damn!" he said. I glanced over and saw that he had stuck his thumb with his hook. Then he picked up a sinker from his tackle box and fumbled it into the water. He got another sinker and dropped it in the water too. He finally got one attached to his line on the third try. Then he tried to tie a knot in his line but made a mess of this too. He kept trying and trying, and I could see a tangled snarl of fishing line developing. You could see his movements getting frantic and sense his growing frustration. He suddenly stood up and reared back as though he was going to give an almighty cast and threw the whole rod and reel out in the channel. It was a powerful throw. It arched high and spun slowly around and around several times before it hit the water with a gentle splash.

He stood there on the granite, his face flushed, and yelled at the top of his lungs, "Goddamn it! No! God, damn *you*! Did you hear that, God? I'm damning *you*. You damned her, and now you're damning me. Well, guess what. It's your turn now. You got that, God?"

He stood there, clenching and unclenching his fists, then slowly collapsed into a kneeling position before slumping back on his haunches. I could see him sag. I looked around, but incredibly, no one else on the jetty had heard—or if they had, they didn't seem to care.

I waited a couple of minutes, then said, "Are you okay, Scott?"

"Yeah," he said. He just sat there. Just when I thought that was all he was going to say, he calmly continued. "She had ALS. She died one year ago. On this day. Fifty-one years. We were married fifty-one years. I'm sorry. I guess I needed someone to talk to. I'm sorry it was you. I don't seem to be getting better. I thought fishing might help. I used to be a useful person. I used to be happy. I used to be competent. Used to be. Used to be. Now I'm just a washed-up surgeon. Good for nothing. Useless."

After a moment, I said, "Are you hungry?"

"You know. As a matter of fact, I am. Throwing fishing poles in the Gulf will apparently give you an appetite."

"Come on. Let's go to the Three Bees. Brenda makes a mean burger." If I ruined my appetite, I figured Dolly would understand.

"Brenda. So that's her name. So, why do you suppose she doesn't just tip over?"

"That's a topic for greater minds than mine." I dumped the rest of the shrimp in the water and picked up my rod and tackle box, and we walked off toward the base of the jetty. "By the way, do you know any good jokes?"

Brenda did make a mean burger. I had a Dr Pepper, and Scott had a Lone Star. We finished, and Scott insisted on picking up the tab. He left Brenda a generous tip. Tight T-shirt with no bra was a wise investment decision on her part.

As we walked out, we saw a small crowd standing in a circle just beyond the surf. There were about twenty people. One of them, a young Hispanic woman, was crying.

We walked over and, in the middle of the circle, saw a young Hispanic man lying on his back on the sand. He was not moving. The whole group was just standing there.

"What happened?" Scott asked.

"He must have stepped in a hole," a man said, still catching his breath. "His wife here says he can't swim. I saw him floating in the surf and went and got him just a minute ago."

Scott knelt beside the man and felt for a pulse in his neck while watching his chest. He pointed to one of the women in the group. "Go tell Brenda in the Three Bees to call an ambulance. Tell her to tell them he's not breathing, and I don't feel a pulse. Do it *now*!"

The woman ran off as Scott knelt over the man and began thrusting on his chest with both hands, one on top of the other. He told me to take off my shoe and slide it under his neck. Puzzled, I did what he said, and this forced his chin up as it bowed his neck.

"Now watch what I do," he said. With that, he rapidly moved to the man's head and pinched both nostrils with one hand. He slid the fingers of his other hand under the man's chin and pulled up. Then he leaned over, opened his mouth, and breathed into the man's mouth. The man's chest rose. He did this three times and then went back to his chest and resumed thrusting away.

"When I stop the compressions, do what I did and give him three quick breaths. Got it?"

"Yes." I was petrified and wondering how I got dragged into this. I did it anyway.

Every so often, Scott would stop and check for a pulse and watch to see if the man was breathing. Still nothing. The man's wife was still crying. Fifteen minutes later, there was still no ambulance, and Scott was still at it.

"Do we quit?" I asked.

"No. We do *not* quit!"

Three cycles later, I gave him the first of the three breaths, and as I inhaled to give him the second breath, he vomited right in my mouth. I fell back and spit as much of it out as I could. Your own vomit was pretty noxious to taste, but someone else's was several levels more disgusting.

Scott stopped his compressions and turned the man's head to one side and felt for a pulse again.

"We got one!" He was exultant.

"Scott," I said. "He's breathing too."

The man threw up again. We sat there in the sand and watched as his wife sat down beside him and stroked his hair. *"Querido. Querido,"* she whispered over and over.

The ambulance came at last, and they loaded the man and his wife in the back, and, siren wailing, off they went.

All the onlookers but one wandered off. The one remaining was Dolly. She came over, knelt down behind me, and put her arms around me, her long, blonde hair spilling over my shoulder. Brenda came over too. She sat between Scott and me and handed Scott a Lone Star and me a Dr Pepper. "These are on the house," she said. We both smiled at her.

"Scott," I said. "That was unbelievable. You were unbelievable. The whole thing was unbelievable. When he threw up in my mouth, that was about the happiest moment of my life."

Scott laughed. "You did well, son."

"I did, didn't I? But you. You were fantastic. The way you took charge when everyone else was just standing there watching. The determination on your face, the fact that you didn't give up. You were dead wrong about one thing though."

"What's that?"

"You are very definitely not useless."

Dolly and I said goodbye to Scott and sat in my car and watched the water. We saw my four classmates swimming back across the Ship Channel. From where we sat, I could tell that the current was swift and they were having to work harder than usual, but they were going to make it. A bit later, they walked by us, Mack proudly holding a big tarpon. "Nice fish," I said.

"Thanks. See you Monday."

Dolly and I sat there and watched the sunset. "I'm not hungry right now," I said.

"Me neither."

"Maybe we could have that walk on the beach and just get some pizza on the way home?"

"Fine with me."

We left our shoes in the car and began to walk along the shoreline hand in hand. A soft summer breeze was even softer when it was experienced with little waves lapping at your bare feet. The water changed color from blue to gray to black. I told her about Scott. Neither of us said anything for a while.

Finally, I said, "I found out something about myself today."

"What?"

"I found out what I want to do with my life."

Chapter 14

Mrs. Moore

Forward

I stared at the chart in the chart rack outside the door and blinked twice. It still read "Mable Moore." She was the last patient of the day. Earlier that day, a buck, apparently seeing his own reflection, had charged through the floor-to-ceiling plate-glass window of the office foyer. He'd scared the hell out of the patients in the adjoining waiting room and then had the gall to bleed all over the foyer before retreating. In his defense, it was mating season. He probably didn't like the look of himself in his territory. Oh well. Boys will be boys. Especially when there was a girl involved. Far worse than that, Anita had just called. Rebecca's husband had called home, and she was in the ER in Dallas. She was six months pregnant with her first child and had developed some bleeding the night before. They weren't sure yet what was going on. I was worried and distracted and petulant, and now I had to see one of my least favorite patients.

The patient had sent me a letter a few weeks ago. It read:

Dr. Carson,

I am planning on having my cataract surgery in March.

I did not like it at all when you would not tell me what all that was under the big *E*. While I was fixing potato salad at 8:15 this a.m., it dawned on me why you refused. After I have the surgery, you would test my eyes and see if I could tell you then. I did not tell you this, but to me it looked like a bunch of chickens had come together and put all the scratches on there.

Have a good day.

Your patient,

Mrs. Moore

PS. Please excuse the slanty writing. I cannot see the lines.

I had done her cataract surgery the day before, and I was now standing in the hallway, looking at the door. I sighed and opened the door, and there she sat—hands clasped in her lap. I smiled (as I always did), looked her in the eye (as I always did), and repeated her name (as I always did). I got to do this quite often, as she had glaucoma, and I was her ophthalmologist. This meant I saw her on a regular basis—and would see her on a regular basis until she died. This time was different. Since it was a one-day-post-op visit, it should have been quick. The nurse had removed the eye patch, and I asked her how she was doing. She said fine, as she should have, since her vision was perfect. I did my exam, told her everything looked great, and counseled her on what eye drops to use and all the usual things a doctor tells a routine post-op patient. I left the rest of it to my assistant, who had by then entered the room behind me, and I headed for the door. I was in a hurry. I needed to get home.

As I opened the door and was about to make my getaway, I heard her say, "Dr. Carson?"

I sighed but turned around and said, "Yes, ma'am?"

"I want to ask you something."

"Yes, ma'am."

"Yesterday, when you were finishing my operation and you were putting the patch on my eye, did you say, 'I love you'?"

Well, that was unexpected. Of course I hadn't said "I love you." I didn't even like her. But I was ready to leave, I was at the door, and a "no" would have seemed a bit rude and might lead to a lot of questions. So I opened my mouth, and a "yes" foolishly came out. Then I was out the door and on my way home.

The next day when I came to work, her chart was on my desk with a note from the staff. "Dr. Carson, please call this patient. She has a question for you. She says to let the phone ring about fifteen times, since she has a hard time getting to the phone."

At the end of the day, I called her and let the phone ring fifteen times (I counted). She picked up the receiver, and after I told her who it was and asked how I could help, she said, "Dr. Carson, these drops you gave me. One of them has a gray top, and one has a white top. What if I get the tops mixed up? Is that bad?"

"No, ma'am. It won't hurt a thing." Man! That was a dumb question!

"Oh. And one more thing. I love you, Dr. Carson."

I was glad I was on the phone and she couldn't see me, since I put my palm on my forehead, dropped my chin, smiled, and said, "I love you too, Mrs. Moore."

Three days later, there was her chart on my desk again. There was another note. Same as the first one.

At the end of the day, I called again and let the phone ring. She must have oiled the wheels on her walker since it only took fourteen rings that time. "Dr. Carson?"

"Yes, ma'am."

"My vision seems to be doing fine."

"Glad to hear it, Mrs. Moore."

"Guess what?"

"What?"

"I haven't gotten the tops mixed up a single time. I thought you'd like to know."

"Thank you, Mrs. Moore."

"Dr. Carson?"

"Yes, ma'am?"

My suspicions were correct, since the next thing she said was "I love you."

"I love you too, Mrs. Moore." I smiled again.

That night at dinner, I confessed to Anita about the new love in my life. She interrupted her feeding of table scraps to Scooter, our terrier, looked up, and said, "So now I'm third?"

"What do you mean 'third'?"

"Well, it's obvious, isn't it? Mrs. Moore is number one. Scooter is number two, and I bring up the rear at number three."

"You're forgetting about my pickup."

"Oh. That's right. So I'm down to number four, right?"

The next thing I did was really dumb. I told the staff. They had a great time with this tidbit. I began to get valentines on my desk with love notes in handwriting that didn't look anything like Mrs. Moore's "slanty" scrawl. I got invitations to parties telling me to BYOB. I even got a small box of cheap chocolates. Well, at least someone was having fun.

A week later, she came to the office for her second post-op visit. Again, she was doing well, and we went over the new eye drop schedule and arranged for the last surgery follow-up visit. I got up to leave, and she held out her arms for a hug. I gave her as small a hug as I could. Then I placed my hand on her shoulder and pushed down a little, hoping to keep her in the chair long enough for me to get out of the room, and told her I would see her in four weeks. Before I could get out the door in time, she turned her face up and said, "Dr. Carson, I love you." What might have been a tiny smile played across her face for a moment.

Well, there was nothing for it now but to carry on. "I love you too, Mrs. Moore." I had, after all, brought this on myself.

After that, I continued to get notes to call her on a regular basis, and each call was as unimportant as the last and always ended with the same professions of ardor. Funny thing was that I began to mean it. But only a little bit. It was fair to say I didn't hate her.

Then the notes quit coming. I got nothing for about two months. One day, her chart appeared on my desk with another note. But this one was different. She had fallen and broken her hip and was in the rehab facility, which was affiliated with the hospital. She wanted to see me. First, I was relieved. Then, I was aggravated. Crap! It was a fifteen-minute drive to the hospital and then, of course, a fifteen-minute drive back. So that was a half hour right there. Then the trip up to her room and then a visit and, well, crap again! If she just hadn't said "I love you" so many times, I wouldn't have done it but, well, crap. So I went. Hit every damn light on the way over too. Then my doctor's card wouldn't work in the parking thingy, and so I had to park with the peons and go in the damn front door to boot.

When I got to her room, I shoved the door open and bustled in, feeling like a pissed-off martyr. I had done my damn duty, and so there! Her bed was empty. And, ominously, it was made up like when the bed was being readied for a new patient. The pissed-off martyr made a hasty exit to be replaced by a human being. A suddenly chastened human being, who sank down in the nearest chair. Then the toilet flushed, and Mrs. Moore came tottering out of the bathroom, leaning on a cane. She looked up and saw me and actually smiled. I stood up automatically.

"Oh hi, Dr. Carson. What's the matter with you?" She glanced at her bed and said, "Well, I see they finally got around to cleaning up my mess." She climbed in. "So how are you doing, Dr. Carson?"

"Fine," I said as I sat down again in the chair next to her bed. "Where is your walker? Why the cane?"

"I forgot it at home, and the nice folks at the insurance company wouldn't get me another one. I guess they're running low on cash. So I'm using this thing for now. The doc says it's okay to go without the walker for a while."

"What happened to you? Were you behaving yourself?"

"Nope. I've found out that's no fun. I was in the backyard, and I saw Mr. Bigs just sitting there in the yard, looking down, and so I went over to see what was going on. And he—"

"Who's Mr. Bigs?"

"My cat. Anyway, as I was saying before you interrupted, he was just sitting there, looking down at this rattlesnake, who wasn't doing nothing. Just lying there. He wasn't even rattling. I guess maybe his bunions were bothering him. Well, I yelled at Mr. Bigs, but he just ignored me like he always does. So I went in the house and got some ant spray. And—"

"You got some ant spray? Why?"

"Why, to get the snake, honey. So as I was saying before you interrupted me again, I got my ant spray and went over and sprayed that sucker right in the eyes."

"What did he do?"

"Nothing. Remember that, if you ever see a rattlesnake in your yard. Ant spray don't do nothing to a rattler. So I went and got my baseball bat. Beat the thing senseless. Just smithereened him. Ant spray is worthless, but a baseball bat works just fine."

"So you hurt your hip swinging the bat?"

"No. When I was going back in the house, I tripped over a hose and landed on my hip. Hurt like the dickens. Couldn't move. Just lay there. My next-door neighbor found me four hours later by accident. All my screaming didn't do no good. Anyway, that's why I'm here. I wanted to see you because I got a present for you."

"Mrs. Moore, you don't need to give me anything."

"If I want to give you something, I'm gonna give you something. Hand me that bag over in the corner."

I handed her the bag and sat down. She reached in and proudly pulled out the most God-awful afghan I had ever seen. It was mainly purple. There was a zigzag pattern in the background and, in the middle, a huge squirrel with slightly crossed eyes. I was amazed and once again proud of myself for not laughing.

"It's an African. I made it for you. I wanted something with eyes on it, you know. Your staff told me about Elvis once when I was here. Sorry, but I don't think I got the eyes quite right."

"Wow and wow again. This is the most spectacular, uh . . . African I have ever seen."

"Well, you flunked that test."

"What do you mean?"

"I mean that I know it's an afghan. I just wanted to call it an African to see if you would call it an African or an afghan. So, anyway, you flunked."

"Well, African or afghan, this is the most interesting gift I have ever gotten. I can't wait to show it to my friends."

She reached over with her cane and jabbed me with it. She meant it to be an affectionate gesture, but she got me right in the ribs, and I am perhaps the world's most ticklish person. I squealed and twisted ninety degrees. I saw her eyes light up, and she jabbed me again. This time in the stomach, and this was even worse (for me—apparently better for her). I squealed again and reached for the cane, missed it, and knocked over the water pitcher on her bedside table. She was too quick for me and struck again and made a direct hit right in my armpit. By then I was roaring with laughter, and then she started in with what proved to be a laugh.

Eeeeeeeeee-heeeeeeeeee-heeeeeeeeeeeeee was the best imitation I could do. It started with a long *e* sound, followed by two more sounds, both of which started with an *h* sound. They always came in a series of three. The volume and the length of the sounds varied, but otherwise it was the same every time. It was so ridiculous I started laughing at her laugh.

The cane was coming at me again, so I got out of the chair to defend myself and slipped in the water just as she jabbed again. She got me in the middle of the chest, and I fell backward, butt first into her wastebasket, and got stuck.

EEEEEEEeeeeeeeeeeeHHHHHeeeeeeeeeeeeeeeeeeeeeee-HHHHHHHHHHHHHHHEEEE.

I couldn't get out of the damned thing and tried kicking like a madman.

EEEEEEEEEEEEEeeeHEEEEEEEEEEEEEEEEeeeHHHHHH-HHHHeeeeeeeeeeeeeeeeeeee.

I managed to tip the thing over on its side and slid out and lay there on the floor, laughing, until I was finally able to climb back in the chair. I said, "Oh my God! Oh my God! Oh my God!"

"Glad you like my gift, Dr. Carson."

"Best gift *ever!*"

"Dr. Carson, have you ever tried laughing without smiling?"

"No, ma'am. And I doubt anyone else has either."

"Anyone else don't include me, 'cause I have. It don't work very well. Kind of like ant spray on a rattlesnake. But I recommend you try it sometime. Preferably when you're alone. People will think you're crazy if you do it in public. In fact, I think there's a lesson there somewhere. Not sure what it is though. But I do think laughter is one of the three things that separates us from animals."

"Laughter and what else?"

"Music, and, of course, toilet paper."

I laughed. "You have a special mind."

We said good night, and I stood up, kissed my forefinger, and then touched her forehead. As I headed for the door, she said, "Dr. Carson, there's something you oughta know."

"What's that?"

"You've got butter stuck to your butt."

I reached around behind me, felt something, retrieved a pat of butter, threw it in the trash, and headed for the door again.

"Dr. Carson, there's one more thing you should know."

"What?"

"Your butt looked better with butter."

I closed the door, and as I turned to walk down the hall, I heard a faint *Eeeeeee-heeeeee-heeeee.*

I went downstairs and got in my car. I started it up and tried laughing without smiling. She was right. It was no good. Kind of like ant spray on a rattlesnake.

From then on, she always brought baked goods with her for every office visit. So, naturally, she became a real staff favorite since they got most of the goodies. One day, there was a note stuck to her chart: "Dr. Carson. Today is M. M.'s birthday." And so it was.

I did my exam and then said, "Well, happy birthday, Mrs. Moore."

"Why, thank you, honey," she said.

I liked the "honey" part. No one had ever called me that before except my mother. "Eighty-five, eh. How does that feel?"

"Same as eighty-four. What a dumb question!"

I laughed a little. "Well, how does eighty-four feel?" I was running behind again but found I was in no hurry to get to the next patient.

"Good. Just good. If your body is a temple, then my foundation is cracking a bit. Maybe the Lord ought to be a little worried. But the control center seems okay. Of course, that's just my opinion. But, yeah, that's a lot of years. I just wish I knew where I was going to die."

"Why is that?"

"Well, I just wouldn't go there."

I wasn't sure whether she was kidding or not, so I didn't laugh, and that didn't seem to upset her. But it was sobering. I got up and kissed my first two fingers and touched her forehead and left.

It was a week before Christmas, and it was cold. Cold for Central Texas anyway. Now it was my turn. I had a present for Mrs. Moore, so I called her and asked if I could deliver it to her house. I wouldn't be seeing her in the office for another two months. She seemed quite excited and said that was fine but that she had been in bed for a couple of weeks because she'd been feeling weak. Rebecca, who was home for the holidays with her husband and new baby, had learned of my plan and asked if she could go too. I asked Mrs. Moore if it would be okay if my daughter came as well, and she seemed even more excited.

I got her address, and we drove to her house. She lived on a caliche street, and I parked, and we walked past the mailbox with a pink flamingo painted on it and up the front walk. There was a flock of fading pink plastic flamingos standing guard in the far corner of the yard. There were flower beds near the house but no flowers that time of year. I knocked, and a young woman answered the door. I told her who we were, and she smiled.

"Come on in. I'm Donnelle. Gran's in here." She led the

way. It was a neat little house with knickknacks of all kinds covering every conceivable surface. Animals and knights and big-eyed children and cartoon characters and, of course, lots and lots of Elvises. The linoleum flooring and space heaters gave the place a sad feel—at least to me.

Donnelle led us into Mrs. Moore's bedroom, and she was sitting up in bed. I introduced Rebecca, and Mrs. Moore told her how pretty she was. For once, she didn't have her bobby pins in place, and I saw why she always wore them. It looked like she had been caught in a tornado and then stuck her finger in a light-bulb socket. She looked sick. She smiled anyway. She had lost weight, and her cheeks were sunken. She had a faded chenille bedspread pulled up under her chin. I sat down on the edge of the bed since there was no chair. Rebecca stood at the foot of the bed. It was hard to look at Mrs. Moore. I fingered a loose thread on the bedspread.

I said, "So how are you doing?"

"Better than you, looks like."

I smiled. But only with my mouth. My eyes weren't in the mood to participate. "Have you been to the doctor?"

"Yes."

"Uh . . . what did he say?"

"What makes you think he's a he?"

"Oh, well then, what did she say?"

"She's a he, and he said not to talk to nosy people about it."

"Oh. So I came over to give you a present."

"Oh, honey, you don't need to give me anything."

"Mrs. Moore, if I want to give you something, I'm going to give you something."

Rebecca handed me the bag she was holding, and I reached in and removed Mrs. Moore's present. I handed it to her. "Merry Christmas, Mrs. Moore." I had wrapped it myself, and while I could wrap a present competently, I was no good at decorating one. Rebecca had made a beautiful fluffy red bow and had tied it on expertly.

"Can I open it now?"

"Of course."

She opened it and revealed a framed photograph. It was a picture of the squirrel, our Elvis. I had photoshopped it to uncross his eyes.

Eeeee-heee-hee.

"I operated on him."

"That you did. And did a fine job too. Put it on my bedside table. And don't knock stuff over like the last time you got near my bedside table."

I looked down at the linoleum. "You know, Mrs. Moore. You make me feel ashamed."

"Well, honey, why on earth would that be?"

"Because you're a better person than I am."

"No, honey, I'm not better. Just plainer."

When I got up to leave, I bent over and kissed her gently on the forehead and told her I loved her. Then we left. Out of the corner of my eye, I saw Rebecca dab at her eye.

***

Mrs. Moore died two weeks later. I went to the funeral. There were only a few family members present. Donnelle was there. I sat in the back—the very back. I told myself it was so I wouldn't intrude on the family, but the real reason was so the family wouldn't see me cry. She once told me she was lucky to have known me. I think I was lucky she had bad hearing.

Chapter 15

The Bully

Backward

One of my very favorite things was walking home from school with Richard, my best friend. Unfortunately, Richard had moved to Austin a month earlier. I had been feeling sorry for myself ever since. We had been best buddies for a couple of years. Momma had been trying to get me to make new friends, but that wasn't easy. You couldn't just stand up in class one day and say, "Hey! Anybody want to be my new best friend?" At first, I thought maybe Dolly could be my friend, but that didn't work out, to say the least.

I looked ahead and saw three of my classmates, Mack, Bill, and Charlie, pestering poor Jerry. Those three were always together. They called themselves the Three Musketeers. Jerry had a deformed face, and people teased him all the time. I didn't want to be party to that.

I crossed the street and turned off, heading to my house at 321 Elizabeth Street. I was sorry Jerry had a problem, but I had my own problem. I had Dolly to deal with. Not only did Dolly turn out not to be a friend—she proved to be an enemy. Today I had to apologize to her for something that wasn't my fault. Life was so unfair.

****

Dolly had moved to 323 Elizabeth Street a couple of weeks ago. She was in my grade at school but not in my class. She was much bigger than I—but then, most kids in my class were. She was a tomboy. She always wore her long, blonde hair in pigtails. They flew behind her when she was on her bike, and it seemed like she was always on her bike.

Momma and Daddy, d/b/a Santa Claus, had given me a bike last Christmas, but I was slow learning how to ride it. I'd had trouble keeping my balance and eventually gave up after a few accidents. That was when I got my trike, and I loved that thing. You never fell off a trike. It was an unusual tricycle. It had a twenty-inch front wheel and twelve-inch back wheels. I didn't know where Daddy found it, but it wasn't in a toy store. He said he had been told it was once used in a warehouse. I wanted to be a policeman, and I loved to play cops and robbers on it. I had gotten Daddy to attach a little hand-cranked siren on the right side of the handlebars and a light (which I never used) on the left side. I had hand-painted the word "Police" on both these additions and on the front fender. You could hardly read the front fender "Police." We lived four blocks from the bay, and what was capable of rusting had already done so. Salt air was great if you were trying to get something to deteriorate quickly. The leather had been worn off the seat long ago, and the metal seat had also begun to rust. I was too big for it, and I was too old for it. I knew that but just didn't care. It was my favorite toy . . . ever. Hands down.

I met Dolly for the first time the day after she and her

family moved in. I was riding my trike on the sidewalk when Dolly rode up behind me, skidded to a halt, and said, "Wanna race?"

"No. I don't think so. It wouldn't be fair. You'd beat me."

"Not if I give you a head start."

"How big a head start?"

"We'll race to the end of the sidewalk. You'll start here, and I'll start at the other end of the sidewalk."

That seemed fair. I thought I could win this one, so I said, "Fine."

She went to the far end of the sidewalk, and I got ready. She was sitting on her bicycle and yelled, "Ready. Set. *Go!*" and we both took off.

I was pedaling like a madman, and I was flying along. The end of the sidewalk got closer and closer. I was just a few feet away. I was going to win! Then she flew by me, bounced over the curb, and skidded to a halt in the middle of the street.

"I won! But barely. You can really make that thing fly."

"Thanks." For lack of anything more intelligent to say, I came out with, "Do you like cookies?"

"What kind?"

"My mother makes the best chocolate chip cookies in the world."

"They're my favorite."

We rode to my house and went in through the back door. Momma had gone to the grocery store, Daddy was at work, and Frankie was at his violin lessons. We sat down at the kitchen table. I took the lid of the cookie jar off and shoved the jar over to her. She took two out and shoved it back to me. I took two, and we sat there munching away.

"You're right. These are really good," she said.

"Do you want some milk? I do."

"Sure."

I got up and poured us each a glass. Chocolate chip cookies and milk. What could possibly be better? Well, actually, to answer my own question, what could be better was chocolate chip cookies and milk and a new friend.

"I gotta go," she said. "My mom doesn't know where I am."

As she reached the door, I realized we had forgotten one tiny detail. "What's your name?" I asked.

"Dolly. What's yours?"

"Bob."

"How old are you?"

I told her, and she pushed the screen door open and left. It slammed shut behind her.

The next day, I almost ran home from school, anxious to see what Dolly and I could do. I had big plans. Maybe she would be interested in some police activity with me. She seemed an adventurous type.

I got my trike out of the garage and pedaled to the sidewalk. I went by her house, but she wasn't around. I thought about knocking on her door and asking if she wanted to play, but I didn't know her well enough yet to try that. So I decided to just ride around the neighborhood for a while. She was bound to show up sooner or later.

I was halfway to the far corner when I heard a bicycle coming up behind me. I smiled and expectantly turned around to greet her. A water balloon got me right between the eyes. She laughed as she went by. I was shocked. I was also wet. But I wasn't mad. I guessed it was a game. Maybe she expected me to go inside my house and make my own. Then she and I could have a water balloon fight.

She had a basket on her bicycle handlebars. Then she came again. She reached into her basket and pulled out another balloon. This time, she got me in the crotch. The whole front of my jeans was soaked. She laughed again, and that time I could tell she wasn't playing. It was that kind of laugh. On her next pass, she got me in the chest and, as she went by, said, "Hey, little boy, looks like you peed in your pants."

Then I was mad. I pedaled after her in a fury. But a trike is no match for a bike. She just sped ahead, then turned around and came again. She got me in the head, then the shoulder, then the ear, then the leg. By the time she ran out of ammo, I was soaked, livid, and totally humiliated.

I sneaked through the back door of my house and went up to my bedroom. I changed clothes and hung the wet ones up in the bathtub to dry. I hoped Momma wouldn't find them until they dried and I could just put them in the hamper. There was no way I was going to tell this story to my mother or my father . . . or my little brother. Frankie and I had been told countless times to resolve our own problems. Momma and Daddy would step in when they needed to. Besides, this was really embarrassing.

The next day, I was ready. I had armed myself with water balloons that I had put in a tote bag I found in Momma's closet. When I got home, Dolly was already out and around on her bike. I got on my trike and hung my ordnance on my handlebars. I mounted up and rode out to do battle.

She saw the bulges in the bag and correctly judged the contents. She rode around me in semicircles just out of range and began her taunting.

"What's a penny made of?" Then she answered her own question. "Copper."

I got off my trike, grabbed a balloon, and heaved it at her. It fell well short of its mark, and she laughed.

"Hey, Copper Flopper, you've got a really weak arm."

I grabbed my bag and began to chase after her on foot. I let loose another salvo. It too fell short.

"Copper Bopper, Copper Whopper. Poopy Copper Popper. Poopy Doopy Poopy Copper."

I actually think I began to see red.

"Hey, little police boy, did you wetums your little bed again last night?"

I threw them all at her, one after another. All I got for my efforts was "Little Copper Mopper, you are pathetic." She rode off laughing, and I was left standing there . . . once again livid and humiliated.

After school the next day, I came home and went straight to my room and closed the door. Momma came up half an hour later, knocked softly, and came in. I was sitting up in bed doing nothing.

"Are you feeling okay, honey?"

"Yes, ma'am."

"You don't feel sick?"

"No, ma'am."

"You don't want to go outside and play?"

"No, ma'am."

"Okay, honey." She kissed me on the forehead and walked out, closing the door behind her.

I stayed right where I was and plotted my revenge. I had a headache when I had to go down for supper.

For the next week, I did the same thing every day after school. Then my mother paid me another visit. She knocked on my door.

"Yes, ma'am."

She came in and sat down. "Do you want to tell me about it?"

"It's hard, Momma."

"Okay. Some things are hard. You can talk to me anytime about it. You know that, don't you?"

"Yes, ma'am."

"But in the meantime, you need to get out of your room and go outside and play. Starting tomorrow."

Well, great. The humiliation was going to resume. I didn't

really have a plan. She was bigger than I was. She was faster than I was. And, worst of all, she was meaner than I was.

The next day, I got on my trike and went out on the sidewalk. I was dreading what I once couldn't wait to do. She was nowhere in sight, thank God. My spirits rose a little. Half an hour later, she still hadn't shown up. I was beginning to relax and enjoy myself.

I neared our house and looked up, and there she was, pedaling full speed at me and holding a broom like a jousting knight would hold his lance. As she went by, she rammed it in my chest. I fell backward off the trike. As I was getting back to my feet, she flew by again and hit me on the back of the head with the side of the broom.

This time, I pitched forward and landed on my face. And then I gave up. I just gave up and ran up the sidewalk to our front door and went inside. We had a big stuffed chair by the front window, and I knelt on it and put my chin on the back. I peered out the window. My trike was sitting right in front of our house on the sidewalk. I couldn't cry. I was trembling. I didn't know if it was anger or fear.

Dolly rode off, and there I sat. Momma was in the back, in the kitchen. She probably didn't even know I was in the house. This was the low point. I couldn't even play in my own yard anymore.

Then I saw her. She rode up on her bike, stopped right by my trike, and got off. She reached in her basket and got out a small sledgehammer. She raised it over her head, and it came crashing down on my precious trike. *Crack.* The seat split in two. She didn't stop there. *Crack.* She hit the siren, and it splintered. *Crack.* She bashed the light, and it fell off the handlebars, bounced off the sidewalk, and broke in two. *Crack.* She turned her attention to the front fender and then the rear fender, and they crumpled and crumbled as a pile of rust fell to the sidewalk. She attacked the wheel and mangled the spokes. *Crack. Crack. Crack.* It was as though she had gone insane.

I'd suddenly had enough. It was my turn to go insane. I opened the front door and walked slowly toward her.

"Hey!" I yelled at her.

She turned around, and I punched her right in the face as hard as I could. It was the first time I had ever hit someone in anger. Blood spurted from her nose. She dropped the hammer and ran down the sidewalk toward her house.

It felt good. I was surprised how good it felt. Later, I would be surprised at how ashamed I was that it had felt so good. This despite the fact that my fist hurt. It was worth it. A human being is a highly complex contraption.

I went up to my room and lay down on my bed, flat on my back. I stared at the ceiling. An hour later, my mother came in. She didn't knock. She sat down on my bed.

"Dolly's mother called. Tell me what happened."

So I did. I left out a few parts. Like how humiliated I was. It was bad enough without mentioning that.

When I was through, she said, "Here's what you're going to do. Tomorrow, right after you get home from school, you are going to go find Dolly, and you are going to apologize. You are going to tell her you are extremely sorry for what you did. Do you hear me, son?"

"Yes, ma'am."

"And after that, you and I are going to have another talk. Do you understand?"

"Yes, ma'am." What else was there to say?

The next day came way too fast. As I neared our house, I saw Dolly riding on her bicycle. She was riding away from me. I wanted to get this over with as soon as possible. I yelled, "Hey, Dolly."

She turned around and slowly pedaled over. She stopped in

front of her house, got off, lowered her kickstand, and started walking over to me. She took her sweet time. Looking back, I'm sure she knew what I had to do and was determined to draw out every last second of her triumph. I had a knot in my stomach. I was holding my books waist high in front of me with both hands. I had a death grip on them.

She came and stood right in front of me. "Yeah, what?" was her opening comment.

"About what happened. You know, yesterday. My mother knows about it. She told me I had to apologize. So I am. I apologize. I'm sorry I hit you. You're a girl."

She drew her fist back and hit me in the face. Right on the nose. Hard. Far and away the most memorable thing about that moment was the look on her face. I had never seen such an expression. It wasn't anger. It was a look of profound, helpless anguish. She began to cry and ran inside her house.

I had dropped all my books and so reached down and gathered them up. I didn't want to go inside and face my mother. For one thing, my nose was bleeding. So I headed toward the big oak tree in our backyard. There were a couple of white wooden Adirondack chairs under it. Nearby was a swing attached to a large limb. I went over to the swing, dropped my books on the grass, turned around, and sat in the swing. I took my shoes and socks off. I wanted to feel the grass under my bare feet. Just like when I was little.

I should have been mad or humiliated again, but I wasn't. I felt sad. Sad for me and, for some reason, sad for Dolly. The look on her face haunted me. It was an expression that was hard to hate.

I sat there and let my nose drip its blood on the grass. I examined a single blade of grass. I had never done that before. It was beautiful. I admired its symmetry. The green of it glistened. The wind rustled it a little, and it moved slightly. A tiny red bug crawled slowly across it. Why had I never noticed these things before? What was wrong with me? Why did all this happen? Was it all her fault? That's sure what I had thought. What if at least part of it was somehow my fault? But how? So many questions. I was confused. What should I do now?

Common sense told me I needed to hit her back. After all, I had hit her, then she had hit me. Now it was my turn to hit her. But then next it would be her turn to hit me and so on and so on. I didn't want that. I was willing to bet she didn't want that either. I couldn't get the sight of her face out of my mind.

And then it happened. I didn't know where it came from, but suddenly my mood got lighter. It was like I had been walking around with a huge, heavy, wet blanket thrown over me for the last two weeks, and now it was gone. I felt exhausted but relieved and somehow proud of myself. It felt like my soul wanted to dance. I hoped she felt as good as I did, though I doubted it. Maybe later. Hopefully.

Our back door opened, and my mother came out and sat in one of the Adirondack chairs, the one closest to the swing.

"Are you okay, son?"

"Yes, ma'am. Actually I am."

"I know what happened."

Mothers generally know what happened. It was one of the many magical powers mothers had. Right then, I needed my mother.

I got out of the swing and climbed onto her lap. It was a tight squeeze. I didn't fit as well as I used to. I curled up and put my head on her chest and cried. Sometimes, when life threw troubles in your path, crying in your mother's lap was the only thing a kid could think of that would help.

She let me cry and rocked me back and forth. When I finally stopped, she said, "Dolly and her family moved here from the Valley. Did you know that?"

"No, ma'am."

"They kind of had to. Her twin brother died. They needed

to move someplace else. There were too many memories in the Valley for them. People would look at Dolly and ask how she was doing. You know, just nice people being nice. But that kind of thing can make things worse for some folks. I guess it's like a constant reminder of what you're trying to forget. Sometimes you just need to start over. You just need to be left alone while you heal. They needed a new place. New people. So they moved here."

"I didn't know, Momma."

"I know you didn't. You weren't meant to."

"When I apologized to her, I didn't really mean it. I said the words, but I was kind of lying. I guess she knew. But if I had to say it now, I would mean it. In fact, I kinda feel like I *need* to apologize again. You know. Get it right this time. I just don't understand all this, Momma."

"That's okay. That's just fine. Sometimes feeling is better than understanding."

"Momma?"

"Yes, son."

"Am I a bad person?"

"Oh, Bob! Of course you're not a bad person. You're one of my favorite people in the whole world."

"What was Dolly's brother like?"

"I don't know. But he was the same age as you. His name was Bobby."

"Momma?"

"Yes."

"I need to learn how to ride my bike."

Chapter 16

The Seventy-Fifth

Forward

January the second. My seventy-fifth birthday. Three-quarters of a century. Anita and I always did something that was fun on our birthdays. It was understood it had to be something we had never done before. The other spouse could not refuse to participate. One year I chose skydiving. Another year Anita chose a fashion show in Dallas. The other spouse couldn't veto the request, and there was a further requirement. The other spouse could not complain about the choice. This year, and for the last several years, there was to be no choice and no fun.

***

It started ten years earlier. About. It was really hard to say. It just sneaked up on us so slowly that I now couldn't figure out when things began to go wrong.

At first, it was little things, and it was funny. One day, she came into the den with a perplexed look on her face. I asked her what was wrong, and she said, "I can't remember what I did with it."

"Did with what?"

She then got a relieved look on her face, pulled a bottle of water from the crook of her arm, and said, *"This!"*

Another time, I was in the kitchen, and she came in obviously looking for something. I asked her what she was doing, and she said she had lost her phone. She had been looking all over the house. About thirty minutes later, she walked back into the kitchen, and I asked if she had found her phone. She said yes. I asked her where she found it, and she couldn't remember.

We laughed a lot about these kinds of things, just a sign of getting old. After all, she was sixty-three then. What did we expect? We did what any sane couple would do to deal with the situation. We ignored it.

***

Then I began to notice the bizarre behavior. She kept buying certain things over and over. I was looking for something in her vanity drawer and found fourteen eyelash curlers. I found twenty-eight packages of pecans in the freezer. She had nine things to scrub dishes with in the sink.

One day, she came home quite upset, and I asked her what the problem was. She wouldn't tell me at first. That night, while lying in bed, she admitted that she had gotten lost on the way home. She was scared. So was I, but all I said was that I thought we should see a doctor. She agreed.

The neurologist said all the tests were normal for anything important. He said he didn't know what the problem was but that she didn't have Alzheimer's. Well, that was a huge relief. He gave her some pills.

The pills didn't help. She got worse. Anita had always been

a kind, sweet-natured person, but then she became too sweet, too agreeable. That might seem like a strange thing to say, but it was true. It made me uncomfortable. It just wasn't right. It wasn't her. Her fire was not gone, but it was sputtering.

We had our happy moments, but happy moments are just that—moments. Like a big glob of cotton candy. It looked great, and when you popped it in your mouth, it tasted sweet, but only for an instant and then *poof*—it was gone, and you were left with nothing but a memory. I supposed that was what memories were for, so that later a smile would touch your heart. But we weren't content. Contentment was like an all-day lollipop. It lasted and lasted. It was part of who you became. It was something to savor.

She tried so hard to be normal. She would lie in bed in the morning after the alarm went off and try to remember things. Anything. Names, places, events. Just to prove to herself she was still normal. That she wasn't losing her mind.

She became clingy. She followed me around like a puppy dog. She tried to do everything for me. I was her knight in shining armor. I could do no wrong. But all I wanted was to be her husband. I wanted my girl back. I wanted to banter with her again. I wanted her to tease me. I wanted her to poke me on the arm just like old times.

One day, we were sitting at the top of an embankment that sloped down to the river. The river there was still and as muddy as chocolate milk. We were looking down at the water, and suddenly a huge crocodile glided halfway out of the water and slid up on the bank. He stopped and eyed us both malevolently. He opened his mouth wide and slowly closed it. Then he slid back into the water. He left no ripples. He never made a sound. That was a recurrent dream I began to have once or twice a week. I never told Anita about it.

In her efforts to be normal, she tried to help me. I gave her simple tasks to do, but even that became more of a problem than a help. I had a stack of envelopes that needed stamps. She wanted to apply the stamps, so I stacked the envelopes neatly and put the stamps next to the pile. When I came back, she had applied all the stamps in the lower-left corner. I thanked her and redid it all that night after she was asleep.

There became fewer meaningful things we could do together. At least we could watch TV, but that caused problems too. Anything with a plot got to be off-limits. She would get confused and then upset. Eventually, all we could watch were game shows.

We still took vacations. I had to watch her all the time. I couldn't let her out of my sight. I figured a cruise would be a good option, so we tried that. She got lost on the ship, and I couldn't find her. I was afraid she had somehow fallen overboard. Eventually, I found her at the front desk in tears. She was trying to get the front-desk clerk to call my brother, Frankie, since perhaps he would know where I was. Frankie wasn't even on the ship.

One of the hardest things I had to do was tell her she couldn't drive anymore. She had hit a couple of fenders in parking lots and then had had a minor collision at the bottom of the hill where we lived.

We were both on the phone, on separate extensions, with a young lady named Maria from the insurance company. She was asking Anita how the wreck had occurred.

She said, "So you were at the intersection and turned. Did you turn right or left?"

"Yes. I was at the intersection. I kind of turned off that way."

"Which way? Right or left?"

"You know. Over there. It wasn't even dark. Then she kind of hit me."

"What did you do then?"

"I screamed and called her a bad name."

"I mean, did you stop and call the police?"

"Oh yes. I stopped, but the police weren't there. The girl who hit me was mad. She had her hair in a ponytail."

Then Anita abruptly hung up, leaving just me and Maria on the line. "Sir, do you think she should still be driving?"

I had to say, "No. I don't."

So I began to drive her everywhere. We went to visit her mother in a nearby assisted-living facility every day. The trip was about ten minutes with a lot of turns. Every single time, she said the same things at the same points in the ride.

"Oh look. There's our old house. I wish they would take better care of it."

"I've always loved that tree. Its shape is so pretty."

"I wonder why they put a stop sign here. They don't need one."

"Those apartments are really ugly. I wonder why they painted them purple and green."

"That's where Rita and Steve used to live."

And on and on and on and on. And lastly, "Why are we parking here?"

It was like watching the same movie over and over. It never changed. There was nothing I could do to change it. I was just a minor character whose role and lines never changed. And I couldn't escape.

We saw other doctors to try to get some help. Some reason to hope for better days. We went to Houston, then Baltimore, then New York, then Florida, then Chicago. And that was where they told us. It *was* Alzheimer's. I didn't remember much of that day, but I did remember standing on the street outside this huge building. A group of three young girls were walking down the street. They were happy and laughing with their high heels clicking on the pavement. As they passed by, one of them was saying, "I saw it on TV last night! There's a new mascara that is just fabulous!"

I hated them all instantly. Silly, vacuous, gourd-headed girls! They had it all. Youth. Happiness. Health. And a future. And they didn't deserve any of it. And my girl, my wonderful girl, had this . . . this monster.

Then they were gone, and there we stood, the wind whipping our clothes. A newspaper page blew down the sidewalk in fits and starts. It was gray. It was cold. I didn't know what to say. I didn't know what to think. And I didn't know what to do. We had been living in denial for years. There could be no more denial. There would be no more hope.

***

It got worse. Of course I had to do the usual things I had been doing, but now I also had to do what Anita used to do. On top of that, I had to take care of her. Instead of having one job, I had three. I had to do each one of them quickly and did none of them well. There was no time or energy for anything else. Before this, I'd thought that the worst thing about this disease would be taking care of someone who was increasingly helpless. If that were all there was to it, the stress would be half of what it was. The worst thing was having a front-row seat to the disintegration of the most important person in your world and being powerless to significantly alter it.

She got confused, then anxious, then angry and hostile. I was the only target, and I was always there—always in range. I walked around on tiptoes, trying to avoid setting her off, but it came anyway. She blamed me for everything. But it wasn't her fault. I thought if I said that often enough, I would come to believe it.

The older I got, the more distasteful lying became. I didn't even like little white lies anymore. I greatly resented being lied to. My daddy once said, "A little thing is a little thing, but honesty in a little thing is a great thing." And liars were always,

always found out. Maybe not at first—but eventually. Then trust evaporated. Then you had nothing.

I decided early on that I would not lie to Anita about this situation. So I didn't. Then our much-loved nephew, Crockett, was killed. I got the call early in the morning from his father. It woke both of us up. Anita could tell something bad had happened. "What's the matter, Bob? What happened?"

"Crockett died. It was an accident. It happened last night."

Anita began to sob uncontrollably. She cried all day. I couldn't go to the funeral without her. There was no way she could go with me, and so neither one of us could go. The problem was she wanted to go, but there was absolutely no way in hell she could make the trip at the time. I had to tell Crockett's family we wouldn't be there. Anita kept crying the next day and the next. I finally told her that I had made a mistake. Crockett was okay. It was someone else named Crockett who had died. He was fine.

She stopped crying immediately and never asked any other questions about it. I realized I could have gotten someone to stay with her. Even though I was retired, I could have told her I had to go to a medical meeting, and there would have been no problems. She wouldn't have gotten upset, I would have been able to go to the funeral, and the family would have been relieved that at least I had been there. That was when I started to lie to her about whatever it took to grease the skids.

***

Christmas came. I used to buy one present each year—hers. She bought all the rest. That year, I bought twenty-two. I knew that sounded like a lot, but I did. Nephews, nieces, brother, sister-in-law, friends. I wrapped all of them and decorated them by sticking on adhesive bows. I hid them in an unused bedroom. If Anita saw them, she would get upset. She would want to help or wouldn't understand what was going on. Christmas Eve, after she went to bed, I loaded them all in the trunk of the car and in the back seat, and threw a blanket over them. The next day, we drove to her brother's house in Austin for Christmas with the family. We were on the interstate going seventy miles an hour when she said, "I want to go home."

"We're going to Ronnie's house now. Remember?"

"I don't know any Ronnie."

"He's your brother."

"I have no, you know, person like that. It's not right, you taking me there. There can't be a Tommy. I need to go home."

"We'll turn around in a minute. Okay?"

"No. Not in a minute. I need to go home. Now. I don't like this. Why are we in this car? I don't know this car. I need to go home."

She yanked on the handle to open the car door. At seventy miles an hour, the wind was so strong she had trouble opening it, but she did get it open a crack. Then she tried to squeeze out. The seat belt kept her from being able to jump. She fumbled to release the buckle.

I hit the brakes and swerved from the far-left lane, across two lanes, and onto the shoulder and came to a stop just as she unbuckled the belt and jumped out onto the pavement. I ran around the car and grabbed her. I managed to convince her to get back in the car, this time in the back seat. I buckled her in and hit the child-safety button to keep the back doors locked. Then we drove to Ronnie's house for Christmas. I had wine.

***

We had a glorious spring. Not unusual at all in Texas. Everything was green. It wasn't hot yet—just warm. The bluebonnets were in full bloom, and you got huge carpets of blue undulating in the wind. Gorgeous. Just gorgeous. Texas was the only place on earth bluebonnets grew. You couldn't claim to be a Texan if you didn't have an old picture of yourself sitting in a field of bluebonnets. We decided to go to the lake house.

We packed the car with Sasha, our crippled mutt. She was a godsend. She usually helped calm things down. As I put the car in gear, Anita remembered she had forgotten her crossword puzzle book. She used to do the *New York Times* Sunday crossword puzzle every week in ink. When she couldn't do that anymore, she did the daily crossword in the local paper in pencil. Then she did the simplest of Dell crossword puzzles. Now she couldn't even do those. But she carried the book around with her. We looked in all the usual places but couldn't find the thing. She got angry and stayed that way all the way to the lake.

She calmed down a bit before getting to the lake, then realized she still didn't have the puzzle book and got angry all over again. As she began to unpack, she found it in her cosmetic bag and was happy. As she was unpacking her suitcase, she found a lot of T-shirts in it. I had packed her bags, and she thought I had packed too many T-shirts. She began to pull them out one by one and throw them at me.

I stood there and tried not to feel anything at all. It was one of the ways I tried to get through those moments. I just tried to go numb. I knew this wasn't really her, but that thought didn't help much. It sure looked like her and sounded like her, and I still had to deal with it—or at least endure it. I hated to admit it, but the only thought I had that was any help at all was *This is* not *my fault*. But it wasn't her fault either.

While watching TV that night, she got mad again and thought we were at the wrong lake house. She wanted to go to the old one—the one we had sold seven years earlier. She packed up and decided to take the bus back to San Marcos. There was no bus service at the lake. So we repacked and drove back to San Marcos at midnight. After we returned and unpacked, she wanted to pack up and go to the lake house.

***

We tried changing her meds over and over, looking for that magic bullet. After a while, I couldn't tell how much of her problem was due to the disease and how much was due to the side effects of her meds. We would stop one med and try another and get a whole new set of problems. I was used to facing a problem and fixing it—one way or another. Here, I fixed nothing. It was like punching a fogbank.

I looked forward to the evenings after she went to bed. Mercifully, she retired relatively early and slept well. Then I could sit for an hour and relax. It was a welcome reprieve from the woman I still loved.

One night, as I was sitting in the den shortly after she had gone to bed, I could hear her coming down the hall. I could tell by the force of her footsteps that she was furious.

She came into the room and stood right in front of me. "So that's what you think of me, is it? I can't, you know, put up with you anymore. And I mean it too." With that, she spun on her heels and stomped off.

Five minutes later, she was back. She again stood right in front of me and, with her eyes blazing, said, "So that's what you think of me, is it? I can't, you know, put up with you anymore. And I mean it too." Then she stomped off again.

She did the same thing at five-minute intervals four more times. The last time, she said, "So that's what you think of me? Well, here's what I think of you."

She bent over, picked up my glass of wine from the end table, and threw it against the wall. Then she began to claw at the other items on the table and threw them on the floor. My books, coaster, TV remote, and even the lamp. She left only our wedding photo standing. There we were. Two happy, bright-eyed young people at the start of their lives together. When she noticed it, she threw it on the floor too. The frame cracked. The glass broke. She stepped on it and then kicked it across the room on her way back to bed.

That was it. I had put up with all I could stand. Something snapped. All the frustrations and horrors came boiling up inside me and needed somewhere to go. She was the problem. It was her. Not me.

I jumped up and followed her to the bedroom. The lights were off. I turned them on. Then I screamed at her, "Well, here's what I think of *you*! *You* have ruined my life. *You* give me nothing to look forward to! *You* are hardly a human being anymore! *You* would be better off *dead*!" I turned around and went back to the den, where I cleaned up the mess.

I sat down at the kitchen table. I stared straight ahead for a few seconds. Then I screamed at the top of my lungs. No words. Just a primal scream. I hit the table as hard as I could with closed fists. Something cracked in my right hand. It hurt like hell.

I went back to our bedroom, undressed, and got in bed. I rolled over and whispered, "I'm so sorry, baby. I didn't mean any of it. You know that, don't you?"

"Sorry about what?" she said.

My hand hurt. Good. I deserved it.

***

She had obsessions. One was her purse. It went with her wherever she went. She spent most of her waking hours sitting at the kitchen table, looking through her purse, rearranging things. Taking them out and putting them back, over and over again. One day, she said, "I don't have any friends anymore."

It was true. They had all left. I couldn't blame them. She got mad at them when they would come over. It was embarrassing. They didn't know what to do or what to say. She couldn't really carry on a conversation. Her bridge group continued to ask her over to play bridge long after she could no longer handle it. I appreciated it more than I could ever tell them. Eventually, they left our lives—one by one. Even my cousin David quit visiting. The last one to abandon her was her bridge buddy Raye. Bless her heart. Frankie called from Tennessee every week. That was what brothers were for. Bless his heart.

"I hate my life," Anita said. "All I do is sit at this table all day long. Sit at this table. Day after day."

She began to slam her purse down on the table. "Day." Slam. "After day." Slam. "After day." Slam. "After day." Slam. "After day." Slam.

I just stood there and watched.

"After day." Slam.

There was nothing I could think of to say.

"After day." Slam.

I shed no tears.

"After day." Slam.

As I stood there, I prayed. *God, please help me. I can't do this by myself anymore. I'm not strong enough for this amount of pain. I thought I could handle anything, but I can't. If you won't help her, help me.*

"After day." Slam.

***

We were living in her world now—a world without reason from which there was no escape and no end. Her rules were all that mattered. And her rules were unknowable. Trying to reason with an irrational person was futile. My darling wife was no longer my best friend. She was my enemy, and the beast in her was her enemy, a terrible antagonist, and I couldn't help her fight the battle. The most important person in my world was disappearing by dribs and drabs. I was living with a stranger, but I was really alone.

She was sitting at the kitchen table, looking through her purse again. Just moving things around. Taking them out and putting them back . . . again. I was sitting next to her, reading the paper.

"There they are again," she said.

"Who?"

"Those people."

"What people?"

"In my purse."

"What are you talking about?"

"Those people who are in my purse. I've killed them before. Squashed them. Stabbed them. But they keep coming back. Want to see them? They're ugly and mean."

"Uh, okay." I peeked into her purse. "Oh yeah."

"They tried to kill me last night. But I know where the knife is. I'm going to kill them first."

She got up from the table and came back with the biggest knife in our kitchen. She held it over her head and then swung it down in an arc and buried it in her purse. She raised it again, and again slashed down, burying it in the purse and sticking it in the table. She couldn't get the knife loose at first, so she grabbed the handle with both hands and jerked it free. Then she raised it over her head and said, "And now it's your turn."

She came at me and raised the knife. I grabbed her arm, and she dropped the knife. Then she sat down and glared at me. "I hate you," she said.

I picked the knife up and put it in the sink. I stood there by the sink for a few minutes, trying to decide what to do. I called the psychiatrist she had been seeing, and he said I had no choice. I had to take her to the ER first. There, they would do an evaluation, check her for a urinary-tract infection, and, if it was normal, transfer her to the psychiatric hospital in Austin.

I didn't understand. "Check her for a urinary-tract infection. Why?"

"Because urinary-tract infections can cause psychosis on occasion."

I told Anita we needed to take a ride, and we got in my car and drove to the ER. The doctor was real nice. There was no infection, and so they said they would call the police to take her to Austin.

I said, "The police. Why the police? I can take her myself."

"Sorry, Dr. Carson. It's the law. In these situations, it has to be the police."

They called the police, and two officers showed up. They were very nice and professional. They explained they had to take her in the back seat of the patrol car. I could follow in my car if I wanted, but I couldn't ride with her.

We walked through the back door of the ER, and she got into the back seat quietly. They held her head as she got in. Just like they did for criminals. Then they got out their handcuffs.

"Whoa," I said. "Wait a minute here. You're going to handcuff her?"

"That's the law, sir. Sorry." I must have looked distraught. "Tell you what. We won't close them so they lock tightly at all. We'll just kind of put them in her lap. Okay?"

"Thank you," I said.

I got in my car and followed them out onto the interstate. This was it. The low point, the absolute nadir of this whole unreal, horrible thing. My wife being driven to a psychiatric hospital in the back of a police car in handcuffs.

I thought about what one of my teachers in medical school had said once. "If you could give one gift to a loved one, you would choose, without question, the gift of good health." I'd bet he was speaking from experience.

I felt guilty. I didn't know why. Now I was thinking, *Is this my fault? I can't think how. But it must be. It must be my fault. It makes no sense.* Why did decent people feel guilty about things that common sense told them could not possibly be their fault?

***

She came home three weeks later, and we resumed our routine. We slept in late, or at least we stayed in bed late. I would wake early and just lie there, waiting for her to get up. The later, the better. There was nothing to do, and the later she got up, the less time we had to kill.

She got up, and I helped her to the bathroom. I went into the kitchen and turned the coffeepot on. I had gotten it ready the night before. She sat at the table and sipped her coffee. Sometimes I had to remind her. I read the paper, and we munched on our toast. I wiped the crumbs from her cheek. Neither of us spoke. There was nothing to say anymore.

Then we went back to the bathroom, and I helped her into the shower. She sat at her vanity table, and I put her makeup on. Just like she used to do it. But I couldn't curl her lashes. She wouldn't let me do that. I hummed our song, "It Had to Be You," and she liked that. I could tell. I brushed her hair. Just like she used to do it. Then I leaned over and put my chin on her head and told her I loved her. And I did. And I still didn't know why. I know now, without a shadow of doubt, that love isn't love if it's a noun. Real love is a verb. I told her she was beautiful. But she wasn't anymore. How could you be beautiful with no life in your eyes and no love in your heart? A little lie. God would forgive me.

I walked slowly with her down the hall to the den, and she sat on the couch. I put her glasses on her so she could see her birds. I opened the drapes wider and went out on the patio. I watered her plants, and she watched me. I came in and sat next to her, and we held hands. She liked that. I could tell.

In the evening, after dinner, I gave her meds. One little ineffectual pill after another. Then we walked down the hall, and I watched as she brushed her teeth. I undressed her and put her pajamas on and tucked her into bed.

Later, I went to our closet and sat down on a chair to get ready for bed. Sasha, our big old mutt of a dog, limped over and sat down right in front of me. She sat there not to be hugged but to let me hug her. She knew that was what I needed. I could tell. Then I climbed into bed.

That night, Anita said softly, "I grow small. So small." Then she rolled over and went to sleep.

***

She didn't know me anymore. And then she quit eating. I had visited two different Alzheimer's care facilities but just couldn't bring myself to put her in one. But you couldn't last long if you didn't eat. I got selfish. I didn't want her to die in our home. I had no plans to move, and I didn't want that memory to be part of our house.

The facility I chose seemed nice, and the employees seemed nice. I hired Delia, an old housekeeper of ours, to sit with her during the day. But she was more than a housekeeper. She was a friend. We had invited her to both Cole's and Rebecca's weddings. When it came time to take Anita to the facility, I reached my hand out and Anita took it. I looked down. They still fit together perfectly. We walked through our home. In each room, I told her what it was and what had happened there. "This is Cole's room. This is where he slept. Remember? This is our patio. This is where Rebecca got married. Remember? This is our kitchen. This is where you used to bake chocolate chip cookies. Remember? This is the den. This is where we used to practice dancing. Remember? This is our bedroom. This is where we made love. Remember?" But she didn't remember. Those were only my memories—not ours. It was as if her whole life had simply been erased.

We got in the car, I fastened her seat belt, and we drove to the facility. Happy Acres Eldercare. What a joke. I didn't remember much about leaving her.

I drove home, unlocked the door, went into the den, and sat down on the couch. Sasha came and sat in front of me. I gave her a big hug. She was the only living thing who had stuck with me through the entire nightmare.

I went to see Anita every day. Delia and the staff took good care of her. I didn't worry about that. I never stayed long. I just couldn't. Rebecca, then Cole, came to see her and say their goodbyes.

A few weeks after she was admitted, it was New Year's Eve. Delia wanted to have a New Year's Eve party for Anita—in the afternoon. Delia wanted to spend the day with her own family. She didn't tell me until all the arrangements had been made. She thought it would be fun. I didn't want to go. I knew what it would be like, so I asked what time it would be. I arrived two hours late, hoping it would be over by then. Unfortunately, they had postponed the party until I got there. When I walked in, Anita was in a wheelchair that was pulled up to a table. There were noisemakers and silly conical hats. They all had one on—including Anita. They had the radio tuned to an oldies station. At the end, everyone sang "Auld Lang Syne" and then clapped and cheered.

I couldn't stand it. She had absolutely no idea what was happening. She smiled but with no comprehension. I kissed her on the cheek, but she didn't react. She looked confused. It was terrible. I went home.

She died that night. They called me on the phone, and I drove down to the facility. Everyone was nice. I went in and said goodbye to her and gently kissed her forehead through the sheet. I didn't pull the sheet down. I didn't want that memory. Several years ago, she had told me she wanted to be cremated. I thought of that then as I walked to my car. I remembered the poem I had written for her a few months earlier.

> Ashes are memories of a fire that flared.
> A now pale pile
> Of a loved one's world.
> Who shared our life for a too-short while.
> Now gone. And left a hole.

When I got to my car, I opened the door and gently closed it as I slipped into my seat. I lowered my head and looked down at my hands in my lap. Old, cracked fingernails, stuck on old, gnarled fingers attached to old, splotchy hands. I was old. And now, for the first time in my life, I felt old. Things began to blur. The world looked scary through a lens of tears. I started the car, then stared straight ahead and wondered what to do and where to go. Home? Where was home anymore? Then I blinked.

Chapter *17*

The Rainbow

Backward

I climbed the stepladder, reached up, and pulled on the cord. The folding attic stairs appeared from the ceiling, settling gently on the floor with a soft click. Momma had asked me to get a box of her old clothes, which had been stored in the attic. I asked my little brother, Frankie, to help. I planned on going to Boy's Canyon after this chore to get some more yellow wood. Momma and Daddy let us roam all over town. They never seemed to worry about us, and we sure didn't worry about ourselves. I needed to dye some T-shirts as I only had one yellow one left. I didn't need Frankie to help me with that important job. I briefly considered having him go up to the attic first to check for spiders. I was afraid of spiders and was trying to get over it. I ascended the ladder and Frankie followed.

I turned on the light in the attic and looked around. Momma kept her attic nice and neat. There was a glass object on the floor, which looked out of place. I picked it up and opened the nearest box. The box proved to be filled with old books. I pulled one out. *Adventures of Huckleberry Finn.* One of my favorites. Momma read it to us when we were little kids. I replaced the book, put the glass in the box to get it off the floor, and closed the lid. The box of clothes was in the back, and Frankie and I wrestled it over to the opening of the attic, down the stairs, and into Momma's bedroom.

I thanked Frankie and left the house through the back door. Boy's Canyon was a short walk—only three blocks away. My mission was to gather a few sticks of its famous yellow wood.

Boy's Canyon wasn't a canyon and shouldn't have been there, but it was. No adults or girls had ever been seen there. No one called it Boy's Canyon except boys. Neighbors called it an eyesore. Real estate agents called it prime development land. There were rumors about why it hadn't been developed. It was about twenty acres of wilderness smack-dab in the middle of Corpus Christi. It was very much like the Texas Brush Country usually seen elsewhere in South Texas. The brush was so thick around the perimeter that it was almost impossible to penetrate. But boys knew how.

Inside, there were stunted salt cedar and mesquite trees and bushes. There were grapevines, which could be cut into short lengths and smoked like cigarettes. There was little light and almost no grass. It didn't rain much in Corpus, especially during the great drought of the 1950s. Near the center was a pond that, surprisingly, usually contained water. There were birds of all kinds, especially around the pond, including a family of great blue herons. I had been hoping for a couple of years to find a blue-heron feather. I didn't know anyone who had one. Certainly none of my friends. The canyon was dark and forbidding and mysterious and quiet, and it shut the world out. Boys loved it.

There was a small bush growing there with yellow wood. Boys knew what the bush looked like. Its wood could be put in a pot of water and boiled. The water would turn yellow and could be used to dye a white T-shirt a beautiful yellow color. If you didn't have at least one yellow Boy's Canyon T-shirt, you were a nobody. I didn't plan on being a nobody. I planned on being a somebody, and there was no time like the present to start on that project.

I walked up to a break in the brush and entered. I made my way toward the pond, where I knew the yellow wood would be. I had brought along my big pocketknife to cut the wood. Daddy had given it to me for Christmas the year before. It had a beautiful bone handle, and the blade was razor sharp and locked into position once opened. The back side of the blade was serrated and could be used as a saw. It was a prized possession. I was deep inside the brush and almost at the pond when I looked down, and there it was. A huge, perfect, beautiful blue-heron feather. I held my breath as I reached down to claim it. Then suddenly I heard a heavily accented voice from behind me. "Hey, white boy. Are you lost?"

I stopped and whirled around, dropping my feather. There were three of them. All Mexicans and all bigger than me. They were in jeans and dirty white T-shirts. They had long oily black hair swept back on the sides into ducktails. One of them had a pack of cigarettes rolled up in the sleeve of his shirt. He was the one who had spoken. You could tell. The other two were looking at him, and he was looking at me.

"No. I'm not lost."

"I bet you are. You wouldn't be here if you wasn't lost. You look scared, white boy. You look little too."

"I may be little, but I ain't scared," I said. I have no idea why I said "ain't." Maybe because I was scared and thought a little show of bad grammar might convince him I was a tough customer. The slight quaver in my voice no doubt negated whatever macho impression that pathetic effort might have made.

"He says he ain't scared. Juan, does he look scared to you?"

"Looks scared like a little baby to me," Juan replied.

"Lupe, does he look scared to you?"

"Like he's about to pee in his pants," said Lupe.

"How about it, white boy? Are you gonna pee in your pants for us? I'd kind of like to see that. But I'd also like to see what's in your pocket. What is in your pocket, whitey?"

"Nothing. It's nothing."

"Well, let's have a look at that nothing. Juan, Lupe, go see what his nothing is."

Juan and Lupe came over, and Juan grabbed me from behind. Lupe reached in my pocket, and I started squirming. Juan pulled my arms straight behind me and, standing on one leg, put the knee of his other leg in my back. Again Lupe reached into my pocket and pulled out my knife. He tossed it to the guy with the cigarettes.

He opened the main blade and ran his thumb along its edge. "Nice. Real nice. *Que bonito.*"

"That's mine. Give it back. Now!" I was through being scared. I was mad.

"*Creo que no,*" he said. "You speak Spanish, little boy?"

"*Un poco.* Does that answer your question? Give . . . me . . . the . . . knife."

"Nah. I kinda like it."

I spun suddenly to my left, and Juan lost his balance and his grip on my arms as he fell. I hit Lupe in the stomach by ramming him with my head, and he doubled over. I took off running. I didn't know where I was going, but I was in a hurry to get there. I was disoriented now. The brush was incredibly thick. I crashed through it in as straight a line as I could manage. I could hear the three of them behind me, yelling at each other in Spanish. My Spanish wasn't good enough to know what they were saying, but I had two advantages. First, I was smaller than they were, and so I didn't have to bend over as much to go under the low branches. Second, I was more motivated to get away from them than they were to catch up to me. I was getting scratches and cuts and bruises, but I only found that out later. Right then, I was simply focused on escape. I heard their voices getting closer and closer, and I became even more reckless. I was charging ahead at full speed, and I glanced over my shoulder to see if I could see them. It was then that I ran into the sofa.

I hit the thing from behind and tumbled over it, my head landing on the seat cushions, and kept rolling until my feet hit the ground in front of it. I slumped down with my butt on the ground and my arms spread out to either side, each one on top of the two outer cushions. I was too stunned to move and so just sat there, breathing heavily, not sure where I was.

I heard the cigarette guy's voice. *"Vamanos. Es la casa de Tio."*

My Spanish was good enough to know part of it. *Vamanos* meant "Let's get out of here." That was all I cared about anyway.

I didn't move for another ten minutes, and then I sat up on the sofa and looked around. I was in a small clearing. There were two old wooden chairs with peeling paint and three numbered metal washtubs in the middle of the clearing. There was a clothesline off to one side and a neat, well-tended garden off to the other. There was no grass underfoot. Directly across from the sofa was an old travel trailer. It was rusted a bit and propped up on blocks. There was a man inside, leaning against the doorway, looking at me. He was wearing a cowboy hat and bib overalls with no shirt. He was Mexican, and he wasn't smiling.

He pushed open the screen door and walked into the clearing. He sat in one of the chairs and said, with a heavy accent, "Who are you, and why are you sitting on my sofa?"

I looked him in the eyes and felt better. "I'm Bob. I was looking for yellow wood."

"I doubt you'll find any on that sofa." The corners of his

mouth turned up a little. "Do I need to fear for my life?" he inquired.

"No. I think you're safe. I'm not as dangerous as I look." The corners of my mouth turned up a little too.

"Glad to hear it. So you wanted to dye some T-shirts, huh?"

"Yes. I only have one left."

"Don't tell me you couldn't find any wood."

"I was interrupted. Three Mexican kids attacked me. One of them stole my knife."

"These Mexican kids, as you call them, were they named Joe, Juan, and Lupe?"

"Well, two of them were Juan and Lupe. I never heard the name of the third one, but he seemed to be the leader. You know them?"

"Yes, I do. Answer me this. Are you an American?"

"Yes, of course."

"So are they. They are not Mexicans. To me, you look like an American who looks like an Englishman. They are Americans who look like Mexicans. And they are proud of it too. They are prouder than you."

"I'll bet they aren't."

"Do you live in a nice house?"

"Yes."

"Do you have a mother and a father?"

"Yes."

"Do you have enough to eat every day?"

"Yes."

"Can you go to a movie when you want to?"

"Yes."

"Can you walk into a nice place to eat and not get thrown out?"

"Yes."

"Well, they can't. They live in a shack. They don't have a father. They don't always have enough to eat. They don't have the money for a movie. They can't go to a nice place to eat. But they do have pride. That's pretty much all they have. It makes up for a lot. It has to."

"They were going to hurt me."

"No, they weren't. They were just trying to scare you. They were being macho. It's a very important pastime for a Mexican."

"You mean an American who looks like a Mexican," I said, and smiled.

"You're okay, young American who looks like an Englishman."

"You live here?"

"Yes. I have for twenty-three years. I used to work for Mrs. Anderson. Back when I could work."

"Who is Mrs. Anderson?"

"Was. Who was Mrs. Anderson. She owned what you call Boy's Canyon. All of it. Her husband was a wildcatter."

"So who knows you live here?"

"Her lawyers know, and they are about the only people I want to know. In her will, she let me stay here as long as I want. And I like it here. So I stay. She was a nice lady. I liked her. She liked me."

"Did she live here too once?"

"No. She lived in town. Her husband grew up in Corpus and went to Boy's Canyon when he was a kid. So he wanted to leave it for other kids for a while. When I die, it'll be sold. The lawyers tell me the money will go to start a free children's hospital."

"She must have liked you a lot."

"Yeah, well . . . like I said, she was nice."

I looked around. "Why do you have three washtubs, and why are they numbered?"

"Number one is to wash my clothes. That's why they call them washtubs. I'm surprised you didn't know that. Number two is to rinse my clothes in. Number three is for my fires. I like my fires in a tub. I like to sit outside and watch a fire and eat marshmallows."

"So you like toasted marshmallows?"

"No, I just like marshmallows. I eat them right out of the bag."

"Why did you number them?"

"I had some extra paint."

I wondered if he was pulling my leg, but he seemed serious. "What do you eat besides marshmallows?"

"Vegetables. I grow my own, as you can see. I don't eat much meat. I don't have nothing against people who do. I eat a little rattlesnake from time to time."

"What does it taste like?"

"A little like heron."

I laughed. He didn't.

"Well, I better be getting home. How do I get out of here?"

"There's a narrow path you'll see out front. It'll dump you in an alley that runs into Santa Fe. Then you can figure it out, I'll bet."

"Thanks. Would it be okay if I come back sometime?"

"Yes. But just you. I don't like a lot of people."

"You mean you don't like a lot of people around here, or you just don't like a lot of people you meet?"

"Both."

"Okay. And I won't tell anyone about you either." I started to leave, then stopped and turned around. "I didn't ask. What's your name?"

"Roberto," he said. "Same as yours."

I went to visit Roberto regularly that summer and never told anyone else about him. Not even Frankie. A promise was a promise. I always looked forward to the visits. I think he enjoyed them too. He sure did tease me a lot. I took that as a good sign.

I must have visited his place almost every day for the next month. I helped him with his garden a lot. There had been a rainstorm over the bay one afternoon just before I was ready to leave. I looked over toward the east and saw the most vivid, complete rainbow I had ever seen.

"Look at that, Roberto!"

"That's a pretty one, isn't it?"

"Momma loves rainbows. She says a poem whenever she sees one."

"Do you know it?"

"Some of it . . . 'My heart jumps up when I behold / A rainbow in the sky: / So it was when my life began; / So it is now that I'm a man.' Then something about getting old. I forget the rest of it."

We stood there looking at the rainbow. He put his hand on my shoulder.

"It makes my heart jump up too," he said.

"Blue is my favorite color. I wish it was just all blue."

"Nah. You're wrong there. It needs all the colors to be complete. All of them. Just like people. We need all the colors."

One day I asked him how he got around. He said he just walked wherever he wanted to go. He was about seventy and was thin as a pencil. He would work for hours and never get tired. I helped him in the garden a lot, and we expanded it. I tried to buy him some seeds once, but he would not hear of it. In fact, I think it kind of insulted him. He said Mrs. Anderson saw to it that he had all the money he needed, but all he needed was what we were looking at. He said Mrs. Anderson said she wasn't giving him the money. He said that she said he had earned it. And then he got real passionate and said a curious thing. "She said, 'Don't ever let anyone tell you you don't deserve this. You worked hard for every penny of it. Good, honest work. And people like me don't forget.'"

A few weeks later while we were working in the garden,

the screen door to the trailer banged shut, and we both looked up, and there was Joe. Mr. Cigarettes-in-the-T-shirt himself. He saw me and started to turn around to leave when Roberto said, "Where do you think you're going? Get over here."

Joe shuffled over to where we were kneeling in the dirt and began to examine his shoes closely.

"Joe, aren't you going to say hi to my guest? His name is Bob."

Joe didn't look up, but he said a small, soft "hi."

"Hi," I said.

"From what I hear, you two have met. Is that right, Joe?"

"Yes, Tio."

"Do you have anything to say to my guest?"

"I already said hi."

"Don't mess with me, Joe. I think you want to say something to Bob, don't you?"

"Yes, Tio. Sorry, Bob. We didn't mean no harm. I was just showing off. Here." He reached in his pocket, took out my knife, and handed it to me. "Sorry." This time he seemed to mean it.

"Thanks." I pocketed my treasure. I didn't feel as exultant as I thought I would. For some reason, I felt kind of bad for him. "Is Joe your real name?"

"No, but I don't like José."

"Joe's a good name."

"Thanks."

"You know, I really was scared."

"Sorry."

"That's okay. The last time I checked, I seem to have lived through it. Although I must admit the peeing in the pants thing was a close call for a while. I was real proud of myself for staying dry."

"Man! You surprised us. I mean you threw Juan on the

ground and knocked the wind out of Lupe. I think they were both glad we didn't catch you."

"I'm glad you didn't catch me too. So Roberto is a friend of yours too?"

"No. He's my uncle. That's why I call him Tio. It means 'uncle,' you know."

"No, I didn't."

Roberto said, "Lupe and Juan are Joe's friends. Joe is the only person in my family who has anything to do with me. My family knows where I am, but they don't care. They would care if they knew I had money. But I like it this way. I know who cares about me and who don't. Joe don't never ask for no money, so I try to help him out when I can. His father left the family. Nobody knows or cares where that worthless piece of you-know-what is."

"Oh."

No one said anything for half a minute. Then I said, "Where do you go to school, Joe?"

"I go to Miller."

"What is your favorite subject?"

"Shop. I like shop best. English is my worst subject, and I really need to pass it."

"Why?"

"Because I want to be an electrician."

"What does passing English have to do with being an electrician?"

"Because the job I have in the summer is helping an electrician, and I like it a lot. My boss says he'll hire me out of high school and teach me how to be one if I pass. I really want this. I can't afford to go to electrician school myself. I want to be somebody. You know what I mean? I do good in my other subjects, but I don't do good in English. Tio would help me, but he don't read."

"I read. I can help . . . if you want."

"Nah. That's okay."

"Nah yourself. I said I'd help, and I mean it."

"You sure?"

"Yes. I mean it. I could help. But, come to think of it, my mother could help more."

"How can your mother help?"

"She was a teacher for a while. Roberto, if it's okay with you, I could tell my mother, and Joe could come to our house, and she could help him. I'd have to tell my mother where I met him, and that means she'll know about you."

"That would be okay if your mother would keep quiet about me just like you do."

"I'm sure she will. I need to ask her first, of course, but I'm sure she'll say it's okay."

My mother did say okay, and Joe began to come by our house after work. Momma found out what his reading list was going to be the next school year, and she bought the books we didn't already have. She made Joe read them all. I read the ones I could. She made Joe write reports and then graded them and made him do it all over again. He began to quit using double negatives. She bought him a dictionary and told him if he read a word he was unfamiliar with that he had to look it up and write it down. Then he had to show her the list, and she would explain word roots to him. That was where I got my life-long habit of doing the same thing. To this day, it made me mad if I read a word I didn't know. I looked it up so the writer couldn't feel superior to me just because he knew a word I didn't. Momma gave us both vocabulary lists to memorize. She bought him some clothes at Goodwill and would wash them for him. You could tell she was getting fond of him. One night at dinner, she was telling Daddy, Frankie, and me how smart Joe was and how much he had improved. Daddy turned to me and said, "That is a nice thing you are doing for this boy. You need to remember this. If you are nice, some people will take advantage of you." Then he added, "Be nice anyway."

At the end of the summer, we saw him less often, but he came by on the weekends, and Momma would have him bring his work from English class with him. At the end of the school year, Joe stopped by our house one Sunday and showed us his report card. He had passed all his subjects and made a B plus in English. It was his highest grade. Momma asked him if he was going to graduation, and he said no.

"Why not, Joe?" she said.

"Uh . . . I just don't want to."

"Joe, would you go if I were to loan you twenty dollars?"

"Loan me?"

"Yes. You can pay me back later."

"Yes. I would go."

Momma went and got her purse and gave Joe two tens. He thanked her and was at the door when Momma said, "When is graduation?"

"Saturday, two weeks from now at the Coliseum."

The whole family went to the ceremony. Roberto went with us too. When they called Joe's name, we all cheered. We saw him after the ceremony and took him out to eat. He wanted pizza. He didn't want us to drive him home, so we just went to our house. He would walk home as he always did. I let him get to the end of the sidewalk and then ran after him. As I got closer, he turned around.

"Joe. Wait up a sec."

"What's up, whitey?"

"I have a graduation present for you." I reached in my pocket and handed him my knife.

"Whoa. Wait a minute. You're not the one who should be giving a present to me. I should be giving one to you. I will one day, believe me, but right now I can't afford one as nice as you deserve. I can't accept this." He started to give the knife back to me.

I refused to take it. "You're wrong, Joe. I not only want to give it to you, I need to give it to you. You taught me what it feels like to judge a person for the wrong reasons. I found out I wasn't as fine a person as I thought I was." Then I turned around and walked off.

One week later, Momma found a package in our mailbox with my name on it. There was a note that said "I realized I did have something nice enough to give you after all. Joe."

I opened the package. It was my knife.

Chapter 18

The One Hundredth

Forward

I opened my eyes, rubbed them, and looked at the clock on my bedside table. Time to get up. So I got up. Thinking about doing something but not actually doing it was not the same as just doing it. I was excited about tonight. Almost my entire family would be coming for a dinner party. It was my one hundredth birthday. I didn't mind getting older. I just didn't like being old. My family was determined to make a big deal out of the party. I tried to talk them out of it. That was something a real man was required to do. It was not a successful effort. Thank God. I was really looking forward to this.

I bounced out of bed—and, yes, I realized "bounced" was perhaps not the best choice of words, but it just showed you my state of mind.

As I did every morning and evening, I reached over and, with the back of my index finger, lightly caressed my favorite photo of Anita, Cole, and Rebecca. I had photos in frames all over my room. In total, I had twenty-five grandkids, great-grandkids, and great-great-grandkids. Eighteen of them were going to be there that night along with my only friend from the old days, Donnelle. I had framed pictures of all of them scattered about. Before turning the lights out at night, I always kissed two fingers and touched a picture of each of them while telling them good night.

Anita had passed away over twenty years earlier. I had moved to the assisted-living place a few years ago at the insistence of my family. It was tough at first, but I had come to realize it was the best place for me.

My little terrier, Rowdy, slept with me. He woke up, stretched, and came to the edge of the bed for his scratches. He was a lot of company. I talked to him about whatever was on my mind. When I talked to him, he would sit there and periodically cock his head to one side or the other. He and I never had an argument. He thought I was brilliant.

After my shower and morning routine, I got dressed, put a leash on Rowdy, and walked with him out the door. I turned the corner into the hallway, and there sat Betty. She was in a chair and got up as quickly as her cane would allow and smiled. I groaned. I doubted anyone but Rowdy heard. Betty was half-deaf anyway.

I wasn't sure why she was attracted to me. Perhaps the biggest factor was that I was still ambulatory. Or maybe it was the fact that I still had some hair—and some of it was on my head. I had considered shaving my head to see if that would make her go away.

"Happy birthday, handsome."

"Thanks. How did you know?"

"I have my ways."

"Glad to hear it," I lied.

"Care to eat breakfast with me?"

"I can't. I . . . uh, have to walk Rowdy. He gets moody if he doesn't have his morning constitutional."

"Bob, you're so droll."

"That's me. That's what they called me in high school. Bob the Droll."

"I'll bet that's not all they called you."

"See you later." I sprinted down the hall—or at least I tried to sprint. First, I had to bounce, and now I had to sprint. I was getting tired. I exited the side door and left my pursuer behind.

You were supposed to have your dog on a leash there, but I didn't want to do that to him. I took the leash off as soon as we were outside. The powers that be let me get away with it. He was a busy boy. He was a charger. He charged here and there and smelled those smells. I'd have loved to have the nose of a dog for a day. Just to see what it was all about. I wasn't sure why so many things he did made me laugh. Maybe because he did the goofiest things so seriously.

At lunch, everyone at my table wished me a happy birthday. They didn't sing "Happy Birthday," thank God. Anita and I had made an agreement. There were only two grounds for a divorce in our marriage. One was that the other spouse could never arrange to have "Happy Birthday" sung to the other spouse in a restaurant. The other was that we could never go camping. I once read that nature was something you would kill if you found it inside your house. At the table, we talked about politics and religion. Nobody got mad. Nice folks. When people got old, some got meaner, most got nicer. You learned to roll with the punches. If you didn't, the punches would get the upper hand and knock you out.

I went back to my apartment and watched the news, read the paper, and started a new book. Eventually I got sleepy and took a nap.

My family was going to come and get me at 5:30 that night. They had rented the room downstairs and were having the meal catered. I decided I had better spruce up a bit for the party. At least as well as you could spruce up a one-hundred-year-old guy. I didn't mind getting older. I just didn't like being old. Or maybe I already said that.

At precisely 5:30 p.m., Rebecca and Cole came and got me. We took the elevator down to the first floor. Rowdy got to come too. As I walked in, everyone sang "For He's a Jolly Good Fellow" and then a perfectly awful version of "Happy Birthday" with everyone singing off-key just like I had when I used to sing "Happy Birthday" to them. It was a Carson family tradition. This one was not only bad, it was loud. I enjoyed it immensely. The food was great. It was what I liked best. It wouldn't be a birthday without my tacos, refried beans, and flan.

After dinner, I had to open my presents. That was the part I hated. I was the world's worst present opener. I had a hard time acting pleased if I didn't like something. I flattered myself that I was just too honest to lie. Then when I did like something, I didn't want to act more pleased than I acted when I didn't like something. The result was, I was sure, that I seemed to hate everything. Besides, I didn't need any more stuff. I was well beyond the "stuff stage" of my life.

When that ordeal was over, I got a surprise. Twink (not her real name), one of my great-great-grandchildren, who was sitting across from me, inquired if she could ask me a few questions. She said she was on the staff of her middle school newspaper, and when her teacher found out she was going to the birthday party of her one-hundred-year-old great-great-grandfather, she asked Twink to do a story on me. She wanted to know if that would be okay. I said sure. You weren't supposed to have favorites, but she was one of mine. She wore glasses, which she was constantly pushing up to keep them from sliding down her nose. I teased her a lot. She didn't mind it a bit. She thought I was harmless. She pulled out her phone, tapped it, and then deftly swiped her finger on the surface. Next, she set a glowing flat screen on her lap, her fingers poised over the image of a keyboard. Why she didn't use a number 2 pencil and a legal pad, I didn't know. I decided to play dumb.

"You getting ready to call someone? I thought you wanted to interview me."

"Daddy Carson, I'm just getting set up here."

"Aren't you going to need to write something down? You do know how to write, don't you?"

"Yes, Daddy Carson. I do know how to write."

"Want to borrow a pencil?"

"No, Daddy Carson. I don't want to borrow a pencil. Okay, I'm ready. Are you ready to start?"

"Yes, ma'am."

"Daddy Carson, what is your earliest memory?"

"As I recall, I stunk a lot."

"Daddy Carson! This is serious."

"Sorry. I'll be good." I paused and then said, "I was three. I remember that because my mother and my brother and I went on a train trip. My father was working in Washington State at that time, and we went to see him. I remember a few things about that trip. I recall sleeping in what was called a Pullman car. A Pullman car was basically where you went to sleep. My little brother wanted to sleep in his own bunk, so he was in the lower bunk, and my mother and I were in the upper bunk. The engine was an old steam locomotive with the smoke coming out of the smokestack. You could hear it chug and see the puffs of smoke when you were going around a curve. I recall lying there with my mother's arms around me, listening to the clickety-clack of the wheels on the track and feeling safe and loved and drifting off to sleep. I also remember driving with my family through Yellowstone National Park, stopping the car, rolling the window down a couple of inches, and sticking Hershey's bars out the window and having the bears take them out of my hand. I'm sure you could be arrested for that now."

"What was it like growing up with Uncle Frankie?"

"Mainly we got along great. I was the big brother, so I beat him up a lot. Well, I didn't really beat him up, just held him down and, I guess you could say, physically aggravated him. He didn't tattle on me though. And I was protective of him. Nobody else better 'physically aggravate' him. I took my job as his big brother very seriously. He got me back once pretty good though. My mother was in some kind of club. I believe it was a sewing club. All the ladies were over at our house. One of them had brought her daughter with her. Her name was Suzie. Frankie was sitting on the front stoop, hammering something, and I was playing in the driveway. Suzie came out on the stoop and began to talk to Frankie. He later told me that the conversation went something like this:

"Suzie: 'What are you doing?'

"Frankie: 'Hammering.'

"Suzie: 'Throw the hammer at your brother.'

"Frankie: 'No.'

"Suzie: 'Go on. Throw the hammer at your brother.'

"Frankie: 'No.'

"Suzie: 'Go on. Throw the hammer.'

"Frankie (weakening): 'Okay.'

"He said he could still see the arc of the hammer as he followed its flight toward my cranium and make a perfect landing, immediately followed by a gush of blood from me and a scream, also from me. I ran into the house filled with a bunch of ladies calmly sewing. I was clutching my head with blood spurting everywhere.

"My mother: 'Oh my God, Bob! What happened?'

"Me: 'Frankie hit me with a hammer!'

"That marked the end of the sewing club. I moaned a lot to maximize the sympathy. You'll be relieved to hear Uncle Frankie got into trouble for that one. Suzie did not. Probably grew up to be an attorney."

Twink quit her typing, pushed her glasses up her nose, and said, "What do you remember about Christmas?"

"Daddy, Momma, Uncle Frankie, and I would go to a Christmas tree lot, where Frankie and I would be allowed to choose the tree. We always chose the biggest tree in the lot. Then we would tie it to the roof of the car and drive home. Daddy would have to cut the upper third of it off so it would fit in our little living room. This made it look more like a rectangle than a triangle—just like a big bush. Then Daddy would wrestle with the Christmas tree stand so that it would be in a roughly vertical position. Sometimes we would tie it to a doorknob with a rope so it wouldn't fall over. Even that didn't always work, particularly when our cat decided to climb it. Then we would decorate it. The last string of lights to go up was a string Daddy had when he was a little boy. If even one bulb was burned out, the whole string wouldn't light. We crossed our fingers when Daddy would plug it in. If it didn't light, you had to unscrew each bulb and replace it, going one at a time to find the culprit. Then we would put the angel with golden hair on the very top of the tree and sing Christmas carols. On Christmas morning, Frankie and I would get up early and go into Momma and Daddy's room and wake them up. Then we would open the door to the living room, and there the presents from Santa would be. One year, there was a new shiny red bicycle in front of the tree for me. From Santa himself. It was a magical moment. It was the greatest present I ever got in my life. It wouldn't have been the same if Santa hadn't given it to me. I mean, I loved my parents, and they gave me nice presents, but Santa's presents had magic in them that theirs didn't."

"What do you remember about your father?"

"He chewed tobacco, and he had good aim. Frankie and I would go barefoot in the summer, and Daddy could hit the top of our bare feet from six feet away. Then we would have to drag the tops of our feet in the grass to try to wipe it off.

It always left a brown stain no matter how hard you tried to wipe it off. Daddy would laugh and laugh at our pathetic efforts. But then, Daddy laughed at a lot of things. Even stories where the joke was on him. The four of us would go for long drives on Sundays in the summer. Daddy driving and Momma in the front passenger seat. There was always a lively competition between Frankie and me to see who had to sit behind Daddy. All the windows were rolled down since there was no air-conditioning, and Frankie and I would put our arms on the edge of the door and our heads on our arms to try to catch a little breeze. Suddenly, and at unpredictable intervals, Daddy would turn his head to the left and spit tobacco juice out his window. The wind would carry some of the stuff back into the face of the kid sitting behind him, unless that kid, usually Frankie since he was smaller, was paying attention and could jerk his head back in time. When we asked Daddy where we were going, he would always say, 'Oh, we're looking for Cousin Joe.' We never found him."

"So you didn't have a cousin Joe?"

"No, but we never figured that out."

"What do you remember about your mother?"

"She was from Louisiana. She read to us a lot. In the summer, my brother and I and, a lot of times, neighborhood kids, would lie on the floor in the living room and listen to her. *The Adventures of Tom Sawyer. Paul Bunyan. The Wind in the Willows.* You name it and she read it. I read a poem once that goes like this: 'You may have tangible wealth untold; / Caskets of jewels and coffers of gold. / Richer than I you can never be— / I had a mother who read to me.'"

"So she read a lot?"

"She did. Classics. Poetry. You name it. About poetry, she used to say you had to slow way down when you read it. She said you had to 'fondle' the words. She didn't have a college education like Daddy did. So he bought a bookstore for her to manage. When he handed her the keys to the store, he said, 'Here are the keys to your college education.' Looking at old photos, I see now that she was beautiful. I didn't think so as a child. She was just my mother. Whether she was beautiful or not never occurred to me. And my mother loved her boys. One time when I was a little kid, I remember I was playing outside by myself and having a great time. I heard her calling me and telling me to come home. I didn't want to go home. I was having too much fun. So I hid behind some bushes until she went back inside the house. I continued to play, but eventually I got hungry and so I went home. She of course was there waiting for me, and she said, 'Bob, didn't you hear me calling you to come home?' And I said, 'Yes, ma'am.' She said, 'Why didn't you come home?' Well, it was a good question, and I didn't have a good answer, or any answer at all for that matter. I didn't say anything. Just stood there, looking pathetic. She said, 'Go outside and get me a switch off the tree and bring it back in here. I'm going to give you a spanking.' So I went outside and got the switch and came back inside. She was sitting on a bed, and I handed the switch to her. She took it and sat there looking at me for a moment. Then she suddenly dropped the switch and threw her arms around me and kissed me. I felt awful. Just awful. But in a good way."

"Do you remember your first girlfriend?"

"Yes, I do. I'm surprised you asked me that one. You're not trying to blackmail me, are you?"

"No, sir. Not unless you want me to." She could be a little impish sometimes.

"She was a dark-haired beauty. Her name was Sarah Shapiro. She was my girlfriend in the fifth grade. For some weird reason, a classmate of mine decided to have a party at his house and just invited boys. But the deal was, you had to bring a date. Well, I wanted to go, and I wanted to take Sarah, so I asked my mother what to do. She said to just call her up.

So with my mother standing by, I called Sarah up and asked her out. She said yes, and I told her I'd pick her up at three. So I had my first date. That evening when Daddy got home, Momma met him at the door, laughing. She said, or screamed really, 'Daddy! Guess what? Bob has his first date. Guess who with?'

"'Who?'

"'The rabbi's daughter!' And then they both just laughed and laughed.

"It made me mad. I knew good and well Sarah was *not* a rabbit's daughter."

Twink laughed. "I know what a rabbi is, Daddy Carson."

"Yeah, well I didn't, so don't rub it in, Miss Smarty Britches."

"So. Next question. Did you play sports growing up? And, incidentally, you're doing real well, Daddy Carson."

"Why, thank you, Miss Britches. And yes. I played football from the sixth grade until I was a senior in high school. My high school coach was a wonderful person. He was one of the most influential men I ever met. He once told me, 'If I ever get a negative thought'—and then he snapped his fingers—'I eliminate it!' We were good. And by we, I mean everybody but me. At the banquet at the end of the season, I received the award for Most Mediocre Player on the entire team."

I looked up, and Twink had put her hands over her face. She said, "I don't think I'll put that in my story. Where did you go to college, and what do you remember about it?"

"I went to the University of Texas. I was not in a fraternity. I didn't have the inclination or the money to join one. My roommate was a guy named Paul Conners. He was one of the most likable people I ever met. My second semester, I was able to bring my piece-of-crap car to Austin. It was an old beat-up Mercury. First gear didn't work, and it burned oil like a loco-motive. A beautiful white cloud followed me around because of that. Paul had a fourteen-foot wooden boat powered by a forty-horsepower outboard. It had gear problems too. It would not go into neutral or reverse. The only gear that worked on that boat was forward. Once the boat was started, we would drive around and look for a dock where it appeared no one was home. When we found one, we would go by the dock at as slow a speed as we could, and the guy wanting to ski would jump onto the dock. Then the boat would drive off, and on the next pass, the crew would toss a pair of skis onto the dock. Then they would drive off and come back for another pass and throw the ski rope onto the dock to the skier, who would, presumably by that time, have put the skis on. Then the skier would find, or try to find, the end of the ski rope and get ready to absorb the jerk of the rope, and the driver would give it full throttle and jerk the skier either over the water with his skis or into the water without his skis. It was pretty exciting."

"And then you went to medical school, right? Was it hard?"

"Yes, ma'am, it was hard. It was the hardest thing I ever did."

"So tell me what you remember about it."

"I joined a medical fraternity, Phi Chi. It was different from a fraternity in college. For one thing, it was cheaper. For another, it helped you get through school. Most of my friends at medical school were Phi Chis. One of the first orders of business was to get organized for gross anatomy. There were to be four students assigned to every cadaver, and we got a team together. Phi Chi had a deal with a man named Wilbur. He worked at the medical school and was, among other things, in charge of the cadavers. A thin cadaver was highly prized. An obese one was more difficult to dissect. So each of the four of us ponied up twenty dollars to have the privilege of selecting our own cadaver. They were kept in a kind of pool filled with formaldehyde in the basement of the hospital. We went down there with Wilbur, and there they all were, just floating in that solution. It was like a scene from Dante's *Inferno*, without the fire. We pointed out our selection, and sure enough that was the cadaver that we wound up with. The cadavers were in stainless-steel coffin-like affairs filled with formaldehyde. You retrieved them from the depths by cranking handles at either end. The cadaver, on a stainless-steel slatted platform, would come rising up out of this grievous solution. You then secured it into position by flipping an L-shaped lever. One of the fun things to do was to find someone totally engrossed in their work and, as you walked by them, flip the lever and then watch as they followed the cadaver back down into the solution."

The whole group of kids moaned in unison. Then most of them laughed nervously.

I said, "I've got another cadaver story if you want to hear it."

All but one yelled, "Yes!"

I said to the abstainer, "Okay, Steven, you're outvoted. Cover up your ears. So . . . the cadaver of one of the groups was a young female. Students frequently went over to see that group's cadaver since theirs often was the best dissection. Once, they had a particularly good dissection, and I went over to see it. There was a big crowd when I got there. There were two groups. The one at the foot of the coffin could see the dissection, and the one at the head was awaiting their turn. I kicked off my shoes and hopped up on the cabinet at the foot so I could see without having to wait. Just then, the group at the head leaned too hard on the coffin, and it moved forward a couple of feet on its casters and then suddenly stopped. This set up a wave in the formaldehyde solution, and it crashed into the end of the coffin and shot up into the air and soaked the people standing at the foot of the coffin. Of course, the people at the head began to point fingers and laugh until the wave sloshed back in the coffin and hit their end and soaked them. Then the people at the foot laughed and pointed their fingers at them until the wave made a second trip back to the foot, and the process repeated itself several times. Since I was safe and sound on top of the cabinet, I got to laugh at both groups until I got down and found my shoes filled with formaldehyde and pieces of cadaver."

I got another chorus of moans—this time louder than the first. Twink said, "Did you laugh, Daddy Carson?"

"Of course I laughed. Although the list of bad things that happen to other people that are funny is a lot longer than the list of bad things that happen to you that are funny."

"Dad told me you were in the army. How long were you in, and where did you go?"

"I was drafted. So I was in for two years. They sent me to Vietnam. I was a battalion surgeon. It was not too exciting usually, and I don't want to talk about the days that were; however, one day stands out for me. The rule of the United States Army was that the US government had no responsibility to care for a Vietnamese national unless they were injured by a US vehicle. One day, they brought in a little Vietnamese girl, about four years old, who had been run over by a Vietnamese bus. She was terribly mangled but still alive. Her family was with her. She needed surgery, but we had no operating room and no general surgeon. There was a nearby MASH, a surgical hospital. I called a surgeon there, but when they found out that she had not been injured by a US vehicle, they refused to accept her. I wasn't sure what to do. I then called the radiologist there. He was kind of curt, but I thought he was a good guy, so I just called him. I only needed one of the docs to say bring her on over. He said to bring her on over. We loaded her up in a helicopter and took her over to the hospital. They took her to the operating room, and we waited outside. A bit later, they came out and said that they were unable to save her. She had died. We flew with the little girl and her family back to our unit in the helicopter, got a jeep, and drove them to their home. When we got there, the father got out of the jeep and cradled the body of his little girl in his arms. He then said something to our interpreter and walked off. I asked the interpreter what he had said, and apparently, the father had said, 'Thank you.'"

"Oh. That's so sad. I wish you hadn't told me that."

"Sorry. It's just something that always comes to my mind when I think about my time in the army. You forget about a lot of your triumphs, but you sure as hell remember all your failures. And that one hurt. And sometimes the stories of your life are just sad. You can't live a full life without experiencing great sadness. It is a requirement.

"They sent me to Alaska when I got back to the States. We went on winter maneuvers once. We got all this cold weather gear, and one of the things they were issuing was something called Mickey Mouse boots. They were great bulbous boots with all kinds of insulation in them. They looked like Mickey Mouse's feet. Not cool. Not cool at all. I wasn't about to be caught wearing those things. I was going to be stylish when I went into the field. In January. In Alaska. The maneuvers were for a 'war game.' The 'aggressors' were Eskimos. They were tough cookies. I saw some as patients. It was like they were immune to pain. At any rate, we were camped out in the woods somewhere, and my feet were freezing. All the Mickey Mouse people were doing fine. I spent as much time as I could in front of a fire, sticking my feet to what I judged to be just far enough away so they wouldn't burst into flames. My danged feet never did warm up. But I was the best-dressed GI out there. We had set up a trip wire around the camp to warn us if any of the aggressors tried to sneak up on us. That night, we were invaded by a moose, which set off the alarms, and we used up all our blank ammunition repelling the intruders, and so we lost the war, much to the general's dismay. Scared the crap out of the moose though."

"Was the moose hurt?"

"No. He was fine. I got some of his crap and made a little

stick-figure man out of it. I used it as a paperweight for years. Moose crap is hard as a rock. Yours would be too if you ate nothing but sticks."

"Daddy Carson, I don't always know when you're teasing me."

"I know. I like it that way."

"So then you went to school to be an eye doctor, right? Tell me about that."

"We didn't have any money. Still. We had two kids by then. A radio station in Dallas had a contest. The prize was two years' worth of free groceries at the local supermarket. They would read out two slogans a week from products found in their store, and after a few weeks you would mail your answers in. We sent our answers in, and what do you know, we won. Along with six hundred other people. I went to the supermarket and wrote down every slogan of every product in the whole store. Then I took them home, and your great-great-grandmother memorized all of them. There must have been thousands. They had the playoff, I guess you could call it, in a movie theater. It took six rounds, but your great-great-grandmother won. She got them all right. It was a huge deal for us. That was a good memory. This next story is not. In those days, about one in a thousand patients got a post-op infection after eye surgery. Well, I operated on a patient who got such an infection, and this elderly lady lost her vision in that eye. Her family was really mad. I got a letter from her son a few years later, and he said that I had ruined his mother's life and that he sincerely hoped that my life would be ruined too. I saved the letter. I still have it. I take it out and read it when I get to thinking I'm hot stuff."

"But it wasn't your fault."

"No. It wasn't my fault. But it was my responsibility."

"How many patients do you think you saw when you had your eye-doctor practice?"

"Honey, I just don't know. I never kept count. It was thousands and thousands."

"Are there any who stick out?"

"Yes. There was Mrs. Moore, but that's a long story. I'll tell you sometime. Then there was Bill Condit and the Sunny Beaches Lady. Do you want to hear about them?"

"Yes, sir."

"Not long after opening my practice, I was contacted by an agency affiliated with the local hospital to see if I would be interested in participating in a program to screen people for glaucoma. I said yes. One of the first patients we screened was a deaf Black man named Bill Condit. I came to know him well over the years. His eye pressures were sky high. He needed a procedure to lower the pressures. We do it now with a laser, but that was not available in those days. A few years later, he needed a filtering procedure to prevent blindness. A small hole is made in the eye to allow the excess fluid to drain out of the eye. So I did that operation. I also saw his wife. Then she got Alzheimer's and got combative. He kept her at home. She would hit him in the face. She hit him a couple of times in the eye and squeezed way too much fluid out of it. I told him he needed to put her somewhere or he could go blind. He still kept her at home. When she became homebound, he became homebound. He once told me that he could go somewhere, but he couldn't get her wheelchair out of the house without a ramp and couldn't afford a ramp. I got a contractor to just show up one day and build the ramp for him but told the contractor not to tell him who paid for it. After his wife died, he got huge cataracts and could barely see, but he couldn't bring himself to have cataract surgery because he was afraid he would go completely blind. He eventually moved to Lubbock, and I never saw him again. But he could still see well enough to get around."

"What about the Sunny Beaches Lady?"

"One time I came into the exam room, and there standing

before me was a Hispanic Spanish-speaking patient we came to call the Sunny Beaches Lady. She lived in a nursing home. She was not just standing there. She was wildly swinging her arms, boxer-like, and yelling, "Sunny beaches. Sunny beaches." This was her behavior in the nursing home as well. I somehow coaxed her into an exam chair and discovered she had cataracts, and we took them out. The next time I saw her, she was sitting calmly in the exam chair with the sweetest smile on her face."

"Do you have any regrets?"

"Uh . . . just one. There was a lady I saw once who had a fly on her shoulder, and I just stood there. I could have helped her, but I didn't."

"A fly on her shoulder? Why was that so bad?"

"I'm sorry, sweetie, but it's just too painful to talk about. I'll look her up when I get to Heaven and tell her how sorry I am."

"My dad said you and Momma Carson were married for fifty years. What do you think is the secret to a happy marriage?"

"Forgiveness."

"Is that all?"

"It's about all that matters."

"Daddy Carson, I'm twelve years old now. If you could give one piece of advice to a twelve-year-old, what would you tell them?"

"Change your brand of toothpaste at least every ten years."

Twink laughed. "Come on, Daddy Carson. You're teasing me again. I'm serious."

"So am I. You need to change your brand of toothpaste at least every ten years."

"Okay. Why is that?"

"Big companies and the advertising people they hire mostly don't care about folks over sixty. They care about young people.

Why do you suppose that is? It's not because young people have all the money. A lot of young people have no money at all. In fact, they have less than no money. They have debts. Older folks have a lot more money than younger folks. Advertisers care more about young people because younger folks haven't made up their minds about everything. They are still trying to figure things out. Most older folks have tried all they want to try. Their 'truths' get compressed into a smaller and smaller, harder and harder, more impenetrable kernel of smugness and self-satisfaction. No new idea can even be considered. Their world becomes more predictable, less interesting, less exciting. Let me ask you this. Do you like opera music?"

"No, sir. My friends don't either."

"Have you ever listened to it?"

"I've heard it. All that screeching."

"Your friend's opinions don't count. Have you ever sat down and listened to it alone and with an open mind?"

"Well, no. Not like that."

"You ought to give it a try. If you always just do what your friends do, you will, by definition, be average. It's not important that you like it. It's only important that you consider liking it. And that is why you ought to change your brand of toothpaste every ten years. The eyes of our hearts need to be enlightened. And it should be that way until you draw your last breath."

"Okay. Just two more questions. What is the biggest change you have seen in yourself since you were twenty-one?"

"I've gotten a lot more intolerant of intolerance."

"And the last question. It's a biggie. What is the secret to happiness?"

"Some work to do, some people to love, and something, anything, to hope for."

And that was it. She was through. I asked her to be sure to send me a copy of her article. She said she would. Her father suggested she send copies to all the family. Then she came and gave me a big hug and a kiss on the cheek. Then everyone did. One by one. I liked it. I liked it a lot.

I went back upstairs and got ready for bed. Rowdy jumped up and went to his usual spot at the foot of the bed. I went over and scratched him behind his ears and told him what a good boy he was. I went to my forest of frames and said good night to all my grandkids. It suddenly dawned on me, for the first time in my life, that if I hadn't met and married Anita, none of these wonderful people would be here—and, further, none of their as-yet-unborn offspring would ever be born. Then I lay down on my side and caressed the faces of Anita and our two children with the back of my index finger. I turned the light off on my bedside table and rolled onto my back. I stared at the ceiling and thought, *My God. How lucky can a guy get? I've been given all the seasons of life. And the gifts of joy and wonder. What an incredible adventure.* I thanked God for letting me live long enough to learn what's really important in life. You never got too old to love, and you never got too old to need to be loved. Then I closed my eyes.

For the last time.

Birth

Forward

They are standing on their heads. Both of them. Why are they standing on their heads? And why are they wearing masks? I have no experience in these matters, but that just seems wrong. To make matters worse, I am freezing. This place is cold! Also, I am all wet—head to toe. Like I have just stepped out of the shower. And my backside hurts. I understand that. The guy standing on his head had popped me there pretty good a few seconds ago. That must be why I am crying.

The upside-down lady sticks something in my mouth, then—and this is worse—up my nose. Then she rubs me with a towel like she is polishing a bowling ball.

I mean, what the hell? Is my whole life going to be this much fun? I decide to feel sorry for myself.

All of a sudden, everyone quits standing on their heads.

Next, the lady who used to be upside down wraps me up like a mummy in something soft. It is all done quickly and professionally.

Then things get better. She hands me off to another lady. I don't know why, but things change at once. This lady is different. She smells sweaty—but a good kind of sweaty. She begins to talk to me and says something that sounds like "My sweet baby. My beautiful little Bob." So I'm guessing I belong to her, and I'm either a baby or a Bob. She coos over me and sounds so nice and happy. I like it. I like it a lot. For some reason, I feel safe in her arms. Her touch is just different. My backside starts feeling better, and I begin to feel warmer. I still have no idea what is happening or what will happen next, but you can't have everything. And that is something I am to find out over and over again. You seldom can have everything, and sometimes you can't have anything at all. I decide to take a nap.

***

I am alone again and in a big room with bright lights. For some reason, my head is down below my feet. I don't like that. I'm hungry. I don't care for that either. I decide to announce that to the lady wearing the funny hat who is across the room. She hears me crying and looks up and then goes back to writing like I don't even exist, so I just quit crying. Finally, she saunters over and takes me down the hall to Sweaty Lady, and I am allowed to dine.

This place is boring. Same thing, day after day. I'll bet three days pass before the routine changes. On that day, Funny Hat comes and gets me. She takes me to another room and strips me naked. This room has even brighter lights. Then she begins to wash those three things down between my legs. I have no idea what they are for or what they are called. I have personally named the little finger guy Quincy and the two round guys Roly and Poly.

When she is done, the door opens, and a man dressed in white comes in, washes his hands, and pulls on some stretchy gloves. He has a short white stick dangling from the corner of his mouth. It is smoking, and the end of it is red. It stinks. He reaches inside a tray and pulls a funny-looking metal thing out and takes hold of Quincy. He somehow screws the thing on, and that's when the pain starts. It takes me completely by surprise. I haven't done anything to him. I begin to cry. Perhaps "shriek" is a better word. The pain is just awful. Then I notice him taking another metal thing out of the tray, and he begins to cut on Quincy. I had thought there couldn't possibly be any pain worse than the screwed-on thing, but I was wrong. He doesn't just cut one time; he cuts and cuts and cuts and cuts again. He is laughing about something Funny Hat says when the very end of his mouth stick falls onto my leg. Either he doesn't notice or doesn't care, and so it is left to smolder. I am in agony, and he won't stop. I shriek as loudly as I can and begin to flail my arms and kick my legs as fast as I can. All to no avail. He takes his sweet time. Finally, he takes the metal thing off, and I glance down. I can see blood all over Quincy and spilling onto Roly and Poly.

When he is through, he strips off his gloves and drops what is left of his stick in a sink, where it sputters and fizzles. Then he leaves. I am thinking, *I'm just a little baby, or perhaps a little Bob. Why did you do that to me?* Funny Hat bandages me up and takes me to see Sweaty Lady. She is so sweet. I think I'll change her name from Sweaty Lady to Sweet Lady. She tries to make it all better, but I am too upset to eat. It is the worst day of my entire life.

I had been in exquisite agony, and anyone who thinks this is funny has never had their Quincy carved on without anesthesia. Just because you don't have a voice doesn't mean you can't hurt.

Birth

Backward

My ass hurts. That's the first thing I can ever remember. My ass hurts, and I am upside down. And I'm crying. You would be too if someone hit your bare bottom five times as hard as they could. I don't cry the first four times. I am trying to tough it out. At least he quits hitting me after I have enough sense to start crying. And cold! Man! This place is cold! I decide to keep crying. I am just in one of those moods. Nothing is going well so far. I mean, what the hell? If this is life, I sure hope it's not all going to be this much fun.

Then things get better. They wrap me in a blanket. It is all done very quickly and professionally. I get handed off to another lady, and this one is better. A lot better. She smells sweaty—but a good kind of sweaty. I like the way she looks too. She begins to talk to me and coos over me and tells me how beautiful I am. I like it. I like it a lot. My ass starts feeling better, not normal, but better. I begin to feel warmer. Still, you can't have everything. And that is something I am to find out over and over again. You seldom can have everything, and sometimes you can't have anything at all. I decide to take a nap.

***

I am alone again and in a big room with bright lights. I find out later that they say I wasn't supposed to see at that age. Well, "they" are wrong, and as I would also discover later, "they" are wrong quite often. I advise ignoring the "theys" of the world.

For some reason, my head is down below my feet. I don't like that. I'm hungry. I don't care for that either. I decide to announce that to the lady wearing the funny hat who is across the room. She hears me crying and looks up and then just goes back to writing like I don't even exist. She doesn't even have the decency to make eye contact or say something like "Be with you in a minute, sir." I decide to cry a little louder. She gets an irritated look on her face but stops her scribbling and saunters over. She takes me down the hall to Sweaty Lady, and I am allowed to dine.

This place is boring. Same thing, day after day. I'll bet three days pass before the routine changes. On that day, Funny Hat comes and gets me. She takes me to another room and strips me naked. It is embarrassing. This room has even brighter lights. Then she begins to wash those three things down between my legs. I have no idea what they are for or what they are called. I have personally named the little finger guy Studley and the two marble-like guys the Dude and the Duke.

When she is done, the door opens, and a man dressed in white comes in, washes his hands, and pulls on some stretchy gloves. He has a short white stick dangling from the corner of his mouth. It is smoking, and the end of it is red. It stinks. Why in the world would he make everyone else in the room smell that thing? He reaches inside a tray and pulls a funny-looking metal thing out and takes hold of Studley. He somehow screws the thing on, and that's when the pain starts. It takes me completely by surprise. I haven't done anything to him. I begin to cry. Perhaps "shriek" is a better word. The pain is just awful. Then I notice him taking another metal thing out of the tray, and he begins to cut on Studley. I had thought there couldn't possibly be any pain worse than the screwed-on thing, but I was wrong. He doesn't just cut one time; he cuts and cuts and cuts and cuts again. He is laughing about something Funny Hat says when the end of his stinky stick falls onto my leg. The pain gets worse. Either he doesn't notice or doesn't care, and so it is left to smolder. I am in agony, and he won't stop. I shriek as loudly as I can and begin to flail my arms and kick my legs as fast as I can. All to no avail. He takes his sweet time. The stick makes his breath smell terrible. You can only take so much. Despite the pain, I get furious. This is so unfair. What have I ever done to him—or anyone else for that matter? If I knew how to talk, I would ask Sweaty Lady to sue his ass. Instead, I clench my little fists and try to slug him, but he is out of range. He finally stops cutting, bends over, and begins to take off the screwed-on thing. Since suing isn't a viable option and I can't reach him with my jab, I look at his face, make a few calculations, roll my hip a little to the right, take aim, and let 'er rip. Full blast, by God! I get him good. Pissed right in his left eye. Bull's-eye! So to speak. Funny Hat takes three steps back and puts her hand over her mouth to cover her silent laugh.

He says, "Son of a bitch!" I guess he is talking about himself. Just then, the eye piss streams down his face and into his mouth, which he had opened to call himself a son of a bitch. If I knew how to laugh, I would have.

He strips off his gloves, throws them in the trash, wipes his eye with a tissue, flings what's left of the stick in the sink, and leaves, slamming the door behind him. I am thinking, *Well, you're right about one thing. You truly* are *a son of a bitch.* What a way to make a living. Funny Hat bandages me up and takes me to see Sweaty Lady. She is so sweet. I think I'll change her name from Sweaty Lady to Sweet Lady. She tries to make it all better, but I am too upset to eat. This is the worst day of my entire life. It still hurts, and I am really upset. But I am comforted somewhat by the notion that it is better to be pissed off than pissed on.

I had been in exquisite agony, and anyone who thinks this is funny has never had their Studley whittled on without anesthesia. But just because you're little doesn't mean you can't fight back. I think I'll view this little episode as a learning experience. There's got to be more to this "life" thing than what I just went through. I somehow managed to combat something evil. Maybe that's why I'm here. Maybe I can change the world. Who knows? I'm sure as hell going to try.

Acknowledgments

First, I would like to thank the Reverend Doctor Ben Nelson III, who gave me the idea for this book from one of his sermons. Later, another of his sermons gave me the idea for one of the chapters about the young Bob and forgiveness. I would like to thank my brother, Fred, and my friend Chuck Dunleavy, who were my alpha beta readers. Bless your hearts for plowing through a first draft manuscript of a debut novel that wasn't very good. You never laughed at it (as far as I know) and helped make it better. It must've been hell. To Christina Boys, my developmental editor who had numerous significant recommendations on how to make a series of stories into a novel. I would like to thank Mark Malatesta, who was one of the first people outside my friends and family who thought this might be something worthwhile to pursue. Thank you for caring more about me than my money. I would also like to thank the family at GFP for making this project a reality. Thanks to my publication manager, Sara Addicott, my production editor, Kylee Hayes, my editorial manager, Abi Pollokoff, and my marketing strategist, Adria Batt. Lastly, I would like to thank my wife, Suzanne, for letting me alone when that was needed. She listened to my complaints and knew just how many "there, theres" I needed.

Dr. Rex Cole received his undergraduate degree from the University of Texas and his medical degree from the University of Texas Southwestern Medical School in Dallas. He was a practicing ophthalmologist in San Marcos, Texas for forty-eight years before retiring in 2019. He still lives in San Marcos with his wife and their two labradoodles Piper and Rio, who earn their kibble by protecting the family from squirrels, raccoons, armadillos, buzzards and, less laudably, skunks.